THE SIX QU[

CHRISTOPHER ST. JOHN SPRIGG was
in Putney, southwest London, in 1
novels as "C. St. John Sprigg," begin *the Body* (1933), published in America as *Crime in Kensington*. However, it is for his nonfiction writings focusing on Marxist ideology, published posthumously under the pseudonym Christopher Caudwell, that he is best known today. He died in 1937, killed in action while serving in the International Brigade during the Spanish Civil War.

By C. St. John Sprigg

Pass the Body (1933) (AKA *Crime in Kensington*)
Fatality in Fleet Street (1933)
The Perfect Alibi (1934)
Death of an Airman (1934)
The Corpse with the Sunburnt Face (1935)
Death of a Queen (1935)
The Six Queer Things (1937)

C. St. John Sprigg

THE SIX QUEER THINGS

VALANCOURT BOOKS

The Six Queer Things by C. St. John Sprigg
First published by Herbert Jenkins, London, 1937
Reprinted from the 1st U.S. edition, published by Doubleday, 1937
This edition first published 2018

Copyright © 1937 by C. St. John Sprigg, renewed 1964 by Doubleday

All rights reserved. In accordance with the U.S. Copyright Act of 1976, the copying, scanning, uploading, and/or electronic sharing of any part of this book without the permission of the publisher may constitute unlawful piracy and theft of the author's intellectual property. If you would like to use material from the book (other than for review purposes), prior written permission should be obtained by contacting the publisher.

Published by Valancourt Books, Richmond, Virginia
http://www.valancourtbooks.com

ISBN 978-1-943910-69-4 (trade paperback)
Also available as an electronic book.

All Valancourt Books publications are printed on acid free paper that meets all ANSI standards for archival quality paper.

Cover: Reproduction of the original dust jacket of the British edition. The Publisher is grateful to Mark Terry of Facsimile Dust Jackets, LLC for providing a scan of the jacket.

Set in Dante MT

Contents

CHAPTER		PAGE
I	Michael Crispin	7
II	Voices of the Dead	25
III	On the Borderline	48
IV	The Night of the Mind	72
V	The Man-Woman	83
VI	The Six Queer Things	93
VII	The Mare's Nest	104
VIII	"Something Damned Queer Has Been Happening"	116
IX	The Night of Delusions	128
X	Disappearance of a Suspect	140
XI	The Escape	150
XII	Death of a Doctor	162
XIII	The Dreadful Factory	173
XIV	The Bond of Release	184
XV	Who Is the Director?	194
XVI	Home Comforts	203
XVII	The Wax Goat	216

CHAPTER I
Michael Crispin

Marjorie's uncle was a fat, white-whiskered accountant who was a popular figure at the Bilford Liberal Club. A real good sort, always ready with a joke or a greeting—this was the impression he gave to his numerous friends. Marjorie wondered why these friends had never noticed that her uncle's eyes were small, like a pig's, and set close together; and that even when his pudgy face wrinkled in a genial smile, these eyes remained unsmiling, and as hard as bits of china. She wondered how men who met Samuel Burton every day could avoid seeing his meanness and his basic inhumanity.

But then they did not have to live with him. Marjorie did. Ever since her parents had died, she had lived in Samuel Burton's little house in Bilford, which is one of South London's lesser-known suburbs. She had had a long first-hand experience of his absolute absorption in himself, his pettiness, and the supreme importance he attached to money.

Now that Marjorie was twenty and a junior shorthand typist at the Brixton Cardboard Box Works, she was earning 26/- a week. When she had paid for fares, meals at the office canteen and a few necessities, there was not much left; but it all went to her uncle for her keep. From time to time he would remind her, in an indirect way, of the smallness of this amount.

He was a master of indirectness. If he had been more direct, she would have replied to him that she saved him the cost of a housekeeper. With the help of Mrs Moggridge, she looked after the house in her spare time. Mrs Moggridge, a simple-minded char, loathed Samuel Burton with a simple hatred. Her devotion to Marjorie enabled her to endure Samuel Burton; but it did not prevent her grumbling openly when he came into the room with her. Samuel Burton ignored these expressions of revolt. He was prepared to overlook revolt if it saved money, and he underpaid Mrs Moggridge. He also tried to cut her down in other ways.

"No meals," he would insist. "I refuse to countenance this surreptitious feeding at my expense. I don't expect my employers to feed me as well as pay me."

However, Marjorie saw to it that Mrs Moggridge got her lunch, even though it involved a weekly wrangle with her uncle, when the housekeeping books came to be settled up, because of the enormous consumption of bread and butter.

Often Marjorie had been on the verge of throwing in her hand and going to live on her own. She knew of other girls who managed to make do on as little as she earned. But Samuel Burton was sensitive to signs of rebellion in her, and it was just at those moments that he played another card. He became pathetic.

Marjorie felt certain that the pathos was insincere, and yet, in spite of herself, it touched her. In these moods Samuel Burton painted himself as a lonely, misunderstood old man. Marjorie was the only relative he had living in the world. Tears stood in the hard eyes, and his voice trembled.

"I know I may be a little difficult, my dear," he would say, "but you must try and overlook it. I've done the best I could for you, and none of us is perfect."

Yes, perhaps after all he had done the best he could for her. His words reminded Marjorie of the fact that for ten years—ever since her father's death—he had fed, clothed and educated her. He had some claims on her gratitude. Therefore so far, in spite of bitter moods of revolt, she still stayed on. She did not know whether it was weakness or strength in her.

Perhaps what enabled her to bear it more than anything else was her friendship with Ted. Ted Wainwright was twenty-two and they were going to be married as soon as Ted could afford it. It couldn't be long now. Ted was in the press shop of the Bilford Metal Furniture Company and expected soon to be a foreman. Directly he got the raise they could afford to marry, but not until then, for Ted had his mother to look after.

While she was with Ted, she forgot about Samuel Burton and the housekeeping books, and the hardships of those earlier years when she had been a lonely schoolgirl in the empty house in Bilford Park Avenue. She could look forward to a future spent with Ted. And Ted was looking forward to the day when he could announce to Burton—or "Soapy Sam" as he called him—that Marjorie was leaving. For Ted, from the very first day he had met Samuel Burton, had taken an intense dislike to Marjorie's uncle.

"I'd give a week's pay to clock that bloke," he had said once, after hearing the tail end of a quarrel with Marjorie about money. "The stingy louse!"

"I suppose he is hard up," Marjorie had said defensively.

"Where does he work?" asked Ted sceptically.

"I don't know. He never tells anyone."

Ted had stared at her in amazement.

"*Don't know!*" he had repeated. "What! You've lived with him all this time and don't know where he works?"

"No, I don't!"

Marjorie had become so used to her uncle's secrecy about everything, including his business, that it had ceased to seem odd to her that he had never mentioned his firm's name. He was an accountant; that was all she knew. He had once or twice mentioned his firm's address—a number in Fenchurch Street. Marjorie's answer awoke Ted's curiosity and he began to make enquiries. One day, when in the city, he went to the number in Fenchurch Street, but it had proved a building full of different firms, any one of which might have been Samuel Burton's employers. Marjorie herself had her curiosity roused by Ted's reaction to her confession. Her uncle's reticence was certainly odd, but she knew intuitively that he did not want to be questioned on this subject, and that to do so would only cause a quarrel. Marjorie avoided quarrels with her uncle, for there was something icy and hateful about Samuel Burton in a rage, which made the few people who had roused it anxious not to rouse it again.

The discovery made Ted curious about anything connected with Marjorie's uncle. A point which puzzled Ted was that Burton, in spite of his meanness, cultivated the Liberal Club, his Masonic Lodge and various other expensive social activities. Of course, if he could make a joke or a kind word do instead of a drink or a donation, he did so; but, none the less, he had managed to build up a reputation in Bilford life as a benevolent, hail-fellow-well-met businessman. In the course of a year, this must have cost him something. It was true that these friends were skin deep. He never went to their houses or entertained them at his own, using his bachelorhood as an excuse. But why did he trouble to be convivial at all? Were there two contradictory sides to his nature? Ted gave him up after a time as an insoluble problem, but his discoveries did not make him any fonder of the pudgy little accountant with the ready smile and the hard eyes.

Soon after, Marjorie's growing revolt flared up into a crisis. It happened one Saturday afternoon when, after paying the tradesmen, Marjorie went to her uncle with the housekeeping books. Samuel Burton gave a hollow groan as his eyes skimmed the total. His eyes fixed hers with a hard stare.

"Look at this," he said, "two pounds of butter! What do you do with it? Put it on your hair?"

"No, Uncle," said Marjorie, suppressing a desire to throw the books at him. "We can't manage with less."

"We must manage with less," replied her uncle, striking the table with his fist. "Do you realise what this house costs me—rent, rates, lighting, heating, cleaning, food, repairs and furniture? Do you think I'm a millionaire?"

"No, I'm not likely to make that mistake," replied Marjorie sharply.

To her surprise, the sharpness in her tone had the effect of softening him.

"I see. You think I'm mean," he answered sadly. "I suppose it was my meanness that made me look after you when your mother died, and bring you up and have you educated."

"You know I'm grateful for that," answered Marjorie.

"Well, you choose an odd way of showing it," said Mr Burton plaintively. He pushed the housekeeping books aside. "Don't you think it's about time you started trying to stand on your own feet?"

"What do you mean?" asked Marjorie, surprised. "I've got a job."

Mr Burton smiled paternally. "Come, dear, you can't imagine you're earning your living with a 26-shillings-a-week salary. My dear girl, try to take life more seriously—for your own good.

After all, I'm not a strong man. I might pop off some day." Mr Burton tapped his chest about the region of his heart. "How do you think you'll manage then? You're rising twenty now; you're a clever girl; you oughtn't to be content simply to brew tea in an office and tap the typewriter occasionally. You ought to show initiative!"

For a moment Marjorie was unable to reply to this attack, which was all the more difficult to meet because it was so unexpected. Then, with her cheeks burning, she got up.

"Very well," she said in a strangled voice. "Give me a week, and I won't be a burden to you any longer!"

Without waiting for a reply she rushed out of the room, and experienced the limited satisfaction to be obtained from slamming a door really hard.

Left to himself, Mr Burton became calmer and gazed meditatively at the housekeeping books, flipping them over with his fingers. There was a queer expression of self-satisfaction on his face. Then he got up and went to his desk. Taking a key from his watch chain, he unlocked the bottom drawer. From this he pulled out a bottle of cognac and poured a small portion of it reverently into a broad bellmouthed glass, which he took from the same hiding place. An unusual expression of benevolence suffused Mr Burton's countenance as he sipped the cognac with the air of a connoisseur. Then, putting the brandy away, he walked carefully into the scullery and rinsed the glass. He replaced it with the brandy bottle, locked up the desk again, opened the top drawer and took out some account books. Presently he was immersed in what were evidently complicated calculations.

2

Meanwhile her uncle's words had aroused in Marjorie a cold fury of determination. She was resolved to get at once a better job and not only leave him, but also pay him back for the money he had spent in the past on her upbringing. This repayment would appeal to him strongly, she thought, and would also give her the right to cut short his appeals and reproaches. In return, she would be able to do a little frank speaking.

The immediate problem, however, was how to get a better job, and get it quickly. And even more urgent was the problem of breaking with her uncle. She was determined not to stay any longer in his house. Her first impulse was to wait and tell Ted that evening. But then, she knew what his immediate reaction would be: first, to go and have a stand-up quarrel with her uncle; second, to insist that they get married at once, whatever the difficulties. The first wouldn't be fair to her uncle—at least until she'd paid him back. The second wouldn't be fair to Ted. She must settle this on her own. After all, she told herself, it was only her silly pride. Lots of girls would just grin and bear it. She had accepted her uncle's hospitality and that was the end of it. But she couldn't grin and bear it. Years of stifled bitterness and resentment surged up within her. If it killed her, she'd get a better job.

Unfortunately her qualifications were few. The education about which her uncle so often spoke had not included anything but the barest essentials, certainly none of the accomplishments that would enable her to demand skilled wages.

It was at this moment she took a resolution. The minute she took it, she knew it had been at the back of her mind all the time. This was how the resolution had come there. A few days before she had had a strange experience. She had been sitting in a tea shop in Bilford High Street, waiting for Ted to meet her, when two people had come in, a man and a woman, and sat down near her. Almost as soon as the man sat down, he half turned to her, and looked at her with an expression as if he expected her to recognise him. But she felt sure she had never seen his face before. It was a face one was not likely to forget in a hurry either—a strange, curiously shapeless yellow face, with full red lips—a face that would have been repulsive, if it were not for the eyes. Large, and of an unusual brilliance, these eyes had long black lashes which gave them a depth and beauty that seemed out of place in a man's face. They seemed utterly out of place in the shapeless yellow face of this particular man.

As she waited for Ted, she noticed that the man's eyes repeatedly moved to her face. As Marjorie was pretty and went about a good deal alone, she was used to being stared at by men. But she realised at once that this man's stare was not the ordinary ogling of the woman chaser. Apart from the fact that he was accompanied by a woman, there was a cold, curiously disinterested quality about the stare that guaranteed its honesty.

"He mistakes me for someone else he knows," she told herself.

Then, to her surprise, the woman who was with the man came over to her table. She was a woman in the thirties, with dull hair and tired, drawn features. She spoke in a harsh metallic voice; but she had a kind smile.

"Excuse me," she said with an embarrassed air, "could I possibly ask your name? My brother feels sure he knows a close relative of yours."

"Why, certainly," said Marjorie. "My name is Marjorie Easton."

The woman seemed a little disappointed. "I see. Have you ever heard of someone called Renée de Varennes?"

"Never," answered Marjorie with conviction.

"Then my brother was mistaken," admitted the woman. She hesitated for a moment and then, as if making a decision, sat down on the vacant chair opposite Marjorie.

"You'll probably think we are a very odd couple. But we both believe in acting on impulse, as it is called, and I have not often found my brother's intuition is wrong. He has been very strongly affected by you. It is not only that you bear a likeness to someone for whom he has a great respect, but he feels that you resemble her in other ways."

"I don't quite follow," said Marjorie, on her guard, and unable to make out what the woman was driving at.

"I mean, my dear, that you may have talents of which you are not aware. I know I am seeming very rude and personal, but what is your occupation?"

"I'm a typist," replied Marjorie, beginning to suspect that both of them were a little mad.

"Exactly. Well, you may not be aware of it, but you have a very unusual face. Does it occur to you that you may be wasting your powers?"

Suddenly an idea occurred to Marjorie. The name Renée de Varennes vaguely suggested a film star, and now it occurred to her that this man with the dead face and the live eyes might be a film producer. Marjorie herself, ever since she had realised she was slightly better looking than the run of other girls, had had a secret desire to go on the films. This desire had gradually receded as she reached years of discretion and became more realistic and practical; but it still lay dormant, and now it gave a flicker.

"I had often thought of going on the films," she confessed. "But you haven't a chance unless you've got a pull of some kind."

The other woman burst out laughing. Then, seeing Marjorie's face fall, she said kindly, "No, my dear, we've nothing to do with the films. And, to be perfectly candid, I doubt if you would be successful. You're altogether too frank and simple to be a good actress. You're very pretty, as I expect plenty of people have told you, but it wasn't your looks that impressed my brother. They're not so uncommon after all. It was an idea that you have rarer gifts. Have you ever wanted to draw or write books?"

"Never," answered Marjorie, feeling out of her depth again.

The woman nodded thoughtfully. "No, perhaps it wouldn't come out that way. It really only strengthens our opinion. My dear, I expect you already think I'm quite mad, so I won't say any more than this. If you're contented to be as you are at present, well, that shows that all is as it should be. What things will be, they must be. But if ever you feel discontented, if ever you feel you are wasting yourself, then I want you to come to us. That's all." She opened her bag and drew out an oblong card. "Here's my brother's address. Remember! Don't come to us unless you feel you really want to develop a side of yourself that isn't developed yet."

Before she could answer, the woman had returned to her table, and from that moment the pair did not look at her again, except that the woman gave her a distant smile as they went out. Meanwhile Marjorie studied the card thoughtfully:

> MICHAEL CRISPIN,
> 7, Belmont Avenue,
> Kensington,
> London.

The name conveyed nothing to her. All the same, she put the card carefully in her bag.

A few minutes later, Ted came in. For some strange reason Marjorie, who hitherto had shared every secret with Ted, did not tell him about this conversation. For one thing, she knew that Ted would at once put the worst possible construction on it, and perhaps go over to the pair and be rude. She herself felt certain that whatever motive lay behind the strange conversation, it was nothing sinister.

But perhaps the real feeling that kept her silent was the instinctive knowledge that, directly she told Ted, his sturdy common sense would make the whole adventure seem nonsense. He would dismiss it with some damning phrase, and his common sense, as she knew from past experience, was terribly convincing. But there was something about this incident which made Marjorie particularly anxious not to have it withered in the cold blast of common sense. The belief that these two people had seen something unusual and glamorous about her, something no one had ever noticed before, made her cling to the memory of the incident. She did not intend of course to go any farther, but it was amusing to turn it over in her mind, and wonder what it was about her face that struck them. Once she caught herself regarding her face searchingly in the mirror, trying to see something new and undeveloped in the familiar features.

"Good lord, I am getting foolish," she told herself firmly, turning away. And for a time she really had put the incident out of her mind.

But now, in her sudden gust of dissatisfaction this Saturday, the memory of the incident returned. She took out the card from the corner of the drawer where she had put it and looked at it thoughtfully. After all, perhaps something might come of a visit to Crispin. It couldn't possibly do her any harm, if she merely called to find out what was on their minds, and did not commit herself. As it happened, she was not meeting Ted till nine o'clock that evening, so even after the week-end's shopping had been done, she would have three or four spare hours. She would go up to Kensington and see the owner of the card. But she would ask for his sister, Miss Crispin, she supposed, unless perhaps the sister was married.

3

The house in Belmont Avenue was a small but pleasant house with a shiny black front door and a chromium-painted knocker. Marjorie asked for Miss Crispin and gave her own name. There seemed to be no difficulties. She waited for a moment in the hall, and then the woman she had seen in the restaurant came down the stairs. She did not seem surprised. On the contrary, she fixed Marjorie's eyes with a calm stare and then took her hand and pressed it warmly.

"My brother felt sure you would come today," she said quietly. "He was, in fact, expecting you. Would you please come and see him?"

Marjorie was so taken aback by the calmness with which Miss Crispin made this unexpected statement, that she said nothing, and followed her into a strangely furnished room. The walls were covered with a kind of black, velvety paper, and there was a thick black carpet which went up to the skirting. The ceiling was painted with a deep tone of grey. In the centre of the room was a large table, with a red lacquer top poised on spidery, chromium-plated legs. The windows were covered with thick black velvet curtains which were drawn across, although it was still light outside, and the room was lit only by an unusual system of concealed lighting which was let into the ceiling. Even before her eyes fell on Crispin, her attention was attracted by a heavy black curtain with silver embroidery, which cut off a corner of the room and formed a kind of small inner room.

Crispin was seated at a small black ebony desk, and it was curious that, although his back was towards her, the figure seemed completely familiar. He got up at once and faced her. As he took her hand and said a word of greeting, she re-experienced the strange sensation she had felt in the restaurant when she had first seen him. As before, it was his eyes which affected her, with their keen, disinterested, brilliant stare. He did not smile as he greeted her, and this solemnity, which she afterwards discovered was characteristic of him, impressed her as if the meeting was of special importance. No doubt the atmosphere of the room reinforced the sensation. It gave her a stuffy, closed-in feeling in which even details seemed significant.

"Your sister told me you were expecting me," Marjorie began, in a silence that followed their first few words. "I don't quite understand that. I only made up my mind to come and see you this afternoon."

Crispin waved this aside. "Often our mind is made up before we realise it. Your mind was made up when my sister spoke to you in the restaurant. It was only a matter of time for you to act on it, and I calculated it would take a week."

Marjorie felt annoyed at his cool assumption that he knew her mind better than she did herself. "Actually I intended not to come, but something unexpected happened today which made me change my mind."

"That, Miss Easton, is what psychologists call rationalisation.

"But I see I have annoyed you," he added, with a note of gentle humility in his voice. "Please forgive me. If you are going to work with me, you will find I have an odd knack of sensing the way other people's minds work. You see, we all have large undeveloped sides of our minds and personalities which are hidden from ourselves, but which we therefore turn to other people. I happen to be particularly sensitive to those sides in other people."

"You'll have plenty of examples of that, if you stay with us," interjected Miss Crispin. "You may find it a little unnerving at first."

Marjorie felt the two were making an attempt to commit her to some arrangement in advance.

"I think there must be some misunderstanding," she said. "You speak of my staying here. But I only came to ask why you spoke to me in the way you did. I hesitated a good deal before coming at all."

Miss Crispin smiled. "Michael," she said, "I'm afraid you are alarming Miss Easton. Please try to be a little more normal."

Crispin turned and regarded his sister for a moment with a faint air of resentment. He fiddled nervously with a button on his jacket. Marjorie, who had a habit of noticing irrelevant details, suddenly saw the contrast between his long thin fingers and the short, almost deformed thumb.

"Quite right, Bella," he answered. "I'm sorry, Miss Easton, I'm being very rude. I'd better leave you to tell me in your own way why you came here." His words made Marjorie feel awkward and very young.

"Well, I'm only a junior typist, at present, and not earning much," she explained. "And I want to get a better job. Your speaking to me in the way you did made me think that perhaps you could suggest something. Of course I don't know what you had in mind. It was only a chance shot, coming here. Really I've no right to trouble you——"

"You've every right, Miss Easton," broke in Crispin solemnly.

Marjorie resented the intimate, emotionally charged style in which Crispin spoke to her. She couldn't exactly accuse him of being too familiar. His manner was too formal and solemn. It was rather his assumption of a complete sympathy with her that ruffled her feelings. It was made more irritating by the shrewdness he had shown so far. It was true that she had made up her mind to accept the invitation from the time Miss Crispin had spoken to her. It was equally true that, although she had ostensibly come asking for advice, she had secretly hoped that Crispin would be able to employ her for whatever gifts he saw in her. But it was annoying to have it openly proclaimed. It made her feel as she used to do in front of her headmistress at school—at a disadvantage socially and intellectually.

Crispin nodded.

"Your powers aren't being realised in your present job. You're quite right: you should have a better one. My sister and I are research workers. We need an assistant. That is the task for which I believe you have special powers."

This was an acute disappointment. Marjorie had visualised various possible jobs or careers that might be offered her by Crispin. The room she had just entered, with its general arty appearance, had suggested that Crispin might be a painter. On the other hand, the lighting had put it into her mind that he might be a photographer. Perhaps he wanted a model, she had thought, and while she was determined to refuse the offer, the idea of anything so much out of the rut was in itself romantic. There seemed nothing romantic about being assistant to a research worker.

"I'm afraid I couldn't help you at all there," she answered. "I haven't any scientific knowledge."

Brother and sister exchanged a smile. "The branch of science with which we deal is one about which little is known at present," Crispin explained. "Your ignorance would be less a handicap than you think. In any case, that's my risk, really, isn't it?"

"Well, I shall have to give up my present job," pointed out Marjorie practically. "And it isn't so easy to get another if you find out after all that I'm not satisfactory."

Crispin frowned. "Oh, if you're worried about security of tenure, I'm prepared to give you a three months' trial. After that, say, a month's notice on either side. That will give us both ample time to see that we are suited to each other."

"That sounds fair enough," admitted Marjorie. "But what would the salary be? You see that's really why I want another job. I'm not earning enough to live on at present."

Crispin's slight frown changed to a look of annoyance. "I refuse to regard money as an important relation between human beings," he said angrily. "Why not settle the more important things first?" He got to his feet and, with a swift, catlike tread, walked out of the room. In spite of his evident annoyance, he closed the door quietly behind him.

Marjorie stared at Miss Crispin, too astonished to speak.

Miss Crispin smiled at her reassuringly. "I'm afraid my brother is sensitive and therefore seems odd to you. You will soon get used to him. He can't bear the idea of people working for him for money, or indeed of their working at all for money. It revolts him, he says. He feels that no one ought to work except to express themselves in some way. Money oughtn't to enter into it."

"Well, after all, we've got to live," said Marjorie. "And one has to have money to live. The world would be much easier if it weren't so, but there it is."

"Yes, my dear, of course. It's just that Michael feels we all ought to live only for something worth while. He often says we might as well die as live *only* to live. Please don't misunderstand him. He didn't mean to be rude. He felt in your case that you weren't expressing your full possibilities in your present job. He said that you had a discontented, suffering look. Of course he exaggerates these things," she added, seeing Marjorie's expression, "so when you raised the question of money, he was a little upset."

"Well, I'm sorry, but money is more important to me than it evidently is to him."

"Naturally. It is to any of us. Michael, you see, is a genius. I really believe that, Miss Easton. And you must allow for the ways of genius. He works because he loves his work; it is his life; and he expects everyone else to do the same. Even the servants in the house here he regards as fellow workers. I simply daren't discuss their wages with him; he'd be hurt and upset. He leaves it all to me. The odd thing is, that after they've been with him a little, they get into his way of thinking and regard him as a fellow worker, not as an employer."

"Well, I'm sorry," said Marjorie awkwardly, "but I've simply got to think of wages, because I've no money except what I earn."

"I understand," interrupted Miss Crispin hastily. "Please don't think my brother grudges parting with money. He never even thinks about it. He's the most generous soul alive. If it weren't for me, he'd have given away all his money years ago. He has no sense of its value at all. Of course, you'll get a salary in the ordinary way, but it is always left to me to settle such practical details. I'm not a clever person at all. You'll find me quite easy to get on with. And so let's get down to business. I suggest you start at five guineas a week."

The suggestion astounded Marjorie. She felt she ought to protest, for she knew that her services could not be worth that. As she struggled with her conscience, Miss Crispin apparently misinterpreted her silence.

"I see you're still a little doubtful about us. Well, that's quite natural. But I assure you that I look after my brother's affairs in a perfectly businesslike manner. You needn't be afraid that wages won't be paid regularly or anything like that."

She opened the ebony desk. "I'll give you a little note confirming the engagement now, if you will accept."

"Yes, I shall be glad to try, if you do realise that I have had no experience except office work. I hope I shall be as useful as you hope."

Now that she had followed it up, the incident seemed to have lost most of its romance and become just a job. But as a job it was something to be grateful for.

"When can you begin? The earlier the better."

"Next week," said Marjorie. "I only have to give a week's notice."

"Good! Then I will draft the letter engaging you accordingly. And in case you still have any doubt, I'd better give you the first month's wages in advance. After that, wages will be paid weekly in arrears in the usual way. Of course, you understand that you will have to live in?"

"No," said Marjorie, surprised, "I didn't. In fact I don't think I could do that."

"I'm afraid it's essential. You see my brother works at all kinds of odd times, and he couldn't possibly keep to steady office hours. Sometimes he works in the evenings, sometimes in the day. You'll have more time off actually than the average office worker, but it won't always be in the evenings."

This seemed reasonable, and, after all, living in made her salary seem even larger.

"Well, I think I can manage it," she said.

"That's excellent. By the way, how old are you?"

"Twenty."

"Then I think you had better get your father's permission," said Miss Crispin. "Could you bring a little note with you in writing?"

"My parents are dead," Marjorie explained. "I live with my uncle."

"I see. Well, if he's acting as your guardian, you must bring permission from him. That's all, my dear; and I hope you'll be happy with us. I'm sure you'll be a very valuable addition to our household."

Miss Crispin rose from the desk, took some notes from a drawer in a cabinet, and put them in an envelope with the letter engaging her.

"I suppose you will want a reference?"

Miss Crispin shook her head and smiled. "No, child, your face is your reference. You can fake one but not the other."

As Marjorie was about to leave, she found courage to put the question that had been puzzling her ever since their first meeting.

"Who was that woman you asked me about when we first met?" she said. "Renée something or other? The one you said I resembled."

Miss Crispin looked a little disconcerted.

"She was a great genius and a very fine soul," she answered hesitantly. "I'll explain more when I see you next. She has been a great inspiration to my brother."

Marjorie went home with the uneasy realisation that she had two difficult tasks before her—to break the news to Ted, and to get her uncle's permission. The fact that she would have to live in with the Crispins would make both tasks more difficult. But she was buoyed up by her elation at the size of the salary, and by her curiosity about the strange couple. None of the ordinary humdrum people she had met at Bilford had any resemblance to them. Her job might prove difficult, but it was unlikely to be dull.

Marjorie now realised that by not telling Ted about the restaurant episode, she had unnecessarily complicated her task. One lie always leads to another, and she decided that she would omit the unorthodox and romantic parts of her story, when telling it to Ted and her uncle, and say that she had been answering an advertisement for a research worker. She felt a little guilty about deceiving Ted, but found comfort in the thought that it was for his own good.

As she expected, Ted was doubtful about the new job. He was particularly suspicious about the phrase "research worker."

"It must be some kind of research," he said reasonably. "Didn't you ask what kind?"

"No," she admitted. "I was too pleased with getting the job."

Ted laughed.

"You are a chump! Didn't this Crispin fellow give you any hint about the kind of work you're to do?"

"No, he didn't."

"Then he must be as big a fool as you are. It's the funniest thing I ever heard of," he said, chewing the end of his pipe thoughtfully. "You'll probably find the fellow's crazy, and you're expected to look after him. He can't be sane—offering five guineas without telling you what the job is, or finding out whether you can do it."

"Don't be so mean, Ted," she answered defensively. "I don't see why he mightn't be a bit unusual without being crazy."

"I don't like this living in and working at all hours of the day either. I suppose that means you won't be able to see me evenings."

"No, it won't, Ted. It's only that some evenings I may have to stay in. I'll probably have more time off than I do at present. You know I can never get away before nine because of uncle's dinner."

"Oh well, let's hope so. It beats me, though, why you're getting such a high salary. It's more than I shall get as foreman. I don't see how you can be worth that. It sounds fishy to me."

"I know," she said, deciding it would be more tactful to agree with him. It would be rather awkward, earning more than he did. "It probably won't last long. Luckily I know I've always got you to fall back on. I wouldn't risk it otherwise."

"That's right," he assented, brightening a little. "But how's Uncle going to take it?"

"I don't know. I'm afraid he may be against it."

"Well, don't you stand his nonsense. Would you like me to speak to him?"

"No, thanks!" said Marjorie hastily. "I think I can manage him alone."

Uncle Samuel, in fact, proved to be very much against it.

"It's preposterous," he said at once. "What do we know about this man? He might be a white-slave trader."

"Don't be absurd, Uncle," replied Marjorie heatedly.

"Kindly remember I'm your legal guardian, and a good deal older and more experienced than you are," said Samuel Burton. "I am *in loco parentis*. I feel that this is a most undesirable job, and I think I should forbid you to take it."

"But, Uncle, you told me only yesterday that I ought to get a better-paid job. Here's one more than three times what I'm getting now."

Samuel Burton paused. He found it difficult to dismiss summarily a job with five guineas a week attached to it. Money was money, wherever it came from.

"It's absurd," he said at last. "You can't possibly be worth that. I shan't give you the permission unless Crispin comes here and tells me frankly the whole story, and why he offers such a ridiculous salary. There must be something behind it."

"But you can't expect him to do that," replied Marjorie indignantly. "No employer would."

"Then he won't become your employer, that's flat," answered Uncle Samuel with great self-satisfaction. "I have my duty to your poor mother. That comes before everything."

Almost crying with irritation, Marjorie went round to explain the situation to Miss Crispin. To her surprise she found the woman understanding and sympathetic.

"Of course, it's no use asking Michael to go round," she said. "He wouldn't dream of doing so, and if he did, he'd only be rude. But I'll go round myself and see your uncle."

"Uncle can be very difficult," Marjorie warned her.

"I'm used to managing difficult people," replied Miss Crispin, with an expression which gave a momentary touch of hardness to her kindly face.

Miss Crispin called next evening and spent an hour in conversation with her uncle. What took place at the interview she never knew, but when she went in, her uncle was looking sulky. Miss Crispin was sitting opposite him with a quiet smile. He nodded in her direction.

"Well, I've been persuaded to let you give this job a trial," he said ungraciously, "but I must say my feeling is against it. You're only a young girl, and it's a responsible position. You still want to take it, knowing my feelings?"

"Yes, of course," said Marjorie decidedly, receiving a reassuring nod from Miss Crispin.

"Very well, then. You can go. I wash my hands of it."

A week afterwards Marjorie left for Belmont Avenue; and a new life began for her.

CHAPTER II

Voices of the Dead

Marjorie arrived in the evening at Belmont Avenue with her belongings. She had dinner with Miss Crispin, a quiet meal during which they said little. Crispin was not there. After the meal, Miss Crispin rose. "I expect you will want to go to your room and unpack," she said. "When you have finished, you can either sit in your room, or come down to me in the sitting room, whichever you prefer. Remember, you are one of the family now! Please be ready with your notebook and pencil tomorrow morning. We shall be starting some important work."

Marjorie spent the evening in her room, slept soundly, and got up next morning with a feeling of expectancy. She had no forethought of the emotional confusion the day would bring.

"At last," she thought, "I shall know what my job is."

She dressed herself carefully in a simple dress she had brought for work. After making sure that she looked sufficiently businesslike, she went downstairs and, as arranged with Miss Crispin at breakfast, went with her into the room in which she had first interviewed her employer. The time arranged had been eleven o'clock. If her working day always began as late as this, she was not likely to be overworked!

She was surprised to find that there were several other people in the room and that the lights were dimmed. As the thick curtains were still drawn across, it was half dark in the room and she could hardly make out the other occupants. There were four of them, two men and two women, and they looked at her with curiosity as she came in. Miss Crispin introduced her to them briefly.

"This is our new assistant, Miss Easton."

Marjorie sat down, at Miss Crispin's request, at the ebony desk. She had an inexplicable feeling of suspicion and unrest.

There was definitely a strange atmosphere in the room. Why was Crispin not there, and who were these visitors? It was absurd to be uneasy, and yet Marjorie wished for a moment that she had made more enquiry before she took the job. What was it all about? Why were the lights dimmed? Why was there something conspiratorial in the way everyone sat round and *waited?*

However, after she had looked at the visitors more closely, she felt easier. Two of them, at least, were reassuring. One was a man whom she judged to be a professional man—probably a lawyer. He was dressed in a well-cut black coat and striped trousers, and wore a flower in his buttonhole. He was silver haired, but could not be old, for his face was still pink and firm. His grey eyes rested on hers with a curious, almost ironical twinkle, which reassured her, although he did not say anything. Beside her sat a middle-aged woman, with a wrinkled, jovial face, like a russet pippin, who was engrossed in knitting an enormous coloured scarf as Marjorie came in. As soon as Marjorie had been introduced, she gave her a nod and a smile and then started knitting again.

Miss Crispin walked over to the girl and laid a reassuring hand on her shoulder.

"You are going to see many strange things this morning, Miss Easton," she said, "things that may seem to you odd and even unpleasant. But you must try to regard them in a cold-blooded, scientific manner—simply as experiments. I want you to note down all that takes place here this morning—particularly all that my brother says. Take it verbatim if possible, but I warn you he sometimes speaks rather fast. You must also note down any actions or events that seem to you important. Don't try to interpret them; simply put them down as they *seem* to you to happen. You will find it difficult at first, no doubt. Perhaps I ought to have prepared you; but frankly it seemed to both of us better to let you begin without any prejudices."

Marjorie was more puzzled than ever by these remarks. She could only nod and open her book, her pencil poised ready. Then Miss Crispin moved silently to the wall and clicked a switch.

The already dim lights went completely out. The room was lit only by a single red lamp placed over the heavy silver-embroidered curtain which shut off a corner of the room.

A dead silence followed this action. No one spoke or moved. After a few minutes, however, of what seemed an endless silence, one or two of the visitors started to move and cough. They seemed to be settling down for a long wait. The middle-aged lady, who had stopped knitting directly the lights went out, resumed it again, holding the work close to her face in order to see in the dim red light. The click of the needles sounded strangely loud in the darkened room. The red light suggested photography to Marjorie, and she wondered if they were about to witness a television experiment.

Just when the silence and the waiting had become oppressive, it was broken by a sudden cry, an almost bestial groan, as if from someone in pain. She jumped to her feet, frightened, but Miss Crispin moved instantly to her side and placed a hand on her shoulder. "All right, Miss Easton. Don't be alarmed." The words and the calmness of the visitors reassured her. Whatever was the cause of the cry, it was not unexpected by them. The groans suddenly rose to short, staccato screams, and were mingled with a hoarse, sobbing breathing. Marjorie felt the hair rise on her skin. The sounds were surely not human, and yet they were not animal; they seemed *subhuman*. There was an angry, muffled quality about them. Just when they seemed unbearable they stopped abruptly, and were followed by a curious gabbling noise. By now she had realised that whatever the sounds were, they were coming from behind the curtain.

"She's coming quickly today," said a man near her—a melancholy middle-aged man with horn-rimmed spectacles and a black moustache. He spoke as if everything was happening according to plan. Maybe, thought Marjorie, this was some kind of test of her psychology. Perhaps it was a gramophone record. She suppressed her growing doubts with an effort and opened her book again. She ought to do her job. She made a note of the time, of the groans, and of the remark of the man in the horn-rimmed spectacles.

The noises stopped. Miss Crispin got suddenly to her feet and walked over to the silver-embroidered curtain. She paused in front of it a moment, listening, and then drew it back.

Marjorie was astounded to see the bound figure of a man

seated on a chair. The head was bowed forward, and the white cloth bandages were passed round legs, arms and waist so as to tie him firmly to the chair. A white cloth was over his head.

As Marjorie watched, the man gave a jerk, a kind of convulsive twitch, and his head rolled back. The cloth was shaken off part of his face and she realised that it was Crispin. His expression was completely changed. The face, coloured by the red rays of the light, had not only become more shapeless, but had also softened. It looked oddly feminine, like the face of an old woman. The cloth which had slipped back from his face but still covered his hair, like an old woman's cap, helped the illusion. Marjorie was struck by his eyes, which did not seem the eyes of the same person. They were focussed on a point in mid-air, about two feet away from him and five feet from the ground—yet there was nothing there. The eyes were absolutely devoid of expression, as cold and staring as fishes' eyes.

And now she realised what was happening, and cursed her stupidity for not understanding earlier. This was merely a spiritualist's séance and Crispin was a medium. At first the normal person's instinctive aversion for the abnormal made her in half a mind to walk out. But her sense of curiosity had been roused, and she stayed where she was, and presently her aversion evaporated. She had no prejudice against spiritualism as such. After all, there might be something in it, and she had known people who believed in it and told her that it was a thing in which a good many scientists were interested. In that sense, perhaps, it could be described as a form of scientific research, and the Crispins had not exactly deceived her. They had told her it was a form of research about which little was known, and for that reason they had not required any experience from her.

Crispin was evidently a wealthy man. This was a hobby and there could therefore be no question of trickery or exploiting the credulity of others. The kind of people who were here—the silver-haired man and the woman with the knitting—was a proof of that. She was there as an employee—and a well-paid one at that. Remembering this, she turned over a page in her book and made a further note. Her feelings of suspicion had given place to interest. Was it after all possible that something real and tangible, some outside influence, was producing the extraordinary changes she could see in Crispin? His drooling babble had given place to a clear articulation. This startled her. For there could not be the least doubt that it was a woman's voice issuing from Crispin's lax red lips, which hardly seemed to move as the words streamed through them, clearly and precisely shaped. With this thin feminine voice, Crispin's coarse, yellowish features became even more feminine in looks. It was almost as if a woman had taken Crispin's place and, dressed in man's clothes, now sat in the chair.

As soon as the words became distinct, she started to make a note of them. The speed at which Crispin was speaking made it necessary to give her whole mind to the job, and she was afraid that, in the dim light, the outlines of her shorthand were bad. Seeing her difficulty, Miss Crispin came up to the desk and pressed a switch. It operated a concealed light in the desk which illumined her notebook while leaving the rest of the room in darkness. She concentrated her attention on the Voice—for she thought of it already as a disembodied voice—so detached did it seem from Crispin's ordinary personality.

The Voice said a dozen words, and then the man in horn-rimmed glasses near her jumped to his feet. "Laura," he said urgently, but as simply as if he were speaking to someone in front of him, "I'm here. How are you, darling?"

The Voice began an account of her state. It was a description of another world given just as quietly as one would describe a journey to the seaside. The man took off his horn-rimmed glasses and wiped them. He was crying.

The scene affected Marjorie in an indescribable way. It was chiefly the strange unreality of it—Crispin lying back inert with collapsed features, while the voice, so utterly different from his, streamed from his lips; the man standing up and talking, gazing not at Crispin, but into empty air; the cold red light ... The very unreality somehow made it convincing.

"Don't be sad," cried the Voice. "I am happy. All is well here. One day you will join me. And now I have with me another friend from the other side. She has not been here before, but today a relation of hers is here. She says she was known on earth as Constance."

Marjorie stopped writing. It was impossible, horrible even. Her mother's Christian name was Constance. Of course it was a mere coincidence. For a second the memory of her mother as she had been in her last long illness, always patient and smiling, flashed through Marjorie's mind.

Then happened the thing that was to send a thrill down Marjorie's spine. The Voice changed. It remained feminine, and yet deepened and became hoarser. Her mother's voice had been deep. There was an uncanny resemblance between her mother's voice and the new Voice—even down to the faint touch of Irish brogue. It was horrifying. As if her dead mother was trying to speak with someone else's vocal organs ... It was disturbing, dreadful—and yet Marjorie listened absolutely spellbound. Unlike the other Voice, this one spoke in snatches, as if interrupted:

"I know you are here. Madge ... little Madge ... At last I am able to speak ... Do not be afraid ... We shall meet again over the other side ... It is happier here, far happier ... Imagine ... Now I understand everything ... All that seemed dark and evil is explained ..."

Marjorie felt her cheeks flush. It seemed agonisingly painful —this voice from the past—in public. They were all watching her ... Surely there was a trick; and yet it seemed impossible, unimaginable that another voice could speak and yet conjure up such intimate memories of her mother.

For the Voice spoke with a hesitating stammer on the longer words, which Marjorie always remembered as characteristic of her mother, particularly at moments of emotion or nervousness. She stared at the shapeless waxen mask of Crispin's face and gave a little cry.

"How can I know it's you?" she cried.

"It's difficult ... believe ... know ... Marjorie ..." The Voice seemed to be fading away. "You must try to believe. Faith ... mountains ... It is not easy for us ... a kind of barrier ... a dreadful effort ..."

The Voice stopped. Crispin started to move and then gave a groan and muttered a few words. They were in his normal voice. The contrast to the Voice was so disturbing that in that moment it did seem to Marjorie that her mother had really been speaking, but now she was slipping away from her, past the difficult barrier that those from the "other side" must pierce to reach the world of clay.

"Can't you give me some proof?" she said desperately. The words were said in such a low tone that they could hardly be heard by anyone else in the room.

Crispin became motionless again. Then, with a queer reverberating quality, as if speaking from infinitely far away, the Voice sounded again. It had a muffled, strangled tone, as though someone were trying to speak through a gag or veil.

"Marjorie ... when I was dying ... the ring ... No one saw." There was another pause, and then, as if with a final terrific effort, "In the blue envelope ... the bottom of your trunk ... your case now." Marjorie had to move forward to catch the last few words. But it was enough. It was proof—final, conclusive proof. Marjorie remembered vividly how, only an hour before her death, her mother had made a sign to her and lifted one hand. Marjorie had caught it in hers, and she had shuffled off the wedding ring that was then so loose on her emaciated fingers.

"For you, dear," her mother had sighed. "We were so happy..."

Marjorie had never been able to tell anyone about that incident, so intimate and sacred it had seemed. Ever since then, the ring, with a photograph of her mother, had been her most treasured possession. At Bilford they had lain, tucked in a blue envelope, in a corner of her trunk, and then, on her move to Kensington, she had put them in her case.

From that moment Marjorie no longer doubted. She knew. Impossible, incredible as it seemed that her mother could be able to speak to her from beyond, she now knew it to be a fact. Yet this violent upsetting of all her ideas left her with a strange, confused feeling. She believed with one half of her mind—the other half ignored it.

Crispin began to moan in his normal voice again. The sitters began to talk among themselves in whispers. Presently Crispin opened his eyes. She looked at him curiously. It seemed impossible that he could not have shared, in some manner more intimate than hers, in this conversation of her mother's. Her mother's spirit had used his lips to speak.

But Marjorie soon saw that Crispin's mind was blank of recollection. He looked tired and bored, and there were beads of sweat on his forehead, as if he had been engaged in violent physical exertion. His eyes had returned to their normal brightness and life, and with the return, his face seemed to lose its shapeless sexlessness, and no longer appeared repulsive.

The man with the silver hair and pink face, who had caught her attention when she first came in, went up to Crispin and undid his bandages. He stretched himself slowly.

"I feel very tired," Crispin said. "Has anything interesting happened?"

"I feel we have perhaps had something evidential," said the man in horn-rimmed glasses, turning his eyes on Marjorie. "There was a message for our new young friend here."

"Well, I didn't get a message," interrupted the middle-aged woman, putting down her knitting with a sigh. "Others can believe what they like, but I shan't be convinced until *I* get a message for myself. . . .

"Please don't be offended, dear," she added with a smile at Marjorie. "I saw that something came to you that was very precious."

Marjorie tried to bring herself back to reality. She looked down at her empty notebook.

"I'm sorry," she said with an effort, "but I forgot to take notes towards the end."

Miss Crispin went up to her and patted her on the shoulder.

"Of course you did. I am sure it was upsetting for you. Our first experience in these things always is. I expect you'd like to go away and think this over. We can carry on without you."

Marjorie accepted gratefully. "That's kind of you. Yes, I don't somehow feel like going on with this for the moment."

Marjorie walked upstairs and went straight to her case. She took out her mother's ring and photograph. . . .

Meanwhile, the man she had placed as a professional man, and who was in fact a doctor, went up to Crispin and felt his pulse.

"Well, Doctor Wood," said Crispin with a smile, "have you seen anything this evening you regard as convincing?"

"It's not my place to be convinced," replied Dr Wood quietly. "Only to observe. I'm afraid we scientists have a rather different conception of evidence than yours in any case."

"But, Doctor!" exclaimed the man in horn-rimmed spectacles. "I know absolutely and positively that my wife speaks to me."

"I'm not denying it," said Dr Wood good-humouredly. "After all, you are in a better position to judge of that than I am." He took out a stethoscope, loosed Crispin's coat, and applied the instrument to his chest. Then he took out a notebook and made a few entries.

"It's interesting the effect this trance has on you physically, Crispin," he said, as he wrote. "Your pulse drops and gets fluttery, your rate of breathing slows, and your blood pressure is low for about half an hour afterwards. Even your temperature is half a degree below normal. Do you feel depressed?"

"Not so much depressed as generally fagged and listless," answered Crispin, greedily drinking the glass of water his sister had brought him. "And I always feel terribly thirsty afterwards, as if I had been in a fever.

"I suppose," added Crispin ironically, "you're a little disappointed to find there's anything real about my trance—even if it's only a few physical symptoms. I believe you're still hoping to find a nigger in the woodpile, Doctor."

"No, I give you credit for absolute sincerity, Crispin," said Wood seriously.

"Meaning that I'm self-deluded?" pressed Crispin sharply.

The doctor gave an enigmatic smile. "We know so little about the dissociation of personalities that I should prefer not to use either the term 'self' or 'delusion.' I prefer to keep to matters of objective behaviour, which can be observed and photographed." He looked at his watch. "Well, I must get back. Thanks for a very interesting morning, Crispin!"

"I like that man," said the middle-aged woman with the knitting, after he had gone out, to the company at large. "At any rate he doesn't come here *expecting* to be convinced." She looked significantly at the man in horn-rimmed glasses who stared at her sulkily.

"If you are referring to me, I was quite as sceptical as he was once. Besides, these scientists are all the same—except for Lodge. Even if they were convinced, they wouldn't admit it."

Crispin smiled coldly, and went to the wall to switch on the lights.

"Wood is a great deal nearer making admissions than you suppose," he remarked thoughtfully. Then he turned to an ugly, grey-haired woman with a red nose, who had waited expectantly throughout the séance, but had received no message.

"I'm sorry nothing came through for you from your husband."

"It's all right, Mr Crispin," said this woman resignedly. "Albert was just the same when he was alive. You could never rely on him. And I suppose we can't really expect people to change their characters in the other life."

They got up to go.

"There will be a full séance in the big room on Monday," announced Miss Crispin at the door as she showed them out. "We are hoping the whole Immortality Circle will attend. Bring your friends if you can, even if they are sceptics. You see, we welcome sceptics, for we know that if they are honest, they will not remain sceptics long."

The middle-aged woman with the knitting twinkled at Crispin as she said good-bye. "I must say for you, dear, you're the first honest one I've met. And, goodness knows, I've met hundreds. I don't know why I go on. But there it is—something tells me there's something in it. I'm blest if I don't believe you'll convince me yet. Mind you, I think it's a pack of nonsense all the same!"

Marjorie, upstairs in her room, had taken out the blue envelope with her mother's photograph. She stared at it thoughtfully. The gentle, sensitive face seemed strangely living now. After all, if a mere copy could seem so vital, why might not the soul itself live on and be able to speak to her through the body of another? A queer sensation of mingled gladness and sadness made the tears start to Marjorie's eyes, even while she smiled at the portrait. Then she kissed it quickly and put it away.

A strange fate had led her to this house. Whatever happened she was determined to follow this strange path to the end. It was her duty to her mother and herself.

2

From that day a new existence began for Marjorie. Gradually Crispin's amazing personality began to fill her whole life. She realised now why it was that his sister had spoken of him always in such reverent tones. There was no doubt that he was entirely, and in every way, different from the ordinary run of men she had met. None of the things that interested them seemed to have any meaning for him. His whole life was centered round the next world, that strange shadowy abode with which he believed—as simply as a scientist believes in the operation of the force of gravity—that it was possible for human beings to get into touch.

Beside his faith, and that of his sister—and hers was of a simpler, and therefore for Marjorie more understandable quality—such of her doubts as still lingered imperceptibly melted away. So real was the spirit world to these two that, even at table or in casual conversation, their looks showed that to them the room was filled with spirit presences groping, as through a veil, for contact with earthly things.

It was no question of secondhand evidence. Marjorie had had firsthand proof at that amazing séance. Since then Marjorie's mother had spoken again and again, and with each appearance there had been fresh evidence, old childish memories, intricate details of family history—a thousand questions, answered without hesitation, and in a way that dissolved all doubt from Marjorie's mind.

Crispin was primarily a trance medium with a voice "control", but he was able occasionally to produce materialisations. In one of these materialisations Marjorie had clearly seen an image which, as in a cloud of smoke, dimly reproduced the remembered appearance of her mother. The strangest and most indisputable evidence of the reality of the experiences Marjorie was undergoing was a photograph which was taken of Marjorie at a séance, under control conditions. When developed, the photograph quite clearly revealed a spirit "extra." The extra was her mother—dim, transparent, blurred, but unmistakably her mother—of this there could be no possible doubt.

As the weeks passed, she discovered that Crispin was well known in the spiritualistic world but that he had always been isolated from it.

"Quite frankly, Miss Easton, fifty per cent at least of the better known mediums are simply tricksters," he said to her once. "It is inevitable, I suppose, as long as science maintains its obscurantist attitude to psychical research. It is the official scientific attitude which makes the most important task of the human mind the quack's happy hunting ground. Science has only itself to blame. All the same, we serious investigators have got to recognise the situation. Because of it I steer clear of the current body of organised spiritualism. It is the only way I can be sure of keeping my activities absolutely above suspicion. For the sake of the people I serve, I must do that."

None the less, Crispin was the centre of a band of loyal adherents. These ranged from sceptics to enthusiastic believers, and also included some of the people in the "convinced against their will" class. Marjorie had not seen again the doctor who had attended her first séance, but she enquired after him curiously, and Crispin told her his story. He was a doctor with a fashionable practice as a psychiatrist.

"And a very brilliant one," admitted Crispin. "His facility for reading other people's minds is uncanny. Half Mayfair goes to him for its spiritual troubles. And he probably clears up more awkward emotional tangles than any other man in Great Britain. I've a great admiration for him as a man, although he clings desperately to the materialistic scepticism of science. If I were in serious difficulties, there is no man in England I'd go to sooner."

"He's sufficiently honest, at any rate, to admit he does not understand the phenomena you produce, Michael," said his sister.

"Yes, and it fascinates him more than he likes to admit. He's got a passion for psychological mysteries, and he feels I am a challenge to him. I shouldn't imagine he's often baffled in his ordinary work. He understands human beings better than I do, I admit. I've often told him that if he were a detective, there would be no unsolved murder mysteries."

"He looked a little wistful when you said that," interrupted

Miss Crispin, smiling. "I've a feeling he'd rather like an opportunity of trying his skill on that kind of problem, instead of the fussy little neuroses of his society patients."

The woman with the knitting was another interesting member of the circle. She always turned up at séances, and Marjorie was unable to make out whether her attitude of amused scepticism was real or acted. Once or twice Marjorie had noticed that, even when she appeared to be busy with her eternal knitting, she was, beneath its cover, paying a close attention to what was going on. Marjorie had tried to draw her out, but had soon found that Mrs Threpfall was no fool and had, in fact, enough worldly wisdom for two. As the weeks went by, they struck up a friendship, and Marjorie realised that behind Mrs Threpfall's air of indifference was a warm and perhaps lonely heart. For though Mrs Threpfall often spoke jokingly about her husband, dead now for twenty years, it was obvious that life had never been the same for her since his death. She had no children.

Most of the other enthusiasts were of a different kind. Some of them were, as she could see quite plainly, almost on the borderline of insanity. Some of them seemed almost over the borderline. After an emotional and evidential séance, one or two would be in a state where they were unable to control their thoughts, and spoke loosely and disjointedly. At first this had worried her, for it seemed to her to throw doubt on the value of her work, but Crispin, with his calm, logical mind, had been able to show her that it was inevitable.

"New truths are rarely perceived by the normal person. Genius is always unusual—that is generally admitted. Eccentricity and the abnormal are the characteristics of all pioneers of thought. The normal mind is rooted in normal happenings. When one has had a great shock of some kind, one's mind is turned from normal happenings to those happenings in which we, as spiritualists, are concerned. But the very shock which produces a turning away from material things may have other effects."

"Why is it," asked Marjorie, "that so many mediums have weak characters? You have often mentioned it, but it seems to me the spirits would be repelled by this kind of people."

"A character of this kind is the easiest medium for spirit conversation. Just because it is not firmly attached to ordinary events and is loose and weak, it is easier for those from the other side to use it. None the less, it is a poor instrument. We shall never have perfect intercourse with the world beyond, until ordinary, normal people of strong character are able to adapt themselves to the new vision. Weak people are easy mediums, but they are not good mediums."

This conversation explained to Marjorie why Crispin, with his powerful, dominating personality and keen intellect, made such a good medium. He stood out in contrast to his followers who were enthusiastic believers and yet, seemed abnormal and even silly. Just because, in spite of his intelligence, he had been able to grasp the new vision, he obtained results so convincing and wonderful as those Marjorie had seen. It seemed right to Marjorie that her mother, who had been so fastidious in her personal relationships, should use for communication Crispin's own acute and powerful personality, instead of some of the scattered and pretentious characters she had met in the movement.

Marjorie soon began to realise that she was becoming strongly influenced by Crispin. She was accustomed to being frank with herself; and she had to admit that no man had ever previously influenced her in the way Crispin was affecting her. She had been friendly with men—there was her love for Ted—but in all those cases, even her relationship with Ted, she had been, as it were, on equal terms with the man; it had been a give-and-take arrangement. She realised that her relationship with Crispin from the start had been entirely different. He was superior to her in intelligence and force of personality; it seemed to her that he gave her everything, and she could give nothing in return except her admiration. Even this was so much the natural thing—his sister, other members of the household and his disciples all seemed to have the same attitude towards him—that a simple admiration appeared to Marjorie a matter of course. Crispin did not ask for it. On the contrary he was inclined to brush it impatiently aside, if he noticed it at all.

Marjorie asked herself whether she was being fair to Ted in devoting herself so wholeheartedly to Crispin. But she was able to answer this query with a clear conscience. Her relations with

Crispin were entirely impersonal. Apart from the fact that he was so much older than herself, it was a curious fact that she never seemed to think of Crispin as a man, but only as a personality. It was, in fact, difficult to imagine any woman falling in love with him. His whole attitude towards life isolated him from any such emotion. Even his appearance—the shapeless yellow face and large magnetic eyes—seemed to express this reserve and isolation. He never seemed interested in feelings or emotions. There was an impersonal, reserved tinge in everything he did or said. It was just because of this, because there was no element of the normal relation between man and woman in their friendship, that Crispin's influence over Marjorie was the more powerful and one-sided.

At the same time she realised that she would have difficulty in explaining this to Ted. From the very start he had been resentful of her regard for Crispin. He cross-examined her frequently about the man and the household, and it was obvious that he had distrusted the whole business from the start, before he knew anything about it. She soon decided that the wisest course to take was to say as little as possible, and merely confess that the job interested her very much, and that Crispin was a considerate employer.

Ted, however, was not content to let it rest at that. He had a violent prejudice against spiritualism, although on his own admission he knew nothing about it.

"And I don't want to, either," he would add defiantly, after an argument about it. "As if it's any good mucking about with that kind of rubbish! You must be crazy to think there is anything in it."

This did not prevent his attacking it in their conversations. Although at first she had intended not to be drawn into an argument, she naturally drifted into defending it, and long and aimless wrangles used to follow.

Another thing that had made Ted suspicious was her salary, which was more than he was earning. He said once that she could not possibly be worth it, and that "there must be something behind it." Marjorie, somewhat irritated, had replied curtly that this was the real cause of his attitude—she was earning more than he was, and it was just jealousy on his part. The remark had a sting, and she saw that she had hurt Ted. She regretted it directly she said it.

Before the evening was over, they had made up the quarrel and determined never to discuss the subject again. It was impossible to keep such a resolution. Again and again, in her evenings off with Ted, the conversation came round to the same perilous subjects of Crispin and spiritualism, and always it left behind a faint flavour of bitterness and wounded feeling. What made it worse was that sometimes Crispin, who worked at all hours of the day, would suddenly decide to work on the very evening she had promised to meet Ted. She would be unable to turn up, and sometimes could not even get a message to him. Of course this made Ted dislike her job and Crispin even more, and there were times when she felt that something hard was creeping into their relations. It affected her attitude towards Ted. It was so difficult sometimes when with Ted not to compare his limited interests and simple mind with Crispin's subtle and intelligent personality, so different from anything she had ever encountered before.

3

Presently matters got worse between Ted and herself. It dated from the discovery by Crispin of her mediumistic powers. Crispin had let slip in conversation that the Renée de Varennes, whose resemblance to her had brought about their first meeting, had been a young French girl medium who had revealed remarkable powers. Unfortunately she had been killed in a car accident at an early age, six months after her gifts had been discovered; and so she had passed to another sphere before evidential use could be made of her unquestioned ability. This conversation led Marjorie to ask whether Crispin thought she herself had any psychic gifts. Crispin said he believed she had and for the first time asked her whether she would like to try her powers.

There followed a period which had a lasting effect on Marjorie's life. Crispin explained that psychic powers could rarely be developed unaided. He had invented a special technique to achieve that suspension of the medium's individuality which would enable other disembodied personalities to use the body of the medium for self-expression. Crispin explained this to her carefully. He wanted to be sure, he said, that she understood what the step she was taking entailed.

The first stage was to produce the trance state. Marjorie was unable to go into a trance naturally, and therefore she had to be hypnotised. Crispin explained to her that hypnotism was completely misunderstood by most people. It was not that if one had a sufficiently powerful mind one could overawe someone with a weak mind. On the contrary, he remarked, it was impossible to hypnotise mental defectives. The will power of the hypnotist did not enter into it.

"You really hypnotise yourself," he explained. "The hypnotist only helps you to do so. It is you who concentrate on falling asleep. It is impossible to make a person who is hypnotised do something which, were he awake, would be contrary to his moral sense, whatever the general opinion may be. It is possible to make a subject do ridiculous things but not crimes. Of course this is not a discovery of us spiritualists. It is a part of ordinary psychological science."

The first few hypnotic trances into which Marjorie was put— at séances where three or four of Crispin's followers were present —were without result. Marjorie was disappointed. But, after a time, they began to get results.

Marjorie knew nothing of them. When she woke from her trances she had only a confused memory of what had happened, like that of a dream we cannot recall. Sometimes she was extremely tired. At other times she was refreshed and happy after each trance.

These results at first took the form of simple voice productions and automatic writing. Some of the messages were remarkably evidential; and as the evidence accumulated, Marjorie began to have an enthusiastic following among the Crispin circle.

Dr Wood had for the moment given up coming to the séances, owing to pressure of business, and so he did not see Marjorie's emergence as a medium. Marjorie was disappointed at this, for she had been impressed by the man in their brief meeting. She knew that some words of belief from him would be worth all the enthusiasm of the followers of Crispin. But Miss Crispin declared that nothing would make him give those words of belief. He would always be sceptical. It puzzled Marjorie how anyone could remain obstinately sceptical in the face of all the evidence Crispin was able to produce.

Mrs Threpfall watched Marjorie's rise to fame as a medium with ironic amusement. It was plain from some words she let drop that she had doubts about the genuineness of the phenomena. She had the tact to avoid suggesting that there was any insincerity in Marjorie's efforts.

"But you mustn't suppose these things are as simple as they seem," she added, pursing her lips up over her brightly coloured knitting wools.

"Well, what do you mean?" Marjorie would ask a little sharply. "Surely our beliefs are simple and well founded enough."

"You'll soon understand what I mean, if I'm right," Mrs Threpfall answered, with an enigmatic look. "And if I'm wrong, what does it matter? There, dear," she added, seeing she had upset Marjorie, "I don't want to talk like an old fogy. Why shouldn't youth have its beliefs? It's the time for them!"

This was not encouraging. It was not surprising, therefore, that a certain coldness crept up between Marjorie and Mrs Threpfall. This plunged her still more into intimacy with the Crispins. Any formality in their relations had long ago vanished, and she was not an employee but a member of the household on equal terms with them. Indeed she had never been more friendly with a woman than she became with Miss Crispin. She confided in her and told her the whole story of her early life and her unhappiness with Samuel Burton.

"I can believe you," agreed Miss Crispin. "I thought Mr Burton was a most objectionable man the moment I spoke to him. I wonder you put up with him for so long."

With Crispin her relations were of course always more formal, for Crispin maintained a certain formality with everyone—even his sister. He never seemed to unbend, to become human, to demand pity or affection. Marjorie came to realise that this coldness and reserve were the price of his unique personality, and of his absorbing interest in the activity to which his life and fortune were devoted. It was as much an essential part of him as the more attractive traits in his character.

As her tuition in the art of mediumship progressed, they began to get still more remarkable results at her séances. The phenomena included spirit "extras" on photographs, voices, rappings and several genuine materialisations. The strangest feature to Marjorie at first, although she afterwards became accustomed to it, was that all these events occurred outside her knowledge. She was the principal actor in them, and yet they all happened when her conscious activities were suspended, and she was deep in the world of trance.

This development in the quality of her productions gradually gave Marjorie a growing fame in the band of spiritualists in close touch with Crispin and his followers. She had found that the believers in spiritualism were divided among themselves into cliques and schools. The Crispin clique was fairly extensive, and was in touch with the best minds of the movement. Among these Marjorie was known under the name of "M", which Crispin had given her to spare her any undesirable publicity. "M" became one of the fashionable mediums. Perhaps her looks and transparent honesty gave her part of her cachet. Marjorie could not help becoming affected by this fame.

She found the development of her newly discovered powers coincided with a strange change in her mind. Before, she had been a fairly normal girl of her age and type. She had been sensitive and easily hurt by other people. She had been optimistic, looking forward cheerfully to the next day. She had always been interested in life, curious about other people, and liking to be among scenes of brightness and animation, among crowds or at shows.

Now this normal personality of hers underwent a gradual change. She began to become more isolated and withdrawn into herself. People no longer seemed so important; they became slightly unreal and, at the same time, lost the power to hurt her. The outside world ceased to be attractive and important: she now found she had ample resources within herself. She was often quite content, when there was no duty to be done, to sit for hours by herself, doing nothing except dreaming vaguely. It no longer seemed of immense importance what she should do tomorrow.

This change of mood seemed welcome to her, because it made her independent of others. She supposed that it was in some way a reward for the work she was doing. The change of mood was not permanent. At times it was disturbed by strange moods when she was easily upset, and a rough word would make her break into tears or, perhaps as easily, burst into uncontrollable laughter. At other times these disturbing moods were marked by intense and causeless depression. She had had a horrible experience in one of these moods. It seemed as though some alien and inexpressibly evil power were struggling to obtain possession of her soul. Her body started to tremble with dread and she could feel the hairs rising on her skin. After a short struggle and an incoherent prayer, the feeling had passed.

Crispin explained to her that this was a common experience in the early stages of mediumship. Elemental powers struggled to obtain possession of a developing personality. She need not be afraid. It would soon pass. Her "control" would see that no harm came to her. He explained in the same way the nightmares from which she sometimes suffered. She woke from these paralysed with fear, her forehead damp was sweat, but yet with no clear recollection of what had caused her fear in the dream.

At first she had tried to hide her mediumistic experiments from Ted. She had realised that he would be angry at her dabbling in what he regarded as dangerous trickery. But she had been forced to tell him the truth owing to an accident. Now that her trance abilities were fully developed, she was inclined to slip automatically into unconsciousness if she let her mind go blank. One evening she was sitting by the fire with Ted at his house, and neither had been speaking for some time. The next thing she knew she was lying on her back on the couch, her face streaming with water. Ted's face, pale with alarm, was bent over her.

"What is it, darling?" he asked anxiously. "Are you ill? You fainted."

"Oh, it's nothing, Ted," she said quietly, sitting up.

Ted saw that she was concealing something. Eventually, as he was insistent, she saw that she would have to tell him everything.

Ted was almost speechless with surprise when he heard her story.

"Good God, Marjorie!" he exclaimed. "Do you realise what you're doing? How could you be such a damned fool? What's happened to you? How could you have been taken in by that dirty old swindler? I'll tell him what I think of him."

This annoyed Marjorie, who was already on the defensive.

"Mr Crispin is a friend of mine, Ted," said Marjorie hotly. "And please realise that you are talking about something which is very precious to me!"

"But listen, Marjorie," said Ted urgently. "Don't get on the high horse. Just think what you're doing. Why, it's the kind of thing that makes people crazy."

Marjorie turned away impatiently.

"You're very narrow-minded, Ted. It's really useless arguing with you. I've explained everything again and again."

"But you can't go on with this business, Marjorie. It's affecting your health! You'll go nuts if you aren't careful!"

Marjorie smiled.

"You're being just silly, Ted. You don't understand it at all. I've got certain gifts and it's my duty to develop them."

Ted laughed sardonically.

"Oh, that's the stuff they've been handing out to you, is it? Well, I'm surprised a girl of your sense should be taken in by it."

Marjorie began to lose her temper.

"I'm surprised you should take up such an attitude. It's just pigheadedness. You've never even met Mr Crispin."

"No. I don't need to. I know enough to see that it's all a swindle, and I'll darn well see it's stopped now!"

"How do you know it's a swindle?"

"I just know, that's all," said Ted woodenly.

"If you'd seen what I've seen, you'd think differently. And if you'd met Mr Crispin, you'd be more sensible. He's certainly not a swindler."

"Well, I shall be seeing him soon," said Ted calmly.

"What do you mean?" asked Marjorie, alarmed by his tone.

"I'm going to call on him this evening and tell him that if he doesn't stop monkeying about with you, I'll push his bleeding face in."

Marjorie jumped up.

"Don't you dare, Ted. If you do, I'll never speak to you again!"

Ted looked at her sulkily.

"Here, you don't think I'm going to let you go on with this spiritualistic business, do you, after what happened today?"

Ted's obstinacy and cold, possessive tone raised Marjorie's mood of irritation to white heat. All the bitterness and wrangles of earlier conversations rose to the surface. She was fed up with Ted. He had to be taught a lesson. She took off her ring with a trembling hand.

"You haven't got the right to speak to me like that. It's just as well I found you out in time. I suppose you think I mustn't have any independent existence at all. Well, you'd better find some other girl who'll stand for that."

"Here, what does this mean?" asked Ted, absolutely astonished. He stared at the ring in his palm as if he couldn't believe it.

"It means that I don't want to see you again!" said Marjorie coldly. "And I mean it," she added, her voice sounding a little uncertain as she repeated the words.

She had expected Ted to apologise, or at any rate give her some loophole for softening the blow. Instead he stuck out his jaw defiantly and got up.

"All right, if you feel like that about it," he said sulkily, "you'd better have it that way. Let's be getting back now."

They rode back in the bus in silence. Marjorie waited for a moment at the gate silently, expecting some word of reconciliation from Ted. She had never seen him looking so determined and angry.

"Good-bye," she said, at last, uncertainly, holding out her hand. It seemed strange not to be exchanging a good-night kiss, and yet she was determined not to make the first move.

"Good-bye!" said Ted stiffly. As Marjorie went up the steps it seemed as if the last link with her old, humdrum life had broken. She was stepping completely into a new existence. It gave her at first a strange feeling of loneliness and depression, but presently, when she went into the lighted drawing room and Miss Crispin gave her a cordial greeting, the feeling passed. This was her real self—a life with a meaning and a purpose, which she had at last discovered.

"You're home early, dear," said Miss Crispin, glancing at the clock.

"Yes," answered Marjorie thoughtfully. She had a moment's impulse to confide in Miss Crispin and tell her of her quarrel with Ted, but it passed. "I had a rather unpleasant evening. Uncle was very sulky."

CHAPTER III

On the Borderline

Shortly afterwards, a series of events took place which left Marjorie puzzled and apprehensive. The first occurred when both Crispin and his sister were out. The servant came in to her, looking a little awkward, and said that there was a visitor who insisted on seeing Crispin.

"Have you told him both are out?" said Marjorie, surprised.

"Yes, miss, but still he won't go away," the girl answered. "He says he must see someone.

"He's such a funny gentleman," she added spontaneously. "I thought at first he was a bit drunk, but I think he's only queer."

"All right," said Marjorie, smiling, "I'll come down and see him."

She went downstairs into the waiting room. She was certainly surprised at the Crispins' visitor, used though she was to the many oddities who figured in the Crispin circle. He was a man dressed in seedy black clothes. He wore a bright green tie, and his long hair fell in mangy tufts on his greasy coat collar. When she went into the room, he was lifting up one of the pictures and gazing thoughtfully behind it. He let the picture drop back and turned round with a start when she came in. Then he stared at her for a moment, as if trying to recognise her. He shook his head slowly.

"No, you're not the one," he said mournfully. "I don't want you."

He dropped into one of the chairs and remained silent, his attention withdrawn. He seemed in a kind of reverie.

Marjorie attempted to bring the interview to a normal plane.

"I'm sorry, both Mr Crispin and his sister are out. Can I do anything for you?"

"Nothing," he said, still more mournfully, his head dropping forward on his chest as he stared at his boots. "Nothing can be done for me at all. I must work out my own salvation." He jerked his head up suddenly and gave her a cunning little smile.

"The old devil told you who I was, I expect."

"Told me who you were?" asked Marjorie, puzzled. "I don't quite understand."

"But of course he wouldn't have done that," went on the strange visitor impatiently, ignoring her answer. He cracked the joints of his fingers with one of the nervous gestures that were evidently characteristic of him. She felt awkward and uneasy. She had never met anyone so odd and erratic, and did not at all know how to deal with him.

"Well, what name shall I give Mr Crispin?" said Marjorie, getting up from her chair. "Perhaps you will be back again later?"

"Oh no!" cried the visitor, smiling queerly, and still sitting down. "You can't get rid of me so easily. I'm not hoodwinked as simply as that. Tell Mr Crispin it's no good sending one of his emissaries down with messages like that. I see through his little game! If he's a man he'll come and see me himself."

"I think there must be some misunderstanding," replied Marjorie awkwardly. "I've already told you that Mr Crispin is out. It would be better if you went and returned in two hours time, if you want to see him urgently."

She turned to go, but the visitor made a sudden movement towards her, which surprised her by its stealthiness. He caught her wrist between his fingers firmly, and she was surprised to feel the tensity of the grip, and that the fingers seemed to tremble with some suppressed emotion. He gave a cold, wavering smile.

"Oh, so you're the same, are you? Pretend to be polite until the moment comes, and then you show your teeth."

Marjorie snatched her hand away indignantly and immediately the man changed his manner.

"I beg your pardon," he said, running one hand through his hair. "I'm not in the best of health."

He sat down again and looked up at her shamefacedly, like a dog that is being rebuked. "I feel I've spoken in a way which was, so to speak, unbecoming. Excuse me. I'll wait here quietly until Mr Crispin comes back."

At this Marjorie left the room, with the visitor inside it. She did not like leaving him alone in the room, but she liked even less the idea of staying in the same room with him. She compromised by hanging round in the corridor outside. No noise came from within. Evidently the visitor was waiting quietly inside. After about half an hour, Crispin came in. She told him of his visitor's behaviour.

He looked puzzled by the account and asked for a description of the man. As she described him, she saw Crispin's face turn pale, and a look of alarm come into his eyes.

"I'll go and speak to him. Go down to Hawkins at once and tell him to come to me here immediately. Tell him Lambert's come here. *Lambert*—remember to tell him the name!"

Marjorie hurried downstairs to Hawkins, Crispin's chauffeur. He was a quiet fellow who had a sullen manner and spoke to the other servants as little as possible. He was, however, a favourite of Crispin's. She was surprised by the effect of the message on him. He was sitting in his room, in his shirt sleeves, when she came in and gave the message. He jumped up, rushed to the chest of drawers and took something out of it, and stuffed it into his hip pocket. Then, without another word to her, he went flying up the basement stairs. Marjorie followed him. As she reached the head of the stairs, she saw him fling open the door of the waiting room. Marjorie's heart missed a beat. The strange visitor was standing over Crispin with a raised hatchet in his hand. The visitor had his back to them.

It was a picture that burned into Marjorie's mind. A large red patch showed on Crispin's face, where he had evidently been struck. He was lying back panting against a chair, as if he had just been violently thrown into it. None the less, Crispin was staring into the visitor's face with a tense, concentrated expression.

Even when Hawkins flung open the door and came in, he did not move his gaze. It seemed to Marjorie, from where she was, that in some way this fixed, tense gaze of Crispin's was holding the stranger at bay, for he stood there like a dummy, with the hatchet poised in his hand, without striking. Marjorie, in the keen vision that comes in a moment of crisis, could see the veins standing out on the man's neck, as if he was beside himself with fury, and yet he did not move.

This was only the vision of a moment. For immediately Hawkins pulled his hand from his pocket and she now saw that it grasped a short black object, like a truncheon. He brought it down on the visitor's head, and it made no noise except a dull squashing sound, as though it were an orange striking a wall. The stranger fell with a thin groan, like a child crying out in fear. Crispin got to his feet and swayed unsteadily for a moment, endeavouring to smile. Then, to her astonishment, he turned as white as a sheet and fell into Hawkins' arms. He had fainted. Hawkins lowered him carefully into a chair, and turned to the unconscious stranger on the floor.

While Marjorie was attempting to revive Crispin, Hawkins was methodically binding the stranger's wrists and ankles.

After a short time Crispin opened his eyes, but was still not fully conscious of what was going on. Marjorie went out and fetched some water, but by the time she returned with it the colour was already coming back to his cheeks.

"I'd better ring for the police, hadn't I?" she said to Hawkins.

"No, don't do anything of the kind, Miss Easton," he replied, in a sharp tone she had never heard him use before. "You mind your own business. Mr Crispin will decide what to do."

Presently Crispin was able to get on his feet again. He stood for a moment, supported by Hawkins, looking down at the bound figure on the floor.

"Get the car out at once," he said to Hawkins. "You've tied him up safely?"

"Yes, safe as houses!" replied Hawkins. "He won't get out of that. Still, in case he does, you'd better take this," and he handed Crispin the black weapon with which he had stunned the stranger. Marjorie now saw that it was a short, rubber truncheon.

"Oughtn't we to ring up the police?" said Marjorie to Crispin, as soon as Hawkins had gone. "I suggested it to Hawkins, but he told me to mind my own business, rather rudely, I thought. It seemed to me the proper thing to do."

"Hawkins was a bit overwrought, Marjorie," replied Crispin. "You mustn't mind what he says. There's no need to telephone, however. We can take Lambert to the police station in the car. That will be quicker."

"I never guessed he was waiting to attack you," said Marjorie, as the full danger from which Crispin had escaped began to dawn on her. "How on earth did he get hold of that hatchet? I never saw it when I was in the room."

"He brought it in under his coat, I expect, and hid it in the room when he was shown in here and left alone. When I came in he took it from under a cushion."

Crispin seemed quite calm now. Only a slight pallor showed that he had just escaped from an attempt on his life. "He knocked me down before I had time to speak to him."

"But what on earth is the matter?" said Marjorie. "Is he mad?"

"I'm afraid so, poor fellow," answered Crispin, looking down at him pityingly. A faint twitch of the prostrate figure showed that he was returning to consciousness. "He used to be a great friend of mine. I helped him a good deal one way or another in his early days, and then he had a sudden shock due to the loss of his wife, and it took the form of paranoia or persecution mania. Sufferers from paranoia generally turn against their best friends; and for some reason poor Lambert imagined he had a grudge against me. They had to shut him up eventually, after he had attempted to throw acid over me, and I'm surprised they have let him out. The last I heard of him was that he was getting worse. I'm afraid we shall find that he escaped from the home. He certainly isn't fit to be out in his present state." Hawkins returned, and Crispin bent over the stranger. He groaned gently, but his eyes were still closed.

"I think you'd better go back to your room, Marjorie," said Crispin. "We'll be able to manage alone. I expect it's been rather a shock to you."

He touched her arm gently, and Marjorie went out. Her curiosity, and a still unsatisfied feeling of alarm, made Marjorie halt for a moment on the stairs.

She heard a sudden, frenzied shouting. She recognised in those animal, incoherent cries the voice of the stranger. He had come back to consciousness. Then she heard Hawkins curse fiercely, and there was a sudden cry of pain, followed by a whimpering noise. The whimpering, which was curiously childish, gave her a feeling of uneasiness. The whimpering was broken by another cry, and then there was silence. Presently a shuffling of feet told her that the man was being carried out to the car. She went to her room.

At dinner that night Crispin, still looking a little pale, told her that at the police station he had discovered that his guess was correct. Lambert had escaped from the asylum that morning, and had gone straight to Belmont Avenue.

"It's all settled now. And he's not likely to escape again. There's no need to be alarmed."

All the same, the incident left Marjorie with an uneasy sensation. The cry of pain and the whimpering stuck in her mind and, somehow, it gave her a feeling of pity for the man. She told herself that this was absurd, he was a lunatic, a homicidal one at that, and would not know what he was doing!

2

The incident with the strange visitor soon took a second place in Marjorie's mind, however, for she was faced with other problems. Ever since her quarrel with Ted she had been low spirited and quite unlike her usual self. Sometimes she had felt so miserable that she had sat down at her writing desk and begun a letter to Ted. Always she had thrown it away half finished. She knew that Ted would demand, whatever happened, that she give up what she was doing and return to an ordinary job.

Yet she had to confess that even spiritualism had lost its power to interest her. The séances had become monotonous. Even those she attended at which she was not a medium, and which before she had found enthrallingly interesting, had now become merely tedious. Yet she had seen amazing things—phosphorescent shapes had taken visible bodily form before her eyes; disembodied voices had gradually acquired an ectoplasmic face. She had felt the touch of spirit hands on hers.

What stopped her from writing to Ted was something inside her which seemed to rob her of her will power. It was as if she were quite unable to make a decision which would involve her leaving the Crispins. Oddly enough, just when her will power was weakest, at those moments she began to feel in some dim way resentful of the Crispins. As soon as she was in their presence, this hatred of them vanished. It was impossible not to be touched by Bella's kindness or Crispin's enthusiasm and intelligence.

This curious attitude culminated in an incident which made Marjorie go cold with horror when she recalled it. Indeed she preferred to think of it as something that had not really happened, and in some moods she could almost believe that it had not happened; it was a mere imagination.

She now often had exceptionally vivid and unpleasant dreams, and during one of these she felt she was being pursued by something dangerous and horrible. In her dream it seemed to her that she was awake in her room and now the growing horror appeared to fill the whole bedroom. She got up and wandered down what seemed interminable passages. They all appeared cold and wind swept, and as she moved, the horror came after her—became blacker and more menacing. As she fled from the terror her mind turned instinctively to Crispin. It seemed as if she could quite clearly see his door at the end of the corridor with a light under it. She stumbled along the corridor and flung open the door. Crispin was sitting in a chair by his desk, lost in thought. He did not see her, and even when she shouted he did not take any notice of her.

This filled her with a final pang of terror.

"I am dead," she thought, and she put her hands round his neck to shake him and force him to see her. As she did so his eyes met hers, and they seemed filled with scorn and contempt. A great indignation overtook her and, pressing together her hands, she attempted to strangle him. A terrific cry rang out in her ears seeming to come from nowhere, and at that moment everything in the dream dissolved. When she came to herself again, she found she was in Crispin's room, lying on the bed, with Crispin and Bella, both in their night things, attempting to revive her.

"What's happened?" asked Marjorie in alarm. A violent fit of shuddering passed over her. Bella stroked her forehead, and Crispin exchanged a significant glance with his sister.

"Nothing," he said. "You've been sleepwalking, that's all. You must have been overtired. You'd better go back to your room. Or better still—go back to Bella's."

Next day, when she had recovered from the shock of the event, Crispin told her gently what had really happened. He had awakened in the middle of the night to find Marjorie attempting to strangle him. His cry for help had awakened her. Then she had fainted.

This discovery terrified Marjorie. She had never walked in her sleep before. Crispin attempted to soothe her.

"You must realise you are not well. You've been putting too much strain on yourself. As a beginner, you do not yet realise the tremendous demands psychic activity makes on the bodily powers. You'd better get a tonic from the chemist; and stay in bed for a day or two."

"Do you think it's merely physical?" asked Marjorie thoughtfully. "You don't think my control has anything to do with it?"

"What spirits do you suppose would wish to harm you?" asked Crispin. "Nonsense! You have exhausted your nervous energy."

"Do you think I ought to see a doctor?" she asked.

Crispin smiled.

"My dear Marjorie, you know the attitude of the average G. P. to psychic matters by now. Can you imagine his competence to deal with such a problem? He simply wouldn't believe you were sane."

"Yes, it would be rather silly to consult a doctor," admitted Marjorie, "only I just wondered if there might be something wrong with me. I've a splitting headache this morning." She pressed her hand to her head. Her eyeballs were smarting like fire.

"Lean back and close your eyes." He passed a hand, with a slow, stroking movement, over her temples. His hand seemed uncannily cool, and as it passed over her forehead it smoothed out the pain and left her cool and refreshed. Marjorie felt slightly drowsy.

"There, you see," said Crispin smiling, "I'm a better healer than a doctor could be. Run along to bed now, Marjorie!"

Marjorie went, and for the next week she felt better. She noticed, however, that Crispin himself was curiously preoccupied and nervy. Something was on his mind. She had never seen him like this before, and it surprised her. Often she thought of asking Bella the reason, but Crispin's sister seemed touched with the same nervousness. When Crispin was late in returning, for any reason, she was unable to sit still, and roamed the house restlessly. Marjorie saw that they were both afraid of something or someone and wondered what it could be. Had Lambert escaped from the asylum again?

One afternoon she came into Crispin's study without knocking. He was absorbed in work and apparently didn't hear her until, as she passed just behind him, she accidentally upset a book which was on the edge of a table. The effect was electrifying. He leapt up out of his chair and, at the same time, put his hand into an open drawer on a writing desk. His face was quite white as he turned round.

When he saw it was she, his look changed to one of relief and he seemed a little awkward. He smiled nervously and put his hand back into the open drawer. She now saw that he had taken out a revolver. She expected Crispin to give an explanation of his alarm, but he said nothing, and his stiffness made it difficult for her to raise it herself. She acted as if the incident had been commonplace. None the less it showed her that her interpretation of his behaviour during the last few days had been correct. Crispin was desperately afraid of something.

A solution of some sort—so incredible that she could not accept it—suggested itself two days later. She was going past Crispin's door when she heard voices raised in anger. The door was not completely closed. She stopped and listened. She was not in the habit of eavesdropping, but somehow it seemed justified in this case. Her first reason for stopping was that it had occurred to her that the other angry voice was Lambert's. But immediately, to her amazement, she recognized the voice as that of her uncle, Samuel Burton!

This astounded her. So far as she knew, Samuel Burton had only met Bella, and that for a brief period. Yet, from the tone of the conversation, Crispin and her uncle might have been old acquaintances.

"I tell you what, Mike, you may be damned clever," her uncle was saying, "but you can't get away with this."

"My dear Samuel," said Crispin's clear voice, "your tone is

rather offensive. I'm not sure that I want to discuss it with you. We get on much better by letter."

"Yes, that's why I came round to see you. It's all very well being bold in a letter. You're apt to climb down a bit when we meet face to face. I've found that before and I expect I'll find it now."

Crispin's voice seemed strangely meek.

"Yes, Samuel. I don't pretend to be manly. I leave that to you. But I don't think anyone has ever accused me of not following a line of action to the logical conclusion. All your bluffs and bullying won't alter that."

"You're bluffing now. You wouldn't dare," said her uncle.

"Don't be childish, Sam." Crispin's voice seemed impatient.

"You'd run too great a risk. It's obvious."

"On the contrary. It's a wonderful opportunity to avoid risk. I'm in danger from one or two other quarters. This will clear it up."

"You artful devil. Well, what's your last word? You know the kind of man I am."

"My letter is quite final, Sam. I give you a week in which to decide!"

Marjorie heard a chair being pushed back, and she went back up the stairs. The conversation she had heard seemed absolutely without meaning. What on earth could be the risk Crispin was worrying about? What was it that had annoyed her uncle? What on earth was it they had in common? How long had they known each other, and why had she never been told that they knew each other?

Although she thought it over and over until her head reeled, she could see no solution. Somehow she could not ask Crispin. Apart from the fact that she would have to reveal that she had been eavesdropping, some deeper inhibition prevented her. It was as if she had guessed the truth, and yet did not wish to know it. It was as if, at the back of her mind, the suspicion was ripening that, beneath Crispin's genius, beneath his undoubted powers, there was a curious little kink. She had not lost faith in him exactly—his intelligence and his psychic powers could not be altered by any discovery that she might make. But perhaps somewhere in his character there was a taint. She did not wish to discover that taint. And was Bella, she wondered, mixed up in the mystery too? Could it possibly be that it was *her uncle* of whom they were both frightened?

Shortly afterwards she had another nightmare, but of an entirely different kind from any she had experienced before. She woke up in the middle of the night with a feeling of alarm. Her first intuition was that there was someone in the room with her. She strained her ears and then could distinctly hear something rustling like silk. As usual, she had her window open and her curtains drawn back, and the moonlight flooded the carpet with a large pool of light. Looking at this pool, she saw something move quickly across it. For a moment she thought she must be dreaming, but presently she realised that beyond all doubt she was awake, and that something *was* moving on the carpet. It was a large snake; and it was moving towards her.

She lay paralysed with horror while this Thing moved towards the bed. In a second it had reached the head of the bed, and it climbed up a leg with a swift, encircling movement. She shrank back against the wall on the far side of her bed and put out her arm to protect herself. With a sudden darting movement, the creature wound itself round her arm. As she felt its cold body against her flesh, she gave an uncontrollable scream. It seemed to tear its way out of her body and end in a long sobbing gurgle.

An age seemed to pass before Crispin and Bella came hurrying into her room and turned on the light. Their faces were white with alarm. Shaking with terror, she screamed at them to take the snake from her arm.

"What snake?" said Crispin, looking down curiously at her.

"A snake? Where?" asked Bella.

Marjorie realised that neither of them could see the snake. The next instant it uncoiled from her arm and seemed to vanish under the bed.

"Didn't you see it? Look, there!" she exclaimed, pointing to its tail as it slid under the bed.

Neither of them replied directly.

"That's all right," said Bella soothingly. "You're quite safe now. There's nothing here."

"But didn't you see the snake?" pressed Marjorie.

"It all happened so quickly!" answered Crispin evasively.

Marjorie looked down at her arm, and realised that the stabbing pain she had experienced could not have been imagination. There, on the fleshy part of her arm were two red marks, like needle pricks, about a quarter of an inch apart. Crispin turned pale when he saw them.

"Good God!" he exclaimed. "That's real enough. What has been happening here?"

He exchanged a significant glance with his sister.

"Marjorie," he said, taking her hand, "something is going on here that it is difficult to fight. But we must fight it. We cannot expect to know everything, and it is one of the mysteries of creation that evil is permitted. There is evil here now. Some evil influence is able to affect you, and has even been granted a certain power of materialisation." Crispin's voice became full and vibrant. "We must fight, and meanwhile pray for strength. May the Supreme Good Spirit, and all spirits serving the cause of good, aid us in this struggle."

"Amen," said Bella, her voice trembling with emotion.

For the first time Marjorie's confidence in Crispin's powers seemed to fail her. Perhaps it was because she had seen him frightened. Perhaps it was the strange conversation with her uncle. Whatever it was, she felt she was up against something that baffled him.

But to whom could she turn for help? To her uncle? Of course the idea was ridiculous. To Ted? But even if he was willing to let bygones be bygones, how could he even begin to understand that the things with which she was dealing were real?

3

A solution came to her next day. She was in the Crispins' studio, making notes, when Mrs Threpfall sat down beside her. They got into conversation. Mrs Threpfall looked at her closely once or twice, and was plainly about to say something, but she checked herself. She went on knitting and exchanging small talk. But before she left, she said to Marjorie:

"I wonder if you would mind coming with me as far as the tube station?"

Marjorie looked at her, wondering if she were feeling ill. A glance at her calm face dispelled this. Evidently Mrs Threpfall wanted a private conversation with her.

"I expect you will think what I am going to say is a great impertinence," began Mrs Threpfall, as they walked along side by side. "If so, you must put it down to the foolishness of an old woman. But the fact is, my dear, I have been struck by the difference in your looks since you first came to the Crispins. You look really washed out now; and I can't help wondering whether you are not more ill than you realise. I know what it is like to be in your position—a girl without any relatives she can rely on. I was once in the same position myself. That is why I am speaking to you frankly. If you like, simply tell me I'm an old fool. I won't mind. I know it!"

Marjorie was touched by Mrs Threpfall's kindness. She certainly felt a desperate need to confide in someone. There were few people, after all, more likely to understand her trouble. Although not an avowed believer in spiritualism, Mrs Threpfall obviously felt a deep interest in it, otherwise she would not be such a persistent attender at séances.

Now Marjorie told her something of her difficulties. She did not tell her of Lambert's attempt on Crispin's life, or Crispin's conversation with her uncle. She did not hint at any of the imperfections she was beginning to suspect in Crispin. She told Mrs Threpfall of her tiredness, her depression, the growing sense of evil which had culminated in two terrible incidents—the sleep-walking and the vision of the snake.

"It's not only that," explained Marjorie, trying to make clear her confused feelings, "it's as if I'd lost interest in life. My mediumship and the messages I got from my darling mother don't seem to matter any more. It's a strange thing, but in the last few weeks no messages at all have come from Mother. It's almost as if she can't help me either.

"Don't think that I'm losing faith in spiritualism," added Marjorie. "I've seen too much for that. If you'd had my experiences, you would believe too. But somehow it's as if nothing seems to matter. It's this awful feeling of depression and evil things all round me—the feeling that I'm losing grip on my mind."

Mrs Threpfall looked at her curiously.

"It's as bad as that, is it? I had no idea!"

They had come to the station now, and as they paused, she laid a hand on Marjorie's arm.

"Promise me you'll get help at once. It's not a thing you can deal with alone. Go to a doctor and tell him everything." She emphasised this with a squeeze. *"Everything."*

"But what doctor ought I to go to? How can they understand?"

"Go to Doctor Wood," said Mrs Threpfall. "You saw him, you remember, at one or two earlier séances."

"But he's a Harley Street specialist. Will he be interested in my case? Besides, I can't afford a fashionable doctor. I'm afraid any doctor will laugh at me."

"No, Doctor Wood won't laugh at you," Mrs Threpfall assured her, "for, although he's a doctor, he's a psychiatrist, and he knows there are stranger things in human psychology than the ordinary doctor dreams of. I know he'll be interested in your case. I could tell you stories..."

She checked herself. "Well, never mind about that now."

Mrs Threpfall took a card out of her bag and scribbled one or two lines on it.

"Give this to Doctor Wood. You see, I say you are a great friend of mine, and I want his special help for you. Long ago, when he was a young and struggling practitioner, my husband was able to help him. So I think you'll find he'll do his best for you now without charging you anything. But you must be frank with him."

Before Marjorie could thank her, Mrs Threpfall had slipped into the lift. Acting on the impulse of the moment, Marjorie jumped into a taxi and gave Dr Wood's address. Taxis were one of the luxuries her increased salary made possible. But, she reflected a little sadly, even these luxuries seemed empty and useless now without Ted to share them. Without Ted... Well, she thought impatiently, she had never been farther from Ted in her life than now.

4

It appeared that Dr Wood was not in Harley Street or near it. He had a small flat in Mayfair, very unostentatious, and without even his name on the door. The Crispins' house had always struck Marjorie as smart and well furnished. Directly she was shown into Dr Wood's rooms she realised that here was quite a different level of "smartness." Everything seemed simple, old, inconspicuous and a little dim. But everything was genuine. The antiques were real antiques; the paintings were of the period and school they purported to be; and the rooms had an atmosphere, a refinement, which Marjorie had never seen at such close quarters before.

The manservant who took Mrs Threpfall's card in to Wood did not keep her waiting long. She was shown into his consulting room, which was entirely different from the consulting rooms to which she was used. The only touch of formality in the beautifully furnished room was the bureau at which Wood was sitting. This itself was a pretty gilt bureau, of the Second Empire, which harmonised with the furniture of the rest of the room.

Wood closed the bureau and got up as she came in.

"Please sit down," he said, pointing to a sofa, and he sat down opposite her.

"Do you like this room?" he said with a smile. "I see you look a little surprised."

"It doesn't seem like a doctor's room, somehow," she answered naïvely.

"Well, you see, I'm not an ordinary doctor," replied Wood, smilingly offering her a cigarette. "And I don't believe in the old theory of impressing the patient. The patient oughtn't to be bullied by the doctor; that's a quack's idea. He ought to be led and advised by him. And so this room is furnished to put patients at their ease, not to impress them."

"Well, I think that's a nice idea," agreed Marjorie. "It certainly is a lovely room."

"Yes, it is," he answered, looking round it with evident satisfaction. "Nicer than it need be for my professional purposes. Well, I admit I'm fond of the good things of life—good food, good wine and good furniture."

His friendly manner put Marjorie at her ease. He chatted on, apparently about himself, and she did not notice that, as he joked and laughed, he was watching her with minute attention. Outwardly, it was as if she were paying a social call and not a visit to a doctor.

"Well, I've talked enough about myself," he said at last. "Tell me something about *yourself*."

Marjorie had thought that the telling would be difficult. She didn't really understand it herself or know what exactly was happening to her. Yet, somehow, once she was launched on her story, she told everything easily. She told him of her moods, her depressions, her terrible nightmares, the hallucination of the snake—if it was a hallucination. But as Marjorie told the story, the old horror seemed to envelop her. She seemed to feel while she was telling the story, that she was wasting time. She would never recover the peace of her earlier days.

"I know you don't believe in this," she said, "but I did really have messages from Mother. I actually saw her. It couldn't be just deception or chance. I've seen other things. But now something dreadful seems to be trying . . . oh, I don't know how to express it . . . to *get* at me. Even now I can feel something——" She broke off, and Wood saw that her eyes had become blank and expressionless. She put one hand slowly to her forehead.

"I don't know what it is. I think I'm going to faint."

Dr Wood got up abruptly and sat down beside her on the sofa, looking into her eyes. Then he took out his watch.

"What's the time?" he said sharply, holding it up in front of her.

Marjorie eyes were set and staring. The lids fell.

He grasped her arm roughly. He felt it stiffen in his grasp and her whole body went rigid.

"I can't see the watch," she whispered, her eyes closed.

"Yes, you can!" he urged. "Concentrate! Pull yourself together!"

"I can't see it," the girl replied, leaning back. "I can't see anything . . . anything . . ."

Her voice seemed to trail away. Except for the stiffness in her poise, one would have said that she had become unconscious.

"Miss Easton, wake up!" cried Dr Wood. He put his mouth to her ear and shouted, "Wake up!"

Marjorie made no response. He dropped the arm he was grasping and went to his desk. Selecting a needle from a tray, he wiped it on an antiseptic pad, and then, pinching the flesh of her arm, ran it about an inch into the muscle. The girl made absolutely no movement, and yet, from between her closed lips, came the query in a hoarse, lifeless voice:

"Why did you do that?"

"Did you feel it?" he asked.

"No, I can feel nothing . . . see nothing . . ."

"But you knew I did it . . ."

"No, nothing . . . nothing . . ."

The girl gave a little sigh, and then slid into a prone position on the couch. Dr Wood turned her head to one side, so that she could breathe, and remained for a moment thinking. He sat down at his desk for a while and made some hurried notes.

In the silence the scratching of his pen and the harsh breathing of the girl could be distinctly heard. After about two minutes the hoarseness of the breathing ceased. Marjorie groaned and sat up.

"What's happened?" she asked, puzzled.

"What do you think has happened?" said Dr Wood coolly, continuing to write.

"I don't know. Did I fall asleep suddenly? I do sometimes, nowadays. Everything seemed to go blank, and then I had such strange dreams." Marjorie shuddered suddenly. "My arm hurts too."

She looked at Dr Wood defiantly.

"Why are you looking at me so strangely?"

"I wasn't aware that I was," he said calmly. "No wonder your arm hurts. I stuck a needle in it just now and you did not feel it. You feel it now?"

"Yes! Why didn't I feel it then?" asked Marjorie.

"That's what I'm wondering. Where was it that the snake bit you, or rather where was it you thought it bit you? On that arm?"

"No, on the other one. The mark is still there."

"Let me look at it," he asked.

Marjorie rolled back her sleeve. He looked at the two red marks and pursed his lips. Marjorie tried to read his expression.

"What's the matter with me?" she asked urgently.

"Can't you guess?" he said gently.

She shook her head.

He sat down beside her and took her hand.

"Miss Easton," he said quietly, "what I'm going to tell you is going to be a great shock to you. I mean it to be a great shock to you. You'll be brave, won't you? Unless you face up to the worst of this, at once, we can't overcome it."

Marjorie gazed at him apprehensively.

"What is it?" she faltered, with a dim suspicion of what he was going to say.

"I'm afraid your mind is going...."

She gave a little cry and turned pale.

"There," he said, patting her hand. "Try to understand exactly what I mean. You are not in any way insane. But you must realise what these delusions, obsessions and losses of consciousness mean? They are the preliminaries of a psychosis."

The whole room seemed to swim round Marjorie. She was suddenly filled with a deadly terror. Now it seemed to her that all the time she had guessed this. This had been the dread always at the back of her mind.

"Can nothing be done?" she asked, white with fear.

"Of course, everything can be done! There is no reason why you should not be absolutely your normal healthy self in a few weeks just as you used to be. But you must fight." His voice rang out commandingly. "Do you understand, *fight!*"

"Fight what?" she asked in a low voice.

"This devilry! Don't misunderstand me," he said, as he saw her eyes take on a hard look. "I'm suggesting nothing against either spiritualism or Crispin. I maintain an attitude of scientific impartiality. All I'm interested in is your sanity. Will you fight for it? For to fight for it you must fight yourself!"

"Yes, I'll fight," she said at last. "What do you want me to do? Must I leave the Crispins?"

"No. I said *fight,* not run. This thing is inside you, not outside. Your only chance is to face up to it squarely and learn exactly what it is. As soon as you do that, you will realise how powerless these forces are. The only power they have is your fear of them. Once that is gone, they just wilt away. But if you let them get you on the run, then I can't answer for the consequences."

"But what has happened exactly?" she asked. "Why do I get these strange moods and hallucinations?"

"Although you don't realise it, you are two personalities. There's the one who's speaking to me now, the one who wants to fight and be healthy. And there's the other one, the one who's grown up in the shadow. *She* doesn't want to fight. She wants to pass into a world of dream and phantasy."

"I think I can understand," said Marjorie thoughtfully. "I do feel as if I were two persons sometimes. But what would happen if I went away? Wouldn't a complete change of scene . . ."

"But could it change your mind? Just think! You came here—running from it. What happened? Even as you were talking to me, this other personality came to the surface and interrupted your story. The enemy is inside you. Running away gives it power. But you must make me one promise if I am to treat you."

"What is it?"

"No more séances!" said Dr Wood positively.

"But how can I do that? I'm employed by the Crispins to attend them and make notes."

"I insist on it as your medical adviser. I'll write a strong note to Crispin now, and I know he won't ignore it. For the rest, take plenty of exercise, and I'll give you a prescription which you must take before you go to sleep. It'll help cure those bad dreams. But don't look on yourself as an invalid. Regard yourself as one who is coming back to life and act accordingly. You want laughter and interest. Determine to do things and do them."

"I'll try," Marjorie promised doubtfully. "But nowadays every resolution I make seems to wilt away!"

"Have you anyone dear to you?" he asked. "Some friend you could rely on? There's nothing like being able to draw on someone else's energy in such circumstances as these."

"Well, there's——" Then she hesitated. She could not claim Ted's help—least of all now. "There's no one," she repeated, "except my uncle. And I'm afraid we don't get on well together."

Wood had noticed her hesitation.

"Come, there is someone, isn't there?" he pressed with a smile. "Or *was* someone. You must trust me, you know, or we shall never succeed!"

"Well, there was a boy I was fond of," she confessed. "But somehow we drifted apart. We quarreled really. It's all over now, definitely."

"All the same, I want his name and address," he said calmly.

"Oh, you mustn't speak to him about this," she said agitatedly. "You mustn't!" said Marjorie.

"Miss Easton, I'm your medical adviser," he said with a sudden sternness. "As long as I remain so, it is not for you to tell me what I must or must not do. You can rely on me to be discreet, but the last word *must* be with me."

Ordinarily she would have resented his tone fiercely, but now she felt curiously weak. Without another word, she gave Wood the name and address.

"There is one more thing before you go," he said. "Have you ever heard voices at night? I mean voices *outside* yourself?"

"No," she answered wonderingly.

"Well, I don't think you will now. But if you do, it means that you are seriously ill. If this should happen, you must promise to leave the Crispins at once and come to me."

"But you told me to fight and not run," she reminded him.

"There are some emergencies in which one must run, unwise as it is. Every general knows that. You must promise me this. I hope and believe it won't be necessary!"

"I promise," she said.

She felt unwilling to go—it was like going out into a hostile world—and he gave her a final encouragement.

"Don't be frightened," he said. "The worst is over. You'd be surprised how many people go through these things and then forget them later, when it's all over and done with! It's only now that you're in the midst of it, that it feels so terrible."

None the less, directly Marjorie had gone, Dr Wood looked grave. He sat for some minutes, chin in hand, and it seemed as if various alternatives were passing through his mind. Then he reopened the notebook in which he had written Ted's address:

Edward Wainwright,
18, Stansfield Road, S.E. 19.

He put on his hat and coat and went downstairs to his car. He gave the address to the chauffeur, and presently they were gliding smoothly eastward.

5

"Well, I've violated professional etiquette and decided to come along and tell you everything," admitted Dr Wood, as he sat in the sitting room of Ted's flat. He told the young man, briefly, what he had learned from Marjorie's visit.

Wainwright's first reaction had been one of utter fury. Wood had with difficulty stopped him from rushing straight round to Crispin and half killing him.

"It's not so simple as that, Mr Wainwright," explained the doctor gravely. "Miss Easton is on the thin hairline which separates sanity from mental breakdown. God knows what devilry that man Crispin has been up to, but she is absolutely in his power. In the state of psychic identification with Crispin that she is now in, any injury to him would be felt as an injury to her. Consciously she is critical of him, but her unconscious, the second personality in her, is absolutely identified with him, and any action against him might have the most dangerous effects."

"But surely if we forced him . . ."

"You can't force him. Miss Easton is a free agent. As for using violence on Crispin, he's only got to appeal for police protection. Miss Easton is in the most suggestible state I've ever seen in a girl, and she has this suggestibility only towards Crispin. Her only safeguard is that she does not realise how completely she is in his power. Once she does that——" He gave an expressive gesture.

"But if only we could get her away," began Ted. "Kidnap her if necessary."

Wood shook his head. "Useless! At the moment she is psychically tied to Crispin. Even when she was in my consulting room she passed into what was virtually a hypnotic trance dictated by him. I've no doubt he has suggested that she should become unconscious if any influences adverse to him begin to affect her. That means we've got to play our cards with the greatest caution. The resistance must come from her. Any outside force will only precipitate a crisis. I warn you that that crisis is close, dreadfully close, and once it happens, there is nothing we can do. She will slip out of our grasp into another world—the world of insanity."

"But it's monstrous, abominable!" Ted jumped up excitedly. "I'm not going to let the swine get away with it!"

Wood put his hand soothingly on the boy's shoulder. "Of course you won't. We'll win. But we mustn't blind ourselves to the difficulties. For example, what is his object in doing this? I admit it puzzles me."

Ted writhed.

"My God, if he does harm her, I'll wring his bloody neck. The filthy swine!"

"You needn't be afraid it's because he's attracted by her," said Wood. "In my judgment Crispin is quite destitute of the normal human emotions. In fact, psychologically he's an enigma to me. He's not a simple charlatan. He wouldn't spend so much money on this game if he were. He seems really to believe in this spiritualism."

"Is there anything in it?" asked Ted. "There can't be, can there?"

"Certainly there are no ghosts of the departed," answered Wood, smiling. "It's a deception to that extent. But unquestionably there are psychic forces of which we are ignorant. I do not mean *outside* forces, but forces from our own minds. Crispin knows more about them than I, as a scientific psychologist, altogether like to admit."

"But what's his motive in hypnotising Marjorie?"

Wood shook his head.

"I wish to God I could guess. We must simply hang on and hope to discover the motive."

Ted jumped up impatiently.

"But we can't *just* hang on. We must *do* something."

The doctor looked at him understandingly.

"That's the hardest part, the waiting. All the same, I'm not even supposed to have spoken to you."

"Can't I do anything?"

"Yes, I think I can use you as a kind of counter influence. She's fond of you; there's no doubt about it."

"Then why did she ask you not to see me? Why won't she ask for my help?"

"Just because her normal personality is fond of you, and so this other part of her reacts against the danger of losing control by keeping away from you. This personality takes care to orientate all Marjorie's life towards Crispin and so cut out all the old memories—even those of Marjorie's mother now. This other influence is blotting out all her normal human relations. It's like an illness. But still, in her heart, she's fond of you. And we must use that."

He got to his feet and paced thoughtfully up and down the room.

"I've got it!" he said suddenly. "You must get into the Crispin circle. He'd suspect me. I can't do it myself. You must meet him and try to find what he's getting at. Go under some other name. Pretend you believe everything that's going on. Try to catch him out!"

"But Marjorie will give me away."

"No, she won't see you. She's promised not to attend any more séances for a little while."

"But how will I get in?"

"Mrs Threpfall will introduce you. You see, she's fond of Marjorie, and I know when I tell her what is happening she'll do anything for the girl. But you'll have to act well and conceal your feelings. It's not going to be easy. How are you fixed for off days?"

"I've plenty," he replied sardonically. "We're working half time just now, and I get more time off than I know what to do with now. Troubles never come singly, do they?"

"Well, perhaps both these troubles will end together. Don't get despondent. You must promise me one thing."

"What is it?"

"Not to lose your temper with Crispin! Whatever happens. It's a difficult thing we've embarked on; and you've got to trust me when I tell you that crude violence is useless. It's worse than useless; it's dangerous to her. Will you promise—for Marjorie's sake?"

"If you say so," Wainwright said. "It won't be easy. But I trust you somehow. It's difficult to say, but Marjorie still means everything to me and——"

"If you're trying to thank me," interrupted Wood, "wait till we're out of trouble." He got up. "So long, then! Expect a message from me or from Mrs Threpfall. And remember—hide your feelings! We've got to fight a cunning enemy. So cunning, we don't even know yet *why* he is an enemy."

CHAPTER IV

The Night of the Mind

Ted regarded himself as an ordinary sort of fellow, chiefly, perhaps, because in his life so far he had only had to face ordinary situations. There had been the difficulty of earning his living, of supporting his mother and so on; but these were all difficulties that could be overcome by the exercise of ordinary abilities. They were the usual difficulties of a young man in his situation.

He had looked forward to marriage and family life with Marjorie on equally ordinary lines, although he did not think of them as ordinary, but as extraordinary and pleasant. Marjorie, too, had been of his sort, with more than the usual rightness—surprisingly and delightfully right. He was in love with her. He knew she had been in love with him. And there had been a hundred and one shared memories and enjoyments which had made the love between them solid and everyday.

Then quite suddenly all this had changed. Marjorie had become a different being, living in a world of whose existence he had never guessed. This world had transformed her and brought about their parting. And now Marjorie was in danger. An awful thing, one it was difficult to understand, had overtaken her. He didn't understand it—that was the trouble. Ordinary methods wouldn't succeed. He couldn't go to Crispin, for example, and give him a good hiding. Dr Wood had warned him of the dangers of that. In some unbelievable way, the girl was in Crispin's power and there was nothing he could do physically to help her. This gave him a sick, helpless feeling.

Yet out of the welter of confusion stood the thought of Marjorie in trouble and pain. The interval during which Marjorie had kept silent, not even sending him a line or a word to hint that her abrupt dismissal of him was not final, had been bad enough. Now, when at last he heard of her, it was to hear this: Marjorie was hopelessly under the influence of Crispin.

He refused to admit this. He was determined to get Marjorie back. There was an explanation of everything, once one got to the back of it. It was necessary to get to the back of this. Dr Wood had promised to help him. Wood would give him a chance of meeting Crispin, of understanding what it was all about. Surely it would be possible to help Marjorie, and once he had got her free—well, then he would settle accounts with Crispin.

His resolve began a new period in his life. His friends and his mother both noticed the change. It wasn't a problem he could talk over with anyone he met in his daily work, not even his closest friends. While it lasted he felt alone, and he began to turn in on himself and become morose and sullen. His only ally was Dr Wood. No one else could help, or even understand.

He managed to get through his daily work in the shops without making a mistake, but that was about all. He hadn't the heart even to play football on Saturdays. By the end of a week Ted realised that he was beginning to think of nothing else but Marjorie and Crispin. This only added to his determination to succeed.

He attended Crispin's séances regularly, refusing to commit himself to anything much in the way of statement, but watching everything. The general effect was unnerving. He hadn't expected anything like this. It was all damned funny, and, in a curious way, *convincing*. One knew there must be trickery in it all; and yet, somehow, one couldn't quite see where the trickery came in. Everyone seemed so dead earnest. For the first time Ted realised he was up against something real and dangerous, and also understood at last why Marjorie had been taken in by it.

Crispin made a profound impression on him. Ted had never met anyone like Crispin before. He had formed all sorts of ideas in his mind about Marjorie's employer, but none of them remotely resembled the man he actually met. He had expected some flashy, plausible scoundrel. Why, he could not say, for Wood had emphasised that Crispin was not a swindler in the usual sense. All the same he had pictured him as a kind of loud-mouthed confidence trickster. Instead, he met a man who was almost ascetic in his manner, and distinguished by a sort of inhuman remoteness. The man was sinister enough, but not with the sinister qualities of the villains he had met on the films. Above all, his complete lack of warmth, of virility, of any positive qualities surprised and disconcerted Ted.

"A reptile" was how he described him in his mind. "A cold, snaky sort of fellow." But even this wasn't quite right. In many ways Crispin was as emotional as a woman. Ted had seen him weep once after a séance, when something had upset him, and evidently his feelings were near the surface.

Ted had been afraid that his manner, to say nothing of his hands, would give him away, and that Wood would not be able to palm him off on Crispin as an investigator and assistant. Wood had said, however, that this would be all right; he would invent a story. All Ted would need to do would be to act naturally and say as little as possible. Ted discovered later that Wood had told Crispin he was a bright young polytechnic student whom he had selected for this job, because he thought he would be unprejudiced either for or against psychic investigation. Apparently Crispin had believed this without difficulty.

If this stage had lasted long, Ted couldn't have stood it. Every séance seemed to reveal to him more clearly the strange and difficult obstacles he was up against. Crispin seemed to grow in formidableness and power. Ted began to be affected by the unreal, emotional atmosphere of the sitting and the constant happening of inexplicable things. His work was suffering, and the foreman had had to speak to him sharply several times about faulty work. He was beginning to become nervy and depressed.

He was denied what he was relying on most—a sight of Marjorie. She was somewhere in the house, but although he did his best, he never came across her on any of his many visits to Belmont Avenue. His inclination was to insist on seeing her. But Wood warned him that Marjorie was determined in her refusal to see him, and that it would only complicate matters dangerously if he insisted on doing so against her desire.

He had, however, spoken to Mrs Threpfall several times, for she had introduced herself to him as a friend of Marjorie's. What she told him of Wood made him realise that Marjorie could not be in better hands. He had to trust Wood completely—that was his only hope. Even so, the matter was desperate. Marjorie did not during these three weeks get worse, but was not getting better. Wood could not conceal his alarm at her lack of progress.

"She's better in health," admitted Wood, "but to offset that, she's losing interest in her recovery. She's beginning to think that it was a mistake coming to me, that she was in some way betraying Crispin. Her will power is oozing away. That's the worst sign. If only she'd have the courage to fight!"

"I can't understand that in Marjorie," said Ted.

"It's always the trouble in these cases: you can cure them if they'll cure themselves. If ever the day comes when she tells me she doesn't want to see me anymore——" Wood broke off abruptly. "But we must be determined that this won't happen."

"Isn't there anything I can do!" exclaimed Ted. "Surely she must realise what her position is. I can't imagine Marjorie just letting herself go to pieces."

"She's greatly changed. You would hardly recognise in her character the Marjorie you knew. I can see that, even though I only saw her once before Crispin's influence got to work! The one thing that will cure her is some shock that will shake her out of this coma. But it's damned risky. It might only drive her over the borderline."

"We *must* do something!" exclaimed Ted. "I warn you, Doctor, I'm not going to let things drift on like this forever. I'll wring that devil's neck if anything happens to Marjorie. I will straight!"

Wood laid his hand on the boy's shoulder.

"We must see it doesn't come to that, Ted. Give me another five days."

2

But the five days were not needed. Three nights later, Marjorie awoke suddenly. There was a curious, plashing, *rustling* sound in the bedroom. At first the noise seemed to be in her head—a kind of dream noise. She was still half asleep, and so she summoned all her energy to dispel the noise. But the noise became clearer. It was plainly outside her, in the room.

She sat up in bed. A shaft of moonlight filled the room and fell on the bed of the nurse who now always shared the room with her. The nurse was fast asleep, and Marjorie suppressed her first desire to wake her. It must be imagination. Or there must be some cause for the noise. Perhaps it was the traffic or a wind outside.

But she knew in her heart that it was not so. The noise was in the room. It was a rustling, like the movements of people who trod so lightly that only their clothes made any sound. But it could not be this. Visitors from another world would not inflict their presence on her now, when she was ill and overwrought. They would be merciful.

She tried to send out kindly thoughts, to beg that the other world should leave her alone. Quite abruptly, the rustling ceased. It was followed by a disembodied voice.

"Marjorie," it whispered, "Marjorie . . . Death . . . Madness . . ."

The words were quite distinct and were charged with a dreadful horror. They seemed an echo of all her worst fears. Were the words subjective or objective? Her doubts were set at rest when the room echoed with three horrible peals of laughter. It was certain that sounds so horrible and hateful could never be imagined by her. They were real, *external*. Some *thing* was tormenting her, but although she strained her eyes in the darkness, she could see nothing.

Beads of sweat stood out on Marjorie's forehead. All the illusions she had cherished about the soft, rosy spirit world seemed to shrivel before that hateful laughter and those horrible gloating words. Her thoughts seemed to stand still and wiredraw themselves out to excruciating length. She felt like a trapped beast.

But why hadn't the nurse heard? How could she fail to hear that last outcry of laughter. Cold with fear, Marjorie leapt out of bed and ran over to the nurse's bed.

"Quick! Wake up!" she cried. There was no answer. Trembling with terror, Marjorie seized hold of the woman's shoulder and shook it violently. Still the nurse made no response. Marjorie shook her with all the force she could muster, as if she were attempting to tear the life out of her rather than wake her. Still the woman slept on. Marjorie stopped, rolled her onto her back, and peered into her face. Her features, absolutely set and motionless, looked a ghastly white in the moonlight.

"She's dead," was the thought that passed through Marjorie's mind, and the full horror of this made her legs give way under her for the moment. With an effort, she mustered the remains of her courage.

"I shall go mad . . . I shall go mad," was the thought that raced through her mind. Behind it was the yet more ghastly thought, "I *am* mad."

She staggered to the electric light switch and pressed it. Nothing happened. Just a click, and still there was darkness. As she tried to preserve her wits from this fresh assault on them, she heard that diabolical laugh ring out, vile, mocking, *gloating* . . .

This time it seemed to come from the ceiling, and, looking up, she saw in the darkest corner of the room a few phosphorescent globes of light, looking like squashy, aerial jellyfishes. They moved gently, with a shoving, jostling motion, like a group of cattle pushing their way along. Now, as her eyes got used to the phosphorescent light, she could distinctly see that they were *faces,* wearing expressions of diabolical malignity. They were moving towards her . . .

This last phenomenon, in all its ghastly and diabolical parody of the gracious presences she had seen materialise in the séance room, completed the ruin of Marjorie's world. She was unable to scream, she could only whimper softly to herself as she staggered towards the door.

The only thing that came to her mind was security, help, *Dr Wood.* The memory of his kindly face came into her mind and gave her courage. The door closed and she tottered out into the dark passage.

As she moved down the stairs, she heard a queer, bumping noise and something which was warm and heaving attempted to grasp her bare ankles. Once again, from the room she had just left, the vile, hateful laugh sounded.

Marjorie whimpered again and collapsed on the stairs. She rolled and slid down them, but managed to get to her feet in the hall and run to the door. How she got it open she never knew, but she felt the cold night air on her face and, just as she was, in her bare feet and night things, she rushed out into the road.

3

On the morning of the following day, Crispin was to give an important séance. About twelve people were expected, among them Ted. Ted thought Crispin looked tired and almost frightened. He wondered whether it was imagination, until, as Crispin straightened nervously the silver-embroidered curtain which formed the medium's cabinet, Ted saw his hand tremble. He decided to watch Crispin very carefully....

The usual desultory conversation took place among the sitters round the séance table. Then Crispin's sister came in, looking confused. She went up to Crispin for some moments and held a whispered conversation. Ted edged quietly near them and managed to catch a word or two. "... insists on seeing you..."

"All right," Crispin said, apparently agreeing. Bella went out and, a moment later, a nurse came in. Ted guessed at once that it was Marjorie's nurse, of whom Dr Wood had told him. She was a heavy-faced, dour person, but now she was obviously excited, and Ted distinctly heard her words to Crispin.

"What shall I do, Mr Crispin? She's gone!"

"Gone, what do you mean?" answered the man sharply.

"Her bed's empty and I can't find her anywhere in the house."

"Well, what were you doing, anyway? You're supposed to be in her room."

"Yes, but I slept very heavily last night for some reason. And this morning, when I woke up, she was gone."

"She must have gone out for an early morning walk."

"But, Mr Crispin, that's impossible," said the nurse positively. "She didn't dress."

"Didn't dress!" replied Crispin. "Then she must be somewhere in the house, obviously. Look in the other rooms."

"No, she's not here. I'm afraid she must have become confused, poor girl, and gone out, just as she was. We ought to inform the police."

"Of course we ought, Miss Furnivall," replied Crispin with alacrity. "Go round to the station at once and tell them everything. I'll be along as soon as possible."

As the meaning of this conversation came home to Ted, his heart missed a beat. His first impulse on hearing this news was to hurry after the nurse and find out more about it, no matter what effect this might have on this plan of remaining unknown to Crispin. But he stifled this impulse. He had heard clearly enough what had happened. Marjorie had disappeared. And, what was more, he felt certain that Crispin knew or was at least expecting it. Whereas before the nurse came in he had been nervous and ill at ease, this nervousness had now vanished. He was once again the withdrawn, self-assured Crispin.

What was behind this? What had Marjorie done that Crispin had singled her out in this way for torment? Why had Marjorie fallen into the trap? Why, now, had she disappeared? All these queries rushed through Ted's head while he tried to keep up a calm front. Perhaps she had been forcibly carried off. Or perhaps she had come to her senses completely, and in her horror had hurried from the Crispins. Ted writhed at the thought of his helplessness, at the fact that Marjorie had never asked his help. Was there really anything left of her love for him, in spite of Wood's assurances?

Well, he would show her! He would finally settle matters with Crispin. He was going to go his own way now. Wood could go to hell. What was the good of playing a waiting game? It might be all right for someone who was subtle and clever like Wood, but he knew he wasn't that sort. He'd get beaten at it every time by a clever devil like Crispin. He preferred simple and violent methods. He had half decided to use them a long time ago. He had even prepared to do so. Now he would act. It was his only chance to save Marjorie.

Probably some of his resolve showed in his eyes and chin, for before the séance began, Crispin looked at him closely once or twice and seemed about to speak. However, he said nothing to Ted and presently the lights were lowered, and Crispin went into a trance. The phenomena that followed added to Ted's anger. He knew that it was all fake, but how it was done he did not know. He was irritated by the enthusiasm and the emotion of the other sitters. He was above all infuriated by the cleverness of Crispin. "But he won't look so clever in a moment," he thought.

For some reason the séance was short. There were no materialisations, only voice production, and the messages were brief and uninteresting. Presently the control announced that conditions were bad. Crispin woke. Bella switched on the lights, the silver-embroidered curtains were drawn back, and Crispin was released from his bandages. He complained that he felt unusually tired and ill.

"And dreadfully hot," he said, pressing his forehead. "I had an unusual experience. Usually I am completely unaware of anything in a trance. It merely represents for me a period of unconsciousness. But today I had the new experience of dreaming, and in the dream I had certain clear presensations. They referred to you," he added, nodding at Ted and giving him a meaning glance.

Ted was a little surprised at being forced into public notice in this way. Everyone stared at him. Hitherto Crispin had treated him merely as an observer. He stared back sullenly at Crispin. "You wait!" was the thought in his mind. Crispin seemed to read it without effort.

"You don't like me, do you?" said Crispin with a curious smile. Ted flushed and protested uneasily. Crispin was taking advantage of the situation—the people here with whom he couldn't discuss Marjorie—to make him uneasy and disconcert him.

"Why should I dislike you?" he said woodenly.

"You think I'm responsible for Miss Easton's disappearance. You are a friend of hers, aren't you? I assure you I had nothing to do with it. It astounds me as much as anyone."

The others in the room were puzzled by the conversation, and stared at Crispin and Wainwright. Ted found this scrutiny awkward. He caught Mrs Threpfall's enquiring glance. No one but Crispin and himself could know yet that Marjorie had disappeared. How on earth had Crispin guessed that he was interested in Marjorie; and that he had overheard his conversation with the nurse? How much more had he guessed? Crispin's eyes now wore the black, lidless gaze of a reptile. They were devoid of expression.

Ted maintained a wooden silence. He was determined not to discuss Marjorie in public. And he was still more determined to settle the matter finally. His hands itched to seize Crispin's soft shoulders and shake the truth out of him here and now, but he restrained himself. The other, subtler way was better.

Abruptly the lids dropped over Crispin's eyes, veiling their cold stare, and his face looked human again. The yellow mask seemed to crumple and soften, and he put his hand to his forehead. Then he made a gesture to Ted.

"I feel very thirsty. Would you be good enough to get me a glass of water?"

It was the usual thing for Crispin to be thirsty after a séance. There was a little sink and tap in the corner of the room, used for developing photographs, from which Crispin generally moistened his lips and throat after a sitting. But it seemed impudence to ask Ted to fetch the glass of water. Ted hesitated. What had Crispin guessed? Then he looked at Crispin again. The man evidently was ill; perhaps there was nothing in it. He went to the sink, held the glass under the tap, rinsed it out once or twice and filled it. Then he brought it to Crispin. Crispin took it with a little smile, which puzzled Ted, and drank it.

Almost immediately an extraordinary change of expression came over Crispin's face. It turned a livid colour, and he half rose to his feet. An appalling look of anxiety distorted his features:

"You devil!" he screamed out. "You really have poisoned me!"

The words changed into inarticulate groans, and he doubled up on the floor in front of them. The onlookers stood on paralysed with horror as Crispin writhed on the floor in convulsions like a wounded beast. They seemed afraid to touch him at first. When at last Ted and two or three others tried to hold him, his own struggles made it impossible to do so. In one last terrible convulsion his spine was bent from nape to heels in a deep reverse curve. After this, his struggles became weaker and weaker. By the time the doctor arrived, he was making slight, jerky movements, while two men held him on the couch and wiped the froth from his lips.

One incident in this episode stood out in Ted's recollection. Directly the convulsions began, Bella stepped back from Crispin with a look of terror on her face.

"They've got him," she murmured. Then she turned and hurried from the room.

When the doctor arrived, fetched by Mrs Threpfall, and they looked round for Miss Crispin, she was not in the house. It was assumed that she had gone for the police; but the police did not arrive and so the doctor phoned for them. The police had not heard from Bella.

By the time the police arrived, Crispin was dead.

CHAPTER V

The Man-Woman

Detective-Inspector Charles Morgan, C.I.D., was not an imaginative man. This was no drawback in his walk of life, for, contrary to popular opinion, criminal detection is not a matter of bold and daring theorising, or amazing flights of imaginative deduction, but of the indefatigable accumulation of minor details, according to an inevitable routine. The net is thrown wider and wider —more and more chance scraps are caught in it. Each is minutely scrutinised by the appropriate person, and perhaps one in a thousand of these scraps may point to some time, place, or walk of life connected with the crime. Ten of such pointers, drawn from the scrutiny of ten thousand, may converge on one person.

But on the other hand, they may not. In which case, here is yet another unsolved crime. The most brilliant fancies of the most ingenious individual are not likely to alter by a hair's breadth this collective routine of Scotland Yard.

Morgan's world was therefore inhabited entirely by facts— preferably "cold." He was a fact himself—a solid, stolid fact with a short ginger moustache and a face that was large and rounded without being fat. It was a leathery face. Morgan had a leathery mind. There was no subtlety or sharpness about it, but it was tough, and it liked tough facts to work upon—not fluid theories or aery speculations. No amount of discouragement or error wore it out. There is nothing like leather.

Morgan found the body of Michael Crispin lying in a fantastic-looking room, surrounded by a group of frightened people. The room was fantastic, but the fantasy was a cold fact. Morgan noticed it at once. There must have been something "queer" about the deceased.

How did the deceased die? A few questions to the onlookers soon secured an outline of the process. Crispin had drunk something, and then had died in convulsions. The water had been given to Crispin by a young man named George Robinson, who was pointed out to him—a husky young man with a curiously defiant expression. Morgan was unable to decide what the expression on George Robinson's face meant. But he was able to decide what Crispin's symptoms meant, even before the doctor had finished his preliminary examination.

Crispin had been poisoned.

"Is everyone here who was here at the time when Mr Robinson handed Mr Crispin the drink?" asked Morgan, turning to the crowd who had huddled together in a corner of the room, but had instinctively separated themselves from Robinson who stood defiantly alone in the middle. The crowd assured him that everyone was there.

Morgan made a short examination of the room. When Crispin had rolled on the floor, the glass had dropped from his hands and spilled the remainder of its contents on the carpet. The glass was still unsmashed.

Morgan picked up the glass gingerly, in order not to smudge any fingerprints, and examined it. A few drops of liquid still adhered to the inside. These would be sufficient for the analysis. As an added check, he surrounded the small damp patch in the carpet, where the glass had fallen, with a ring of coloured chalk. If necessary the carpet could be lifted and sent intact to the analyst's office.

He turned round to the crowd. There were six of them, a mixed bunch—he couldn't as yet quite place them, socially or temperamentally. He would have to get a good many more facts before he would be prepared to make any estimation of them, and his aloof voice reflected this reservation.

"This is a serious matter," he told them collectively. "Mr Crispin has just died in unexpected circumstances and if, as I understand is the case, no doctor has been attending him, it means that there must be a coroner's inquest. Before he died, Mr Crispin made a definite accusation."

The inspector consulted his notebook, although the words were clear in his memory.

"He said: '*You devil, you really have poisoned me.*'"

The inspector's eyes rested for a moment on the face of the young man who had handed Crispin the glass of water, and to whom therefore the remark must have been addressed. The young man's face whitened.

"Does everyone else agree that this was in fact the deceased's last remark?"

There was a murmur of assent from the crowd.

"Well, we can't come to any definite conclusion until after the post-mortem, but obviously already there are several suspicious circumstances of which I have to take note. I must therefore ask you all to give me your names and addresses, so that we can follow up the matter and get fuller statements should it prove necessary to do so after the post-mortem."

One by one, the members of the crowd gave their names and occupations—a curiously assorted list:

Major Aubrey Simpson, R. E. (*retd.*).
Mrs Threpfall.
Miss Lamorna Cohen, *artist*.
Mr Patrick Gleason, *insurance agent*.
Mrs Singleton.
Mr Arthur Lewis Bradley, *independent*.

He read their names and addresses aloud.

"Some of you are probably known to each other," he said at the finish. "If so, you can probably vouch for the authenticity of each other's names and addresses."

As it turned out, there was sufficient interacquaintance within the group for each of them to be known to at least one other.

Morgan turned to George Robinson, in his defiant isolation.

"I haven't had your address and occupation yet," he pointed out.

The young man looked uncomfortable.

"I'd like to have a word in private with you, Inspector."

"I see," He turned to the crowd. "Is there anyone who knows this young man?"

The middle-aged woman, Mrs Threpfall, seemed about to say

something, but she checked herself. No one else volunteered to speak.

"Will you wait in another room in the house?" he told them. "I'll have a word with this young man."

They were shepherded by the sergeant into the neighbouring room which Crispin had used as an office, and directly they had gone, Morgan turned sternly to the young man.

"Now then, Mr Robinson! I must have your address and occupation at once."

"Well, that's what I wanted to see you about. You see, my name's not George Robinson."

"Oh, isn't it? And what might it be then? Everyone here seems to know you as George Robinson."

"It's Edward Wainwright, and I work in the Bilford Metal Box Company."

"Why, exactly, are you going under the name of George Robinson?"

"Well, it's a long story," replied the other awkwardly. "The simplest way I can explain it is this. Crispin was a spiritualist, you know, used to hold séances. He'd been holding one today. Now Doctor Wood—he's not here, but I can give you his address—was friendly with Crispin. Doctor Wood was investigating this spiritualistic stuff as a scientist. Now Doctor Wood has been too busy lately to come himself, so he thought it would be a good idea to have me attend on the q.t. to investigate for him."

Morgan's eyes rested on Ted Wainwright's hands, with their roughened palms and black nails.

"Are you a scientist, Mr—er—Wainwright?"

"No, I told you, I work in the Metal Box Company."

"Then why did Doctor Wood choose you for this task of scientific investigation?"

"I don't know—being friendly, and so forth..."

His explanation sounded somewhat unconvincing, and he was aware of this.

"Did Crispin know you were an investigator? And, if so, why did he let you join the séance, or whatever it is?"

"Yes, he knew," answered Wainwright. "He didn't mind investigators at his shows."

"Then why in that case the assumed name, Mr Wainwright?"

Ted realised that he had fallen into a trap.

"We just thought it would be better," he answered unhappily.

"You are sure it was not because Crispin might have been frightened or unfriendly towards anyone of your name?" asked Morgan, shooting out the question with apparent casualness.

"No, I don't see why he should have been unfriendly towards me." Wainwright cursed his slowness of mind. There was a pause, which seemed to him to last for hours.

Then Morgan asked, apparently irrelevantly, "What has all this to do with Miss Easton?"

Wainwright started.

"Why? I mean what makes you think there should be?"

"It's a fairly simple conclusion, surely. This morning we get a telephone call from this house to say a Miss Marjorie Easton has disappeared from it. We get a full description, and a warning that she may be temporarily insane. The next news we get is that someone has died suddenly in suspicious circumstances in this house. Naturally we want to know the connection between these two events."

"I see. Well, I don't know if there is any connection," answered Wainwright stubbornly.

"Do you know Miss Easton?"

He hesitated. "I did know her once," he said at last, "but we hadn't been seeing each other for some time."

Morgan filled his pipe slowly, and then lit it dexterously with one match. "Mr Wainwright, why not be frank?" he said genially, his whole manner changing. "Surely you can see matters can't be left like this?"

"I don't understand what you mean?"

"Surely it's quite clear," said Inspector Morgan more sharply. "Here is a girl who has disappeared. You say you know her. Here is a man who has died suddenly. His last words are that you have poisoned him. It turns out that you have been hanging round this man under an assumed name. Your explanation of why you did so frankly isn't satisfactory. You surely don't suppose we can leave it like that?"

"Well, that's all there is to it. I can't help it if it sounds fishy."

"You refuse to say any more? That's your story and you stick to it?"

"Yes, if you like to put it that way."

"Very well. We'll have to leave it like that until we get the doctor's report. Until then I can't definitely say you're under suspicion, and hence I'm not warning you. It may be that Crispin has died a perfectly natural death. Meanwhile, are you prepared to let me search you?"

"No. I don't see why the hell you should."

"Very well, then, I must ask you to stay here until we get the doctor's report. If it is to the effect that Crispin died a violent death, then you will be arrested and searched in the usual way. If you want to go home today, you'd do much better to let us search you voluntarily."

"I like your idea of a voluntary search," answered Wainwright irritably. "Why not hold a pistol to my head and have done with it? All right, go along. Search me."

Morgan called his sergeant, who ran his hands through Wainwright's pocket. Morgan glanced rapidly through the papers, penknife, keys, money and other small objects which were brought to light. Then he gave a slight exclamation.

"What's this?" he asked, picking a small glass phial out of the heap. He pulled out the stopper and sniffed it gingerly, and then his face changed.

Wainwright stared at the phial with startled eyes.

"Here," he said, "that wasn't in my pocket!"

"Don't be a fool, young man. You saw the sergeant take it out just this minute."

"But I tell you, it wasn't!" insisted Wainwright. "It couldn't have been. Don't I know what was in my own pockets? What's this, a frame-up?"

Morgan looked coldly into the young man's white, agitated face.

"A frame-up," he repeatedly sternly. "You'd better not use that kind of expression with me! You can put the other things back in your pocket. I'm keeping this. Now go straight home. Sergeant Dooney will go back with you to verify your address."

Sergeant Dooney stepped forward.

"You'd better be available at that address," Morgan added meaningly.

"But look here, I swear I didn't have that bottle in my pocket," protested Wainwright anxiously.

"Are you trying to suggest we can't believe our own eyes?" replied Morgan brusquely. "Don't be childish! Cut along now."

Dooney took his arm and Wainwright went out protesting. As the door closed behind them, Morgan turned to one of the plain-clothes officers who was helping photograph the room.

"Here, Macintosh, cut along after those two, and when Dooney leaves Wainwright, see you keep him tailed. I'll send someone else along to give you a relief as soon as I can spare him. Wainwright may try to make a bolt for it, so keep your eyes skinned! If you want any help, phone us."

Morgan walked into the next room, where the late witnesses of the scene were whiling away the time with awkward conversation.

"I shan't want any of you ladies and gentlemen today," he said genially. "Please go home when it suits you. If we want any other information, we will send an officer round to interview you at the addresses you have given us."

He returned to the séance room and, sitting down at the green bureau, made a few notes. When he had finished, he picked up the phial again and sniffed it. Then he handed it to one of his assistants.

"There's not much doubt about that, is there, Keith?"

The other sniffed it carefully.

"Seems a pretty clear case, sir," he said, replacing it. "Lucky you thought to search him!"

"Hm. I should have deserved a good kick in the pants if I hadn't. Cut along and ask Doctor Tremayne if he's finished the preliminary examination yet!"

Keith returned with Tremayne—a short, pale-faced little man with a small silvery moustache and washed-out blue eyes. He had a small silvery washed-out voice.

Dr Tremayne looked at Morgan sharply as he came in.

"You've hit a queer case, Morgan," he said at once. "Very queer indeed. Got a line on it yet?"

"I've got several facts to go on," admitted the policeman guardedly. "I take it Crispin *was* poisoned?"

"Yes, so far as one can tell from the brief examination I've made. There were clear symptoms of it. I shan't be prepared to say anything definite, of course, until after the P.M."

Morgan nodded. "As I thought. What the facts point to, at the moment, is this. This youngster, Wainwright, has been friendly with the girl, Marjorie Easton, who has just run away. From the way he spoke of her, I'm prepared to bet he was in love with her and perhaps still is. She's been staying here with Crispin. I assume our young man is jealous of Crispin.

"Of course we have no facts yet to show what was the nature of Marjorie Easton's association with Crispin, but I think it must have been fairly intimate. Wainwright has been coming here regularly under a false name. This goes to show Crispin knew of his fondness for the girl, but had never met him under his own name.

"Well, the girl disappears. At present we have no concrete evidence as to why she has run away, or where she has gone to. Perhaps she had a quarrel with Crispin. Anyway, she has been seriously ill—so we must leave that part of the story in the air for the moment.

"Even so, we have plenty of solid material to go upon. Ted Wainwright gave Crispin a glass of water. Crispin drank it and was immediately taken ill. He screamed, '*You devil, you've really poisoned me!*' That seems to show that he had guessed who Ted Wainwright was and why he had been poisoned. As luck would have it, we've one cast-iron proof. We found a small bottle that had held prussic acid in Wainwright's pocket."

Morgan tossed the phial over to Tremayne, who sniffed it carefully and nodded. Morgan looked at him triumphantly.

The inspector was a little proud of his ordered marshalling of the facts which, he felt, inevitably pointed to a simple conclusion —Wainwright's guilt. That, in the inspector's opinion, was how a murder case should be—simple, concrete and obvious. He knew that subtle or involved crimes were rare. People were driven to murder for large elementary causes that stood out a mile—or else they were insane, in which case they made no real attempt to cover up their tracks.

Tremayne looked at Morgan with a slightly apologetic smile.

"It all looks extremely convincing," he admitted. "I hardly like to throw cold water upon it. But there just happen to be two facts..."

"Which don't fit in, eh?" said Morgan, nodding his head. "Hm, let's hear them. I think we can find a place for them."

"Point number one, then. Fit it in. That phial undoubtedly contained prussic acid—or hydrocyanic acid, to be more correct. Hydrocyanic acid is a very powerful, pervasive and clinically distinctive poison. That makes it certain that, whatever substance poisoned Crispin, it was *not* hydrocyanic acid. Hydrocyanic acid causes a rapid deoxidisation of the blood which gives the whole complexion a characteristic appearance. Crispin's body had not got that appearance. Also one can generally smell its characteristic odour in the mouth and lips for some time afterwards. There is no trace of that. Finally, the victim of hydrocyanic acid passes into a coma. Crispin died in convulsions."

"Then what the devil was the poison used?" asked Morgan querulously.

"I incline to strychnine, although it is impossible to say definitely without an analysis of the organs. I'll do the post-mortem as soon as possible. Strychnine kills by deranging the nervous system. Its effect on the neural synapses and the chronaxy of the nerves is such that the slightest stimulus overflows into the whole motor system and produces terrific convulsions. The functioning of the body is disorganised, and death results. The description I got from one of the spectators of Crispin's death, and the general attitude of the body, makes it fairly clear that if he was poisoned at all, strychnine was the cause. The only other possible cause of such symptoms is tetanus, but I think in the circumstances, owing to the suddenness of the collapse, we can rule tetanus out. I should say poisoning by strychnine is undoubtedly the cause of death."

"That's an awkward fact, certainly!" admitted Morgan. "I can see things aren't going to be quite so easy as they seemed at first. What was the other fact which you said would not harmonise with my theory?"

"Well, you suggested that the motive was the eternal triangle

—Wainwright's jealousy of Crispin. Unfortunately you've got your triangle arranged wrongly."

"How do you mean?"

"Michael Crispin happens to have been a woman."

CHAPTER VI

The Six Queer Things

"A woman!" exclaimed Inspector Morgan. "That certainly is a surprise!"

"What beats me," went on Tremayne, "is that no one spotted it. Her build is slightly more masculine than the average woman's, I'll admit, but, even so, the broad hips and hairless face ought to have made most people suspicious. She had her clothes cut to make her look as masculine as possible."

"I must find out who her tailor was. Not that it will help much now."

"Is there anything else you wanted to know?" asked Tremayne.

"Not at the moment. I'd rather you went ahead with the postmortem and analysis as quickly as possible. You've left me plenty to chew over.

"You might take that glass," added Morgan, "and get Hitchcock to develop any fingerprints as soon as possible, and then let you have the sediment in the glass for analysis. If there isn't enough liquid in the glass, there's some spilt on the carpet here. I should test it for strychnine first, as that seems to have been the poison used. You'd better take this phial too. Make sure it *has* contained hydrocyanic acid and nothing else. It certainly smells like it, but after these last two surprises, it's impossible to be sure. It may be some fake stuff."

As soon as Tremayne had gone, Morgan began a careful interrogation of the servants. His first task was the questioning of Miss Easton's nurse, Miss Furnivall. She was of that type, useful to the detective and all too rare, which answers questions clearly and does not regard speculation or inferences as evidence. Unfortunately she had only been in the Crispins' employ for a short time. She had been engaged to look after Marjorie Easton because of her experience with mental cases, and had spent most of her time with the girl.

"What exactly was the state of this girl's mind?"

"She was obviously on the verge of a nervous breakdown, and was very moody and depressed. You could not describe her as in any way mad. She was perfectly rational in her conversation and always recognised people and remembered things. She seems to have had hallucinations occasionally, but these were the outcome of her depressed and sensitive state. I think they would have vanished as she became in better shape physically."

"Why do you think she has disappeared in this way? Was it a sudden brain storm?"

"I can't give any reason at all; perhaps she woke up in the night under the influence of some delusion and wandered out of the house. Even so, I can't understand how she was able to get far, seeing she was still in her night things. She would certainly have been noticed in the street; and if she wandered haphazard into a house, it would have been reported to you long ago. So you would have heard of her even if she is in such a state that she does not know her own name and address—which is quite likely, by the way."

"Up to the time I left there were no reports in of anyone answering to her description," admitted Morgan. "It is strange. It is still too early to fear the worst. There may be some quite simple explanation."

"There's just one thing that worries me, and that is why I slept so heavily last night. I am a light sleeper, and I have that special sensitiveness to sickroom noises which all nurses develop. We do not respond to ordinary noises, even if they are fairly loud, but the slightest unusual movement or cry from our patient wakes us at once. I should have thought it would have been impossible for Miss Easton to have got out of bed and gone out of the room without waking me."

"Well, it does happen sometimes," answered Morgan. "People often sleep more heavily than they imagine—a fact our housebreaking friends count on. I don't think you need be worried by that."

Miss Furnivall looked doubtful. "You may think me foolish,

Inspector, but I am certain there is more in it than that. When I woke up this morning, I found my shoulder and neck were bruised. You can see the marks on my neck now."

Morgan examined the reddish-purple contusions. He gave a low whistle.

"Those look like the marks of a hand. Has someone been trying to strangle you?"

Miss Furnivall shook her head.

"No, the marks are at the side of the neck, not round the windpipe. But they are marks where someone has gripped me violently—and this must have happened in the night. Why didn't it wake me? How could I have been sleeping so soundly that these bruises on my neck could have been made without waking me?"

"You mean you must have been drugged?"

"It seems the only explanation."

"Have you any idea when and where the drug could have been given to you?"

"Most likely in the glass of cocoa which is always brought up to me last thing at night. Now I think of it, it did seem to have had a faintly bitter taste, although I should not be prepared to swear to that."

"The Crispins must have had something to do with that. Had you noticed anything odd about them when you were here?"

Miss Furnivall sniffed disdainfully.

"I haven't noticed anything else. Rappings and séances and spirits—it's enough to drive *anyone* mad. Childish goings on! As for the people who come here—well, I've had plenty of patients a good deal saner!"

"I don't mean that kind of oddness," explained Morgan. "I mean the kind that is likely to come in for my attention, not yours."

"Oh, they were law abiding enough, I dare say. I got my salary regularly, at any rate."

Morgan looked at her speculatively.

"What would you say," he asked, "if I told you Michael Crispin was really a woman?"

Miss Furnivall started.

"I should say you were daft, man!" she exclaimed. Then she

hesitated. "And yet, he certainly was abnormal . . . Do you mean . . . Well, I'm blest . . . That walk and those hips of his . . . And the fatness in the wrong places!"

Morgan nodded.

"Yes, Michael Crispin was a woman. How long she had been masquerading as a man I don't know. What precisely did you mean by saying he certainly was abnormal?"

The nurse found it difficult to explain.

"Well, one got a queer impression of him. He had a standoffish kind of manner, very polite and formal. Somehow one didn't think of him quite as a man because of that, but as someone who was neither—you know, emotionally cold. He didn't strike one as effeminate, as some men do. He didn't strike one as masculine. It was an odd feeling, and it gave me the creeps. I can imagine it would have a powerful effect on some people."

"Well, that's interesting, Miss Furnivall. It's all I want to know at the moment. I suppose you will be staying on here?"

"Yes, for another week, at any rate. I'm entitled to a week's notice. Miss Easton may be found at any moment, and she'll be likely to need my help. Has Miss Crispin said anything about whether I'm to stay on?"

"I can't find Miss Crispin. She seems to have gone out and not come back."

Morgan's next task was to examine the rest of the household —cook, parlourmaid and chauffeur.

He found little response from either the cook or the parlourmaid. They both seemed to think Crispin had been a good master. "He" had paid them well and not been exacting. Their opinion of Bella was not quite so high—she was fussy and tyrannical.

As for the "goings on"—they had been scared of these at first. Not everyone would be prepared to work in that kind of house, they said, much less sleep in. But one soon got accustomed to it. It was harmless really.

"Not that I can ever stomach the way the master talks of spirits being in the room at meals when I hand round the plates. It gives me the jumps sometimes," remarked the parlourmaid.

Their surprise seemed genuine enough when they were told that Crispin had been their mistress and not their master. Evidently Crispin had played her role well and at all times. It had become instinctive no doubt; all the same, they admitted she had seemed "odd."

Morgan's final interview was with Hawkins, the chauffeur. He told Morgan that the car had vanished from the garage. It had been there in the morning, for he had been cleaning it. It must therefore have gone soon after Crispin's death. This suggested to Morgan where Isabel Crispin had gone.

"Could Miss Crispin drive the car?" asked Morgan.

"Yes, I taught her, and sometimes on my off day she would take it out shopping herself. She's not a very good driver, though, as she's still nervous of town traffic."

"How long have you been in the Crispins' service?"

"Five years."

Morgan looked in his notebook.

"You're the senior member of the household then? Did you know that Michael Crispin was not really Michael Crispin?"

Hawkins seemed taken aback.

"Not Michael Crispin? I don't quite follow."

"Michael Crispin turns out to have been a woman."

"A woman! Impossible!" exclaimed Hawkins.

Morgan wondered whether his surprise was really genuine.

"Didn't you guess that?"

"Good heavens, no, sir. I never suspected anything of the kind for a moment."

Morgan felt a little suspicious of this reply. It was if anything too sweeping. Miss Furnivall had distinctly said that Crispin had struck her as odd and abnormal. Even the cook and parlourmaid had admitted that there was something queer and unusual about Crispin's manner. But Hawkins, who was obviously intelligent and had known Crispin longer than anyone, appeared to be completely surprised by the discovery. True, as chauffeur he did not have so many opportunities for observation as the parlourmaid, nor had he the experienced eye of Miss Furnivall.

Hawkins was not a man it was easy to disconcert by cross-examination. He was a quiet, dark fellow of about thirty-eight, with that pliancy of manner which often conceals an internal stubbornness.

Morgan sent him away and returned to the question of Isabel Crispin. She still had not returned to the house, and no one was able to give any useful suggestions as to where she might have gone. He got from Hawkins the number of the car and had the Yard send out a general message to pull it in. If Bella Crispin had used it to make a getaway, she would not be able to go far without being pulled up by some sharp-eyed constable burning for promotion.

That evening the car was found abandoned by the side of the London-Southampton road. No one had seen the driver. It was clear that Bella Crispin had made a getaway.

Crispin was poisoned. Marjorie Easton had disappeared. Bella Crispin had run away.... It seemed a curious and unrelated combination of events; and yet they must be related in some way.

Morgan decided that a thorough search of the house might help him.

He spent the next two days on this search. The result surprised him. The average person has in his house an accumulation of material in the way of documents, letters, and so forth, which arises naturally in the course of his daily life. The Crispins' house on the contrary was bare of everything except the most ordinary and necessary objects—hardly any letters, and these nearly all tradesmen's bills or circular letters, which had been filed carefully away. Evidently there was method in this. Crispin had at some time expected a search.

What could it mean? Did Crispin, during "his" lifetime, always keep "his" house in such a way that no clue would be revealed to any searcher? If so, this raised several interesting questions as to what manner of life Crispin led, that she should be so afraid of enquiry into it. Or had everything suspicious been carefully removed by someone else in preparation for Crispin's murder? Or had Isabel, in making her escape, wiped out any traces which might point to something she wished to keep hidden?

This last hardly seemed likely, in view of the short time which had elapsed between Crispin's murder and Isabel Crispin's departure.

Of course there was the possibility that both the latter hypotheses were true—that Isabel had taken away all revealing documents, from a bank passbook to personal correspondence, because she had been connected with "Michael" Crispin's murder. This, however, seemed ruled out by Isabel's involuntary cry on seeing Crispin die in agony, as reported by those present:

"*They've* got him!"

This seemed to suggest that she had fled from the same assailants as those who, she believed, had struck down "Michael" Crispin.

However, all this was farfetched. The facts still pointed to Ted Wainwright, in spite of the inconsistency of the poison bottle and —as yet—the lack of sufficient motive. Even allowing for these defects, he was easily first on the list of suspects. The inspector's reverence for facts forced him to keep Ted Wainwright in the position of most likely murderer.

Before he had left the house, the inspector's search was blessed by a real find. One of the drawers in a chest of drawers was locked—the only locked receptacle he had come upon in the course of his whole search. This in itself had been curious. Most houses have several locked drawers and cupboards. Moreover, a moment's examination showed him that an effort had already been made to open the drawer by force. There were scratches round the keyhole, and an attempt had been made to insert a lever of some kind in the crack and prise the drawer open.

The inspector remembered that a bunch of keys had been found on Crispin's clothes. He sent down for these keys and found that one fitted. He opened the drawer.

The contents were at first disappointing. He had expected to find papers or some revealing object. Instead there was a collection of things that were not only not directly associated, but seemed to have absolutely no relevance to each other. They were so ill assorted that their very irrelevance gave them, as it were, something in common. They lay there in front of the inspector on the table, and challenged him to read any meaning into them. Six of them—the Six Queer Things, he christened them:

(1) A stout linen sheet with several broad, strong canvas tapes fastened to each side. The inspector had never seen anything like it before.

(2) A piece of card, with various pieces of coloured wool in knots stuck on it and marked by different letters. It appeared to be some kind of colour or size chart, and yet there was an odd irrelevancy and amateurishness about the way it was put together that made the inspector hesitate to classify it as a definite chart or sheet of samples.

(3) A number of toy balloons, one of which was attached to a bicycle pump with a special connection. This connection had a tap leading out of it additional to the main connection, and communicated in some way with the head of the pump.

(4) A photograph of a woman. The fashion placed it about twenty years ago.

(5) A box containing a short forked stick, a thin pipe and a number of straws. There was some brownish substance on the end of one of the straws, and a sniff revealed the presence of nicotine.

(6) A small textbook on "Forensic Medicine."

The last article was the only one which gave any satisfaction to the inspector at all. As for the others—well, there was nothing desperately odd about any of them taken alone, but taken together as found in a carefully locked drawer which someone had attempted to force open, in a house where murder had been committed, they were mysterious and challenging. They were facts, cold, solid facts, which one could handle and touch, and yet for the first time the inspector had an unpleasant feeling that facts were not enough, that just because they were facts it would need some wild and extravagant theory to fit them all within the boundaries of one coherent story. He packed them carefully away in a bag.

His search eventually threw light on one of the Queer Things. In his search of Marjorie Easton's room he came upon an envelope containing a faded photograph and a ring. On the back of the photograph were the words: "To darling Marjorie."

This photograph was of the same woman as the photograph in the locked drawer, although it was a different study, taken at a slightly earlier age.

2

"There is no doubt about it, Inspector," said Tremayne to

Morgan next day. "Crispin, or whatever her name was, died of strychnine poisoning. It must have been a pretty strong dose too!"

"What about the phial which we thought had contained hydrocyanic acid?"

"Yes, it was hydrocyanic acid all right. And nothing else! So I'm afraid the phial can't have had anything to do with the woman's death."

"I'm not so sure. It's more than likely that the phial is a device to put us off the scent. If Wainwright thinks that our discovering Crispin really died of strychnine poisoning will be enough to make us let up on him because that phial contained another poison, he's very much mistaken. We've had experience with half-baked smart alecs like him before. What about that glass?"

"The strychnine came out of that all right. There was no need to analyse the carpet! That's all the news for the moment."

When Tremayne had gone, Morgan phoned up the Records Office, where the fingerprints and photographs of the dead woman had been sent. In return he got back a dossier. "Michael Crispin" had a criminal record.

It appeared that she had first been known to the police as Brenda Hartington, and was that rare bird, a woman crook, who specialised in financial confidence tricks. She had swindled two men in a brilliant bogus company transaction. It was the merest accident that she had been caught, and the money had never been discovered. After that the police had kept a close tag on her, and although, ever since her release, shady stories had been circulating about her, there had never been any definite complaint. And then, quite suddenly, about five years ago, she had disappeared. The police had been unable to pick her up again.

The explanation now seemed fairly clear. She had taken on a new role, that of Michael Crispin, and the change of sex had been sufficient to throw the police off the scent. It seemed an odd choice of disguises to Morgan until, turning over the dossier, he saw that Brenda Hartington had been the daughter of a male impersonator, who had made a fortune on the halls, and then gambled and drank it away, to die of dipsomania in complete poverty when Brenda was fifteen. It was a fairly safe assumption that Brenda, as a child, had copied her mother's turns, and in after life the disguise had come naturally to her. The somewhat masculine build was probably inherited.

Morgan examined again the depositions of the various witnesses concerning "Michael Crispin's" death. These witnesses all seemed to agree definitely on one point—that *no one had handled the glass of water between the time it was filled and the time it was given to Crispin except Wainwright.* Nor had anyone been near enough to him to put in the poison without his observing it. Fantastic as such a possibility was, Morgan had considered it.

The poison might have been already in the glass. But this was effectively disposed of by the statement of three or four witnesses, that they distinctly remembered seeing Wainwright rinse the glass before he filled it. This rinsing might have given him the opportunity to put in the strychnine.

Of course Wainwright must have had some container on him, and the only thing found had been the phial of hydrocyanic acid. But still, he had had plenty of time to get rid of a small article between the death of Crispin and the arrival of the police. It would have been perfectly easy, for example, to throw it out of the window in the confusion.

Indeed, now that the inspector came to think of it, the very fact that the phial of hydrocyanic acid was found in Wainwright's pocket seemed to reveal its function as a "blind." If Wainwright really had used prussic acid to poison Crispin, his first act would have been to get rid of the container. But, on the other hand, its retention could be explained by the theory that he had played the bold game of banking on Morgan's surprise when he found that the phial had not contained the poison which had killed Crispin but another poison. Such a surprise might be relied upon to make a policeman regard Wainwright as an injured party, and turn his attention elsewhere. Morgan had to admit, however, that Wainwright hardly struck him as the kind of character who would commit a crime, and then use such dangerously subtle methods to cover it up.

But, come to that, Wainwright did not seem the type to use poison at all, which only showed the danger of indulging overmuch in theories about criminal characters and what people were likely to do. In the inspector's experience, people did what they did and that was an end of it. It was no good being surprised at his time of life at what people did.

He decided that on the face of it enough facts existed to warrant his reporting to his chief that he had found the murderer. There certainly seemed sufficient evidence to convict Wainwright in a court of law. Morgan would not recommend to his chief the immediate execution of the warrant, for four problems still remained unsolved. Why was there still no news of Marjorie Easton? Where had Bella Crispin vanished to? What was the motive of Wainwright's murder? Why, once he had chosen to poison Crispin, had he chosen such an extremely obvious and easily detectable way—in front of a roomful of people, all witnesses to the act?

Inspector Morgan decided to interview Dr Wood. Wood had been responsible for introducing Wainwright to the Crispin circle, under the pseudonym of George Robinson, and he should be able to throw light upon the motives for Wainwright's deed. Until then there were still too many loose strands. As long as they remained, it would be better to leave Wainwright at liberty and keep a close watch on him. He might easily get panicky and lead them either to Marjorie Easton or Isabel Crispin, or to the real motive for "Michael's" act.

Although Morgan hardly liked to admit it even to himself, there was another factor in the case. There was the presence —inexplicable, challenging and ridiculous—of the Six Queer Things.

CHAPTER VII

The Mare's Nest

Inspector Morgan was puzzled by his first impressions of Dr Wood. He had expected to see some twopenny ha'penny medico with a dubious past, who had been drawn—innocently perhaps and yet discreditably—into Crispin's circle. His first glance at Wood's surroundings, however, showed that "twopenny ha'penny" certainly was not the correct description for Wood. He was either a fashionable doctor or a wealthy one.

This impression was confirmed by his talk with the man himself. Dr Wood had all the assurance that comes from success, and the supple temperament and easy manner that makes the ability to enjoy success.

The coroner's inquest had not yet taken place. The papers were not yet blazing with the full details of what was afterwards to become the crime of the season—The Man-Woman Mystery. Morgan hoped, therefore, to have the advantage of surprise in dealing with Wood.

"I suppose you have heard that Crispin is dead?" he said, as soon as he had introduced himself and Wood's enquiring glance had demanded his business.

The doctor looked genuinely surprised.

"No, dead? Really! I didn't even know he was ill! How did it happen? A car accident?"

"I thought you knew him fairly well. Haven't you heard how he died?"

"I shouldn't like to say I knew him well. But I was closely enough associated with his circle to expect to be told of his death. However, I only came back from Ireland this morning, and it may be the news is in my mail, which hasn't yet been opened. I am sure either Miss Crispin or Miss Easton would let me know of any such accident."

"Both Miss Crispin and Miss Easton have disappeared," remarked the inspector. "You evidently have no idea of the seriousness of what has happened at Belmont Avenue."

"I certainly haven't," exclaimed Wood. "Crispin dead and the women disappeared! What on earth has been going on while I have been away?"

"I had better tell you the whole story from the beginning," said Morgan.

"The whole story" was not quite true. His mind was rapidly reviewing it to decide what he would omit. He decided to leave out a reference to Wainwright's guilt in the first presentation of the story. It might put Wood off his guard, should he have any idea of shielding his protégé.

"Miss Easton vanished from the house on Monday night. No one knows where she went, and she has not yet been discovered. The nurse who was sleeping with her heard nothing, and she believes she was drugged."

"Drugged! But surely that is fantastic. I'm surprised at Miss Furnivall."

"No doubt, but it also happens to be a fact. At the séance next day, when Crispin drank a glass of water, he fell on the ground in convulsions; and a few minutes later he died. When we came in, we found that Miss Crispin had disappeared with the car. It was found abandoned halfway to Southampton, but there has been no sign of her or Miss Easton from that day to this."

"Good heavens, what an amazing story!" There seemed somehow less surprise in the doctor's voice than Morgan expected.

The inspector prepared to launch his thunderbolt.

"Doctor, did you know that Michael Crispin was a swindler?"

Dr Wood had already risen to his feet, and was opening the door of a cabinet beside his chair. He stopped for a moment when Morgan spoke.

"Yes, of course, Inspector," he replied smoothly.

"You'll have a drink, won't you?" he added, as if both remarks were equally casual and expected.

"Oh, you did know, did you?" replied the inspector, a little taken aback. He paused. "Well, I don't mind if I do have a drink."

Wood walked to the table with the glasses and decanter on a tray.

"Perhaps you knew that Crispin was really a woman too?" Morgan watched Wood intently.

"Yes, yes, of course," answered Wood with a laugh, pouring out the drinks with a steady hand. "I suppose it was a surprise to you?"

"It certainly was," admitted the policeman, "and, if I may say so, it is a little surprising to find you knew it. How long have you known it, by the way?"

"Well, naturally, as a psychologist I saw that Crispin was abnormal from the first meeting. I came to the conclusion that it was a case of transvestism at a fairly early date."

"Transvestism?"

"Eonism," explained Wood solemnly. The inspector could not make out whether or not he was being chaffed.

"Eonism? Please explain. I am only an ignorant policeman."

"Transvestism, meaning interchange of garments proper to the sexes. It is a not unusual psychological ailment, also called 'eonism' after the Chevalier d'Eon, a woman who once masqueraded as a man with great success at the French court and later in London society. Or he may have been a man who masqueraded as a woman—it has never been properly cleared up, although a great many people lost money on wagers about it. It's a harmless foible."

"Well, it seems a damned silly foible to me. I can't understand it."

"Probably not, but then, if you'll excuse me, you're a policeman and not a psychologist."

"Nonsense, there's no need to bring psychology into it. Crispin was a convicted swindler, and her disguise was intended to keep her out of the hands of the police."

"But if you don't bring psychology into it, how can you explain why her attempt to escape from the eyes of the law should take that interesting and peculiar form?"

"Well, it's not a point on which I wish to argue," replied Morgan sharply. "All this theoretical stuff is all very well for science, but it doesn't get one far in a court of law."

"I agree. In fact I have never found that anything gets one very far in a court of law—speaking as one who has had some experience of being an expert witness."

Morgan felt he was being deliberately sidetracked.

"What I can't understand—if you'll excuse me, Doctor—is how you, a scientist, should go on associating with a man whom you knew to be a rogue and a swindler. For example, I understand you were attending his séances as an investigator. How could you do that, knowing that he was a swindler?"

"All the more, knowing that he was a swindler," replied Dr Wood with a laugh. "You don't suppose we psychiatrists divide spiritualistic phenomena into 'swindling' and 'genuine'? They are all genuine—that is to say, they are all produced by human beings, they are all *psychological phenomena*. You may equally say they are all swindling, inasmuch as the causes attributed to the phenomena, external disembodied personalities, are not real causes. The fact that the conscious mind of some of the mediums is free from the desire to deceive, and all their phenomena are produced entirely by their subconscious personality, whereas in other cases the medium is consciously aware of fraud, is not a fact of great significance scientifically. Naturally it is of some importance in the light it throws upon the integration of personality, and therefore the swindlers are scientifically the more interesting.

"In the case of Crispin you had a conscious intention of fraud, certainly, but you also had a curious personality—strongly ambitious, eonist, and otherwise peculiar, with definitely unusual psychological powers of hyperaesthesia and dissociation. I have a notebook in which I have a fairly full record of the case. I'm sorry, now Crispin's dead, that I neglected lately to follow up his more recent developments. I am a busy man, you see. But, even so, I have some very interesting psychological data which I am using in a monograph I am writing now. Would you like to see the notebook on which it is based?"

"No, thank you," said Morgan, somewhat abruptly. "I don't understand this scientific jargon. I like to call a fact a fact."

"And I prefer to give it a name which indicates more precisely its class among existing phenomena," replied Wood pleasantly.

"The age-old difference between the scientist and the empiricist!"

"No doubt, no doubt. I can't object to being called an empiricist, as I'm not sure I know what it means. The point is that Crispin has been poisoned. Who poisoned her? Where did the poison come from? And how long before Crispin's death was it administered? In the glass of water?"

"Hydrocyanic acid acts fairly quickly, if it acts at all," replied Wood thoughtfully. "How long a time elapsed between the drink and Crispin's collapse? Not that I want to muscle in on your police surgeon's territory!"

The inspector, who was just then filling his pipe, stopped short and gazed at Wood curiously. A silence followed, and in the silence Wood became aware of Morgan's cold scrutiny. His face was expressionless.

"How did you guess that Crispin was killed by hydrocyanic acid, Doctor Wood?" Morgan asked quietly.

Wood, who had a glass in his hand, raised it to his lips. Some moments passed before he replied coolly, "Surely you told me so?"

"I did not."

Wood smiled.

"You must have done, Inspector. I'm a psychologist, not a thought-reader."

"I did not tell you, Doctor. I am quite certain about that!"

"Well, that's curious. I certainly had a distinct impression that you had said so. I suppose I guessed it from the symptoms you described."

"But I told you nothing about the symptoms," persisted Morgan, "except that Crispin went into convulsions. Does that happen to be a symptom of hydrocyanic acid poisoning?"

Wood shrugged his shoulders.

"I couldn't say. That's more your police expert's province. I've been a specialist in psychology so long that I'm afraid I've lost what little general knowledge I had, including my knowledge of forensic medicine."

Morgan grinned sardonically.

"Well, I can tell you then, Doctor, that convulsions are not a symptom of hydrocyanic acid, which on the contrary produces coma and a general collapse. The symptoms are as opposite as they could be."

There was a definite look of uneasiness in Dr Wood's eyes.

"What a silly mistake of mine. Please don't give me away. Every doctor has these areas of ignorance."

"I'm still interested in knowing what put this idea of hydrocyanic acid into your head?"

"Sheer ignorance, Inspector! I'm not afraid to confess it."

"Crispin died of *strychnine* poisoning."

Wood gave a curious smile.

"Just as well in the circumstances! Otherwise it might have seemed a bit fishy, eh, my guessing the poison without being told? It's lucky I guessed wrong. I know what you detectives are when once you're on the trail!"

"Not by firsthand experience, I hope," said Morgan coldly.

"No," laughed Wood genially. "Only from experience as an expert witness trying to save some poor half-wit from your clutches. Well, I'm sorry I can't be of more help. Is there anything else I can tell you?"

"Oh yes. Quite a lot yet. Can you tell us what you know about Marjorie Easton? I understand you were treating her."

"Yes, that is so. Marjorie Easton was a girl who was unlucky enough to fall under Crispin's influence. As a result of submitting voluntarily to hypnotism and automatic writing, her personality was split. Her new subconscious self was completely under Crispin's domination. At the time I saw her she was on the verge of a complete mental breakdown due to her inner conflict. It was a difficult problem medically. To have taken her away from the Crispins would have produced a mental collapse at once. The conflict would have produced a complete disintegration of the personality owing to the strength of the subconscious self.

"On the other hand, it would have been fatal to let her go on indulging in the various automatisms and dissociations that are part of spiritualistic technique. As a doctor, I ordered her to remain at Belmont Avenue, but to keep out of Crispin's influence, as far as possible, by not participating in any psychic activities.

"As you know, we doctors can't do much in these cases. We have to rely on the natural tendency to integration of the higher nervous centres in a normal person. Miss Easton was, in fact, recovering rapidly under this treatment, and I believe she might have been able to leave Belmont Avenue in about a month with her conflict solved. The subconscious personality was gradually being brought to the consciousness and integrated. Frankly, in view of Crispin's attitude, this disappearance of hers sounds ominous."

"What do you suggest is the cause of it?"

"Well, it is possible that Crispin, finding her influence over the girl was waning, may have had her taken somewhere. I can't understand why Crispin would go so far. But then I never saw the motive for Crispin's domination of the girl. It isn't as if she were a rich client he could fleece. It seemed quite altruistic, if you can use the word in this connection."

"If your theory's correct, now that Crispin's dead she ought to turn up again."

"Yes, certainly. Unless Bella Crispin—or whatever her real name is—is keeping her hidden. The alternative is that Marjorie recovered her normal faculties suddenly. In disgust at the situation in which she found herself, she might have decided to leave Belmont Avenue. It's a natural reaction—an impulse to hide herself away from the world. Such sudden recoveries are known. They generally take place after a stupor which may last only a few hours."

"But she left so hurriedly that she didn't change from her night things into day clothes."

"Then that's bad. Very bad. I'm afraid the other theory's more likely. It certainly is a tangle, whichever theory you adopt."

There was a pause.

"Have you ever heard of a fellow called George Robinson?" asked the inspector.

"George Robinson," repeated Wood slowly. "Oh yes, he's a young fellow who helps me occasionally. As a matter of fact, he acted as an observer for me at some of the séances I couldn't attend at Crispin's."

"I see. Queer chap to use as an observer, isn't he?"

"Why?"

"Well, I mean he's not very highly educated."

"Not in the public-school sense, perhaps. But he has a good grip of general principles and plenty of common sense, and that's all we want."

"I understand. Now can you tell me if you know a fellow named Ted Wainwright?"

"Ted Wainwright. It seems vaguely familiar. And yet I can't place it. Why do you want to know?"

"I'm asking you if you know anyone of that name," said Inspector Morgan stubbornly.

"Well, I can't say I do, definitely, at the moment. But I run into so many people in the course of my work. I may remember later."

"I see. You may remember when I've gone," replied Morgan, with a significant look. "I'm sorry you can't remember now. You might be able to help him. But there it is. Since you can't, we shall have to go straight ahead and issue a warrant for Wainwright's arrest for the murder of Michael Crispin—or Brenda Hartington, to give her her real name."

"Good heavens! You can't do that," exclaimed Wood, his whole expression changing. "What evidence have you?"

"The fact that he was in the room with Crispin under an assumed name; that in addition he had a motive for murdering Crispin; and finally that he handed her a glass of water which proves to have been full of strychnine."

"But this is incredible. I can't believe that Wainwright would do that. It's utterly impossible!"

"Ah, you do know him then," exclaimed the inspector triumphantly. "I think, sir, it would have been better if you had been frank with me from the beginning."

"As a matter of fact, I agree with you. I should have been franker. I see that now. I did not realise you knew so much."

"Well, let's have the whole story now," said Morgan. "The *whole* story, please—no reservations, however well meaning!"

"Briefly the story is this: I found out that Marjorie, before she came under Crispin's influence, had been friendly with this young fellow, Ted Wainwright. They were, in fact, engaged. But then they broke it off, largely as a result of Crispin's influence."

"Engaged, were they? Well, it beats me how a normal girl

could have broken off an engagement with a normal young man simply as a result of getting mixed up with this reptile of a woman with her conjuring tricks!"

"Then if it beats you, I can only say, Inspector, that you have a limited knowledge of the intricacies of the human mind. As for 'normal' people, there are no such persons to my knowledge. If I were to find one, he or she would be so unique that he would be more abnormal than the abnormal, if you'll excuse a rather Irish way of putting it."

"Then who are the abnormal? And what are the people we call normal?"

"Only people who happen to conform to the standards of society, by means of suppressing successfully the antisocial or *odd* parts of their nature. These repressed parts still exist and tend to form another personality for which—in certain circumstances and by certain means—hypnotism is the most obvious method; great emotional stress is another cause—can be awakened to life. Then we call them abnormal. We may shut them up."

"Well, it seems to me that Miss Easton should have been taken out of this hypnotic influence..."

"After it had been built up? I can see you have had no experience of a psychic fixation. I have. No, that wasn't the key to her healing. You *can't* drag people about according to *your* will. They have wills too. Those wills must assent, if the mind is to be healed. No, it was a more difficult matter than just moving her physically. It was quite literally a matter of battling for Marjorie Easton's soul. I called Wainwright in—perhaps unwisely, as I now see—to help me. I got him to attend these séances in disguise, so that he could understand what Marjorie Easton was up against and be able to help her without a countermove from Crispin. Frankly Wainwright's first reaction was the very reverse of helpful to Miss Easton. It alternated between a sullen resentfulness, which could only drive Marjorie away from him and had in fact brought about their separation, and a desire to inflict personal violence on Crispin, which would only have put Marjorie still further under Crispin's influence."

"A desire to commit personal violence," repeated Morgan thoughtfully. "That's interesting."

"You must not misunderstand me," replied Wood sharply. "I mean Wainwright had a natural human desire to sock Crispin on the jaw; that was all. The sort of open violence any man might want to inflict on another who had stolen his girl. It is absurd to suggest, as you are suggesting, that it could have gone any farther. As for poison—don't you see how totally impossible that would be for a man of Wainwright's mentality? He had, in any case, got over that violent mood—I had argued him out of it—by the time he attended Crispin's séances. He had begun to see that he must fight Crispin with other weapons. He realised victory was a matter of psychological, not physical, force."

"Granted all that. There are still certain facts you have forgotten. Granted Wainwright saw the necessity of fighting Crispin with other weapons. Suppose, even, that he was beginning to be victorious with those weapons—with your help. You yourself said Miss Easton was growing better. But then suppose that Crispin, on the defensive, started a new campaign. Suppose that, seeing she was losing on the *psychological* plane, suppose she resorted to physical violence and forcibly abducted Miss Easton. With a knowledge of this, wouldn't your model young man decide to fight violence with the same weapon? Miss Easton had disappeared before Crispin's murder. Surely that disappearance was the motive for her murder?"

"But that's preposterous!" replied Wood hotly. "It is simply theorising without facts, in order to back up your prejudice against Wainwright."

"Preposterous or not, it is what the case suggests to me, and no one has ever accused me of undue imagination. You say Wainwright's instinct would have been to sock Crispin on the jaw—as one man would another. Suppose he had found Crispin was *not a man,* but the strange, eccentric thing she was? Mightn't his reaction have been to destroy her—like a reptile—with poison. He couldn't use physical violence on a woman, however degraded. His instinct would prevent that. But it wouldn't prevent him destroying her in that open way like a pest—in order to save the girl he loved."

"The theory is much too farfetched. As it happened, I never told Wainwright that Crispin was a woman. So how could he know? It would need someone unusually observant to guess it."

"Why didn't you tell him?" demanded the inspector sharply.

"Why should I? It's not my business to provide motives for police detectives."

"I should have thought it would have been natural to tell him—except for one reason. It might be that, as a psychologist, you knew what Wainwright's reaction would be. You feared that if he found out, it would lead him to do this very thing he did do. And I firmly believe Wainwright did find out."

"Nonsense. I am amazed at the way you are speculating in this case, with a few bare facts to go on. It's a tissue of fancy."

"On the contrary, it's a tissue of fact."

"In any case, before you commit yourself hopelessly to the tissue of fact, you might at least explain what Crispin's motive was in dominating this penniless girl? You won't suggest, I hope, that her intentions were charitable? She must have thought she could make some use of the girl, to spend so much time, trouble and money on her. What was it?"

"The obvious explanation is that she was making Marjorie Easton into a medium—one of her tools."

"I think that was only a means to an end. What did she want such a tool for so urgently?"

"It is sufficient explanation for me. However, I admit there are one or two things in the case that are still not clear. Perhaps you can help me."

Morgan opened the small case he had brought with him. Inside were the Six Queer Things.

"These were all found inside a drawer in the Crispins' house. It beats me what they can have been used for. Yet the circumstances make it almost certain that they have some significant bearing on the case. Can you make anything of them?"

Dr Wood examined the miscellaneous articles carefully. Then he turned to the inspector. "You have certainly discovered something very remarkable and unique," he said solemnly. "Congratulations."

"What is it?" asked the inspector eagerly.

"A mare's nest," replied Dr Wood. "I have never seen such a fine specimen in all my scientific career."

Blushing slightly with annoyance, the inspector put back the objects in the case. He managed to muster a feeble grin.

"All the same, I think there's something in them!"

CHAPTER VIII

"Something Damned Queer Has Been Happening"

Inspector Morgan went back to his chief and had a long conversation with him.

"Superficially the case is as clear as daylight," he reported. "Wainwright poisoned Crispin. We know Crispin died of strychnine poisoning; we know strychnine poisoning was in the glass which Wainwright handed to Crispin; and we know no one else went near the glass, or had any other opportunity to put poison in it. We know also that Wainwright had a definite motive for getting rid of Crispin."

The chief nodded.

"Well, what's the trouble? It's clear enough."

"There are still a good few facts left that worry me."

"Such as?"

"Why has this girl disappeared? Why has Crispin's sister disappeared? What's behind the whole episode of Crispin's relations with Marjorie? And then the odd collection of stuff in that locked drawer!"

"The Six Queer Things?" said his chief with a smile. "Has it occurred to you that these might have been put there to make it more difficult?"

Morgan only grunted in reply.

"If you really want my opinion," went on the chief, "it seems to me you've trusted our doctor friend too much."

"In what way?"

"About this girl. How do you know she really *was* under Crispin's influence?"

"Well, good Lord, she was staying at his house! Besides, I've seen her uncle, who said she went there absolutely against his consent. He's very worked up about it. He doesn't seem so much worried at losing her, as that she is dragging him into trouble, which may affect his business."

The chief pulled thoughtfully at his little iron-grey moustache.

"But don't you think she might have been deceiving him as well as Crispin?"

"What do you mean?"

"Well, isn't it possible that she was in the plot with Wainwright? It seems darned odd that directly Wainwright does his stuff she disappears."

"You mean Wainwright, the doctor and this girl had a definite plan of campaign against Crispin?"

"Yes."

"It's possible. It certainly worries me that the girl hasn't turned up. But that doesn't disturb the central issue. Wainwright is the only person who *could* have poisoned Crispin."

The chief nodded.

"Yes, I think that's fairly clear. We may be able to drag the whole truth out of them later when we've got Wainwright behind lock and key. You'll pull him in at once, I suppose."

"Yes. There doesn't seem much point in keeping him waiting any longer."

2

As soon as Morgan had left him, Dr Wood called for his car and went round to see Wainwright. He could not fail to notice the burly man in the mackintosh standing just opposite the little house, leaning against a lamppost.

Wainwright was obviously worried. Lines under his eyes showed that he had had little sleep, and he started pacing restlessly up and down his room directly he had let Wood in.

"What the hell do they think they're doing?" he groaned incoherently. "They ask me every sort of damned silly question. Why did I dislike Crispin? Did anyone else handle the glass? As if I cared a damn when Marjorie is still lost! What did that devil do with her before he died?"

"We're trying to find her," said Wood gently, trying to soothe him. "I don't think it's a question of what Crispin did to her. I think her disappearance was definitely an *escape*. But perhaps she temporarily lost her memory and is wandering round somewhere..."

"Then why can't the police find her instead of badgering me?"

"It's not so easy. She may have concealed her loss of memory and have got a job—started a new existence."

"But the papers are full of her disappearance. Surely that should be enough to tell her who she is."

"Not necessarily. She may not connect the girl she reads about with herself."

"I can't help feeling she's in terrible danger."

"You are the one who is in terrible danger," said Wood quietly. The boy was taken aback.

"What do you mean?"

"At any moment now you may be arrested for the murder of Crispin."

"But it's impossible. How could I be arrested?"

Wood told him of the facts that had come to light. Wainwright dropped into a chair and remained silent for a moment.

"I can't get hold of it. Who framed this up?"

"It may be a frame-up—or it may be coincidence. It certainly seems to me too pat for coincidence. There is something strange behind all this which we haven't fathomed out yet."

"But, damn it," exclaimed Wainwright desperately, "surely I can't be caught like that—for something I've not done."

Wood put his hand on the young man's shoulder. "Keep up your courage. There must be some way out. I can see the way Morgan's mind is working. He thinks the case is over. He's got a case that will go to a jury and get a verdict. He won't trouble to investigate further."

"You mean——" Wainwright's face slowly went ashen.

Wood nodded gravely. "On the face of it, yes. Oh, I know," he added hastily, "that we can find some way out. We've *got* to get at the truth. But we can only do it if we have time."

"But how can I get time?" cried Wainwright. "These blasted splits are hanging round outside the house all day long. If I make a bolt for it, they'll get me, sure as hell!"

Dr Wood remained for some time lost in thought. Wainwright

scrutinised desperately the man's face—his soft plump cheeks, silvery hair and strangely young eyes.

"This interests me," the doctor said at last, "and it challenges me. Frankly, I'm baffled. I don't like being baffled. I think you're telling the truth."

He gave Wainwright a keen look which suddenly made the young man realise the extraordinary cold, penetrative power of the man's eyes.

"But someone hasn't been telling the truth. I wouldn't mind taking on for you the task of investigating this. We've got to gain time, though. I need several weeks. Will you be prepared to take a risk?"

"I seem to be running the biggest possible risk already. I'm certainly not afraid of anything else."

"Then go into hiding until I've got the truth of this. It may take two or three months."

"How can I escape? Every step I take now is watched. I've realised that for some time, but I thought it was just suspicion. I didn't know they had a cast-iron case. Even if I could throw off these splits, I haven't any money to live on. I've saved a little, but I must leave that for Mother."

"Just a moment, let me think."

Wood took three or four paces up the room, and walked to the window. Across the road the man in the raincoat stared furtively at the house. Wood half turned away and then paused. He rapped sharply on the window, and the chauffeur, who was lounging against the car, looked up. Wood beckoned him in.

"Here's just one chance. My chauffeur and you are about the same size. Can you drive a car?"

"Sure! My cousin's a lorry driver, and he taught me to drive."

"Good! You change into my chauffeur's uniform in here, and walk out to the car. If I walk out slightly in front of you, it will hide your face, and the plainclothes man will only get a glimpse of you. He'll think you're the chauffeur come out again. When we get into the car, we'll be shielded by it. Don't forget to open the door smartly for me! Then drive straight to this address. It's a little country cottage kept by a patient I once cured, who promised to do anything for me. I often stay there myself. He'll look after you. He can be trusted absolutely. As a matter of fact he got into trouble with the police once, through something he did when his mind was disordered without his being technically insane. So you needn't fear his giving you away. I'll scribble a note for you."

Wood checked the young man's thanks.

"Don't trouble to thank me. I'm doing this out of professional interest. I'm determined to get to the bottom of it."

Half an hour later, the two were speeding down leafy lanes, while the sentinel in the raincoat still remained at his post.

Three hours later, an irate Morgan was reporting to his chief that the bird had flown.

Five hours later, a suave Dr Wood was disclaiming all knowledge of Ted Wainwright's disappearance or of his whereabouts.

"No, I can't imagine where he has gone to. Still, I'm not sorry he escaped. I believe he was innocent. I think before long, Inspector, you'll find the same."

3

"It's an odd collection of stuff," said Dr Tremayne as he fingered the Six Queer Things. "Haven't you light on any of them?"

"Only on the photograph," answered Morgan. "It's a photograph of Marjorie Easton's mother. There's nothing surprising about that. It would be possible for Marjorie to give Crispin a photo of her mother."

"Hello, this *is* surprising," exclaimed the police surgeon, as he shook out the sheet with the broad tapes.

"Why? Do you recognise it?"

"Yes, of course. Any physician with asylum experience would recognise it at once, and I worked in one for two years."

"What on earth has that sheet got to do with asylums?"

"It's a kinder version of the straitjacket. In certain stages of the manic-depressive type of insanity, you have to have some means of keeping the patient quiet in bed. Otherwise they struggle so violently that they are likely to injure themselves and everyone else, and in any case they may tire themselves dangerously. So these sheets are used to restrain them. The sheet is tied over the patient and under the bed to restrain him, and fits tightly round his neck. That keeps him under control."

"It sounds rather unpleasant. I don't know why. As a police officer, I ought not to find captivity particularly objectionable. All the same it makes me feel a little sickish under the circumstances."

"Well, it's for their good. Good gracious, we don't torture them! What else are you to do with manic-depressive lunatics in the manic stage—except the padded cell or the strait jacket?"

"Yes, I agree. But suppose they don't happen to be lunatics?"

Tremayne stared at the police officer for a moment.

"You don't surely think..."

"I think nothing at this stage," cut in Morgan. "I'm only interested in facts. Let's forget the sickishness. The photo was fact number one. This sheet is fact number two. That only leaves us with four more. We're advancing."

He turned the articles over for a moment idly.

"This seems a silly, childish sort of thing," he said, pulling out the balloons with the bicycle pump attachment. "I wonder precisely what amusement Crispin got out of blowing up balloons?"

"It isn't an ordinary bicycle pump," interrupted Tremayne. "See—this attachment is a special fitment."

"I don't quite see the idea of it, though."

"I do. We use something like it in the laboratory. Got a gas stove here?"

"Yes, downstairs somewhere."

The two went down to the kitchen and, under the disapproving eyes of Morgan's wife, the police surgeon demonstrated how the pump could be used for filling the balloons with coal gas.

"The pressure in a gas tap isn't enough to inflate a balloon against the full pressure of the taut rubber. So this bicycle pump attachment has to be used to inflate the thing."

With the concentration of the scientist, so like the engrossment of the playing child, Tremayne pumped a balloon full of gas and tied the opening with a piece of string, supplied by Mrs Morgan, who watched the operation scornfully.

"I'm surprised at you," she said. "Two grown men wasting your time like this!"

The two grown men ignored her protest.

"Now watch her go up!" said Tremayne with a laugh, as he prepared to release the balloon. But his attention was caught by a blotchy smeared painting on the surface, and he examined it more closely. "Funny, there's some design here." He rubbed a sensitive finger tip carefully over the taut surface. "I believe it's luminous paint. Put out the light and let's have a look."

Mrs Morgan put her foot down.

"Look here, if you're gong to play games, you must get out of my kitchen! We take life seriously in here. The dinner's cooking. Go on, out you go."

Tremayne and Morgan were forced to retire to the sitting room again, and Morgan turned out the light. Tremayne released the balloon. It floated to the ceiling and bobbed there, a gently pulsing globe of light which formed itself into a face—shapeless and yet vaguely pitiful, like that of some unfortunate monster.

"Good God," exclaimed the detective. "This Crispin creature seems to have had some nice toys!"

"She certainly does. A pity we can't get a low-down on some of the other things," said Tremayne, as he turned on the light and recaptured the balloons.

"They're beyond me at the moment. But we may do so later. Look here, do you know anything about this fellow Wood?"

"Wood? Who's he?"

"A doctor chap specialising in psychology. He's got a smart Mayfair place."

"There are plenty of doctor chaps specialising in psychology. Let me see—Wood ... Is he a silvery-haired, soft-mannered, man-of-the-world type—the kind of man you instinctively like and feel on friendly terms with from the first meeting?"

"Yes. Do you know him then?"

Tremayne shook his head.

"No, I know the type. The psychological doctors with Mayfair practices are like that."

He sighed regretfully.

"It's nice easy work, and paying too. Better than this lousy job of mine! But I haven't the manner, you see, or the right shade of hair. People don't instinctively like me."

"Do you mean he's bogus then?" asked Morgan, brightening a little.

"All doctors who get on and can afford to live in Mayfair are bogus," replied Tremayne cynically. "At least that's my opinion. Call it sour grapes if you like. I used to want to be a fashionable psychologist—hence my two years' asylum experience. But it just happened I didn't have that soothing effect on the half-witted which is part of the natural equipment of the successful alienist. The nutty find me irritating. Hence here I am carving up corpses. They can't protest. I get on with them splendidly. Your man's all right, I expect. Why did you ask? Is there anything fishy about him?"

"Only that, although I felt friendly towards him in the beginning, I've now got good reason to believe he played me a dirty trick, so I'd like to get something on him."

"Criminally dirty?"

"Not exactly. He's shielding a criminal."

"Against the strong arm of the law? Bad, that! But doctors aren't taught to have much respect for the law, you know. The difference we are supposed to make is between the sound and the sick, not between the law-abiding citizen and the criminal. Still, I'll look up Wood when I get home."

"I've got a medical directory here, if you'd like to glance at it. The qualifications will mean more to you than they do to me."

Tremayne skimmed rapidly through the big volume.

"Here we are. Wood. Yes, he seems all right. Ah, here's his psychiatric experience. That's strange. He was at the same place I was—a year or two after, though. I know some of the old crowd there. I'll get in touch with them, if you like, and find out your man's record."

"Thanks. I'd be grateful if you would. Not that I think you're likely to find anything. He does himself too well to be a shady doctor. I don't know much about wine, but the cigar he gave me was the cigar of an honest man."

4

Morgan's peace next morning was disturbed by an anguished telephone call from Belmont Avenue. There were still servants there. The trustees of what property Crispin had left—Barclay's Bank, appointed trustees by a simple will which left everything to any relatives who could be traced—had managed to persuade Crispin's servants to remain on in the house until Crispin's sister was found.

It was one of them who sent the urgent call for help to Morgan.

"For God's sake, send someone from the copper station," she had cried down the telephone. "There's ghosts or murderers in the house, God knows which!"

Morgan responded to this SOS by going down himself. He found the cook excited but full of fighting spirit. "The other two have gone, the silly little bastards," she explained. "But I've stayed on. I'm not afraid!" She waved a paper dramatically.

"What exactly has happened?"

"Well, one says we're all going to be poisoned, and the other started to see things, and between the pair of them you don't know where you are. Anne came rushing in here to say there was a snake as thick as my leg chasing her down the corridor. When I went out with the poker, I couldn't see a thing. But Anne's hopped off, so she must have seen something. I told her she'd lose her week's wages, but she said she'd rather lose a week's money than be pushing up daisies.

"You follow me," said the cook, leading Morgan into the former séance room. "None of us ever goes in here now except to clean it. Well, May went in to sweep it, and went out to empty the dust with the door left open. When she came back, she found the blessed dog had run inside and was having fits on the mat. Just like the master died—or mistress, as I suppose he was—although it's difficult to get the hang of it. That dog was carrying on and screaming like something human."

"Well, where is he now?"

"Here he is, poor beggar," she said, pointing in the corner.

Morgan removed the sheet of brown paper which had been

put over the animal. Its back was arched in a sharp reverse curve, and its legs were tightly drawn under it as if it were taking a flying leap through the air. The lips were pulled back from the teeth in an agonised snarl, and the teeth were tightly clenched. It was stone dead.

"Had the dog eaten anything?" he asked.

"Just the usual scraps. There they are on the plate, what's left of them. But what frightened May was its dying in the very same room as the other one, just the same way. It put May in such a taking that she rushed out of the house. I thought I'd best ring you up, and I'll tell you straight, I'm not staying long here myself! I'm not frightened, but I like comfort and company, and you won't get either with these goings on."

"I don't altogether blame you," remarked Morgan, wrapping the plate of scraps in a piece of paper. "It's not too pleasant to be alone in a house where these kinds of things happen."

"As for seeing snakes, I'm surprised at Anne," went on the cook. "She's always been a level-headed girl before this, and it's a bit early in the day for her to get lit up. I've known her to drink a drop before, but there—who are we to judge? I like a bit myself."

"Whereabouts did she see the snake?"

The cook took him to a narrow landing, running from the main corridor to a bathroom.

"And there was no sign of anything when you came here?"

"Not a crumb or a smell!"

"How long after would it have been?"

"Well, Anne came flying into the kitchen like a mad thing, and I went straight along. It would be almost at once, a minute at the most."

Morgan examined the small corridor carefully. The bathroom door was closed, but opening off a part of the corridor was the linen cupboard, and he noticed that a pipe came out of it. A hole had been cut in the wood skirting, and this hole was considerably larger than the diameter of the pipe. He went to the head of the stairs, unfastened a stair rod, and poked this cautiously through the hole. Suddenly he felt something soft and leathery which squirmed and slid violently beneath his prod. There was a sinister hiss. He withdrew the rod hurriedly.

With another hiss, a narrow triangular head with two beady eyes shot out of the hole and quivered on the end of a long neck.

"Mother of God!" screamed the cook. "Look at the wicked little tongue of it!"

The head darted out another six inches.

"I think we'll leave it alone for the moment," exclaimed Morgan, retreating. "Let's go downstairs."

The cook needed no encouragement, and a minute or two later Morgan was phoning headquarters. They promised to send him down an expert as soon as possible. After an hour during which he shared some cooking sherry with his companion, a little man with a bag arrived in a police car. He had been dug out of the Zoo.

"It may not be a dangerous specimen," Morgan told him, "but I'm taking no chances!"

The little man went upstairs, Morgan keeping well in the rear. The reptile had taken cover again. The snake expert scraped gently on the skirting and presently the head shot out.

"Very fine," he murmured. "Very fine, indeed. A lovely animal."

"Is it poisonous?" asked Morgan practically.

"Yes. After one bite you'd be dead in three minutes, I should say."

Morgan moved several paces away. The expert suddenly flashed a forked stick down on the snake's neck, and pinned it to the ground. He then inserted a small lever into its mouth.

"I'm sorry, I was wrong. It's not poisonous. Its poison glands have been removed, although the fangs have been left. An old snake-charmer's trick!"

He removed the forked stick, and picked the snake up by the head.

"It can bite, but although painful the bites are not likely to do any harm."

The sight of the little forked stick gave Morgan an idea, and he had a runner sent from the Yard with the attaché case in which the Six Queer Things were kept.

He removed the forked stick, the thin pipe and the straws, and handed them to the expert.

"Yes, a typical snake-charmer's outfit," he was told. "The sort of thing any charlatan can get hold of. You hold the snake down with the stick and make it silly with straws dipped in nicotine, and then you charm it with the pipe. It dances to the swaying of the body, not to the pipe, in a sort of coma, but it's more impressive to play on the pipe."

"Are you sure this snake could not harm anything—not even a dog?" Morgan described the incident with the animal.

"This snake? Good Lord, no. The glands have been completely extirpated! In any case, its bite does not give you convulsions. You get unconscious and die in a coma."

Morgan went home thoughtfully with the Six Queer Things, a dead dog, and some scraps of food in a bag. The snake he presented to the Zoo—subject to recall—as an exhibit. He had some more facts now, but they were getting infernally difficult to sort out! Balloons with spirit faces, snake-charmer's outfits, non-poisonous snakes, dead dogs, strait jackets....

"Something damned queer has been happening at Belmont Avenue!"

CHAPTER IX

The Night of Delusions

When Marjorie had rushed out into the road from her bedroom, her one idea had been to escape to somewhere safe in a collapsing world. This security took the form of Dr Wood. His calm personality and strength of will seemed the only thing which could save her reason.

The street was deserted when she ran out into it. She had only run a few paces when she began to gain more control of herself. How could she get to Dr Wood? It was miles away from here.

Yet she could not persuade herself to return into the dark house—the house of those horrors where everyone had seemed dead, where even her frenzied shaking had been unable to awaken her lifeless nurse.

She stared desperately at the rows of windows, lightless and old, and it seemed to her overwrought imagination that they were *staring* at her, coldly and aloofly. It seemed to her that invisible presences were watching her from behind the window and jeering at her vain efforts to escape.

Her mouth opened and she felt she would start to scream; that once she began to scream she would never be able to stop. But no scream came. Instead her whole body shook with great sobs of terror, and her legs began to give way. She clung to the railings to avoid falling, and everything started to go black in front of her eyes.

At that moment she saw a car moving slowly along the road. In this city of the dead, anything living seemed a beacon of hope. She managed to walk again, and she staggered into the road in front of the car, careless of the strange sight she must have looked. It stopped at once.

"Please help me," she said desperately to the driver. "I can't stay in the house. I can't explain now, but it's *urgent!* For God's sake, drive me to a friend's house. It's not far from here."

The driver's face was masked by the shadow from the roof of the car. He remained immobile while she spoke, and she had a sudden return of panic terror. It was as if she had been cut off from the real world, and its inhabitants could no longer communicate with her, like the nurse she had vainly tried to shake to life.

But after a moment of silence, the man nodded.

"All right, jump in!" he said.

She opened the door, and as she did so, she started back. A man and a woman were seated in the back, but in such a way that they could not be seen until the door was opened. As she moved backwards her arm was seized, and she was dragged forcibly into the car. She felt a rough hand forced over her mouth. After all she had been through, she did not put up a struggle, although she whimpered faintly and stirred when she felt something sharp thrust into her arm.

This was followed by a feeling of lassitude. As they sped through the streets, the car itself, the feeling of constraint from the rug which was tied tightly round her, and the street lights as they flashed into the car and vanished again, mixed into one dissolving, flowing stream of fantastic semiconsciousness. Was this a dream? It seemed like that sometimes. At other times it seemed strangely as though she were mixed up with her dream, and did not know which was dream and which was herself.

After what might equally have been an hour or a day, the car became filled with the cold, ghastly light of dawn. Then the car stopped.

"This way," said a firm voice, and she obediently got to her feet and stumbled heavily up the stairs, as the man guided her with a strong arm. Upstairs she collapsed into a chair and went to sleep.

She came to consciousness again only when someone shook her, and a woman gave her a drink of what tasted like hot soup. Almost immediately after taking it, she dropped asleep again, and her sleep was full of confused dreams, in which she seemed to have no consciousness of being a personality, but everything swam around her in separate, disjointed visions.

Every now and then consciousness returned to her in snatches, accompanied by the persistent idea that she was at a dentist's....

Someone was shaking her roughly.

"Come on, dress!" she was urged.

She made a few efforts to help the woman who put strange clothes on her and washed her face, but after a time she gave it up, and submitted feebly to the process. The woman's face seemed oddly familiar, and yet she could not give it a name.

"Who are you?" she asked wonderingly.

"Your aunt!" replied the woman. "Your aunt Martha. Fancy your asking such a silly question, Marjorie!"

"I don't remember any aunt Martha," protested Marjorie weakly. "And yet I seem to remember you."

"Don't talk nonsense, darling," said the woman, continuing to brush her hair. She gave it a final pat and smoothed it into place. "There! Look at yourself in the glass. All ready to go!"

Marjorie stared at herself in the mirror. For a moment she hardly recognized herself. She was wearing a hideous black costume, designed for a middle-aged woman. The dress had obviously been worn before—it was green at the seams. The ugliness was emphasized by the condition it was in and the slovenly way in which it had been put on. There were splashes of food and grease down the front. Marjorie's hair had been brushed so carelessly that tangles flopped into her eyes and straggled over her ears. She shuddered at the sight.

Yet such was her weakness and general state of confusion that she could only stare at herself dully in the glass. She put up a hand to smooth back her hair for a moment, and then let the hand drop back without doing anything. She turned away from the mirror.

"That's right, my darling!" said the woman encouragingly. "You're feeling better already. I said your holiday by the sea would do you good."

"By the sea?" asked Marjorie, puzzled. "I don't remember any sea."

"Listen to this, Sam," shouted out the woman. "Marjorie says she doesn't remember the sea!"

The man came in from the next room. He was a large red-faced man with broad hands. As he laid his hand on her arm, she noticed the hairy backs and had a moment's feeling of aversion.

"Silly little thing!" he said in a coaxing voice. "You've not been well! Never mind. Auntie's right. You're looking worlds better for your holiday by the sea."

The woman nodded and got up.

"Well, now we must get off, dear! We've a call to pay. Your uncle will help you out."

"He's not my uncle," shouted Marjorie suddenly, in a high voice which seemed to have got beyond her control. "I can manage all right, thank you!"

She got to her feet and walked towards the door.

"What ideas she does get into her head, to be sure!" said the woman good humoredly. "There, give her a hand, Sam. You can see she can't manage it!"

Her momentary flare-up had exhausted her, and she made no resistance when the man took her arm and guided her into the car.

After a short journey, she was taken up some steps to another house—a large one, standing in its own grounds. They waited a moment and then were shown into a room where three men were already waiting.

They looked at her in a strange way as she came in.

"What is your name?" asked one enquiringly.

"Marjorie Easton!"

"We've just came back from the sea," volunteered the man. "It got worse there. My niece has never been what you could call really right."

"He's not my uncle," exclaimed Marjorie furiously.

One of the three men, a man with a grey pointed beard, looked surprised.

"Not your uncle? Then who is he?"

"I don't know!" she answered helplessly. "I'd never seen him before I got into his car."

The woman gave an exclamation of surprise.

"Marjorie, how could you say such a thing about your uncle Sam!"

"Do you know this woman?" asked the bearded man, pointing to her.

Marjorie looked at her.

"Yes, I know her, but I can't place her somehow. I know I've met her before, but I can't remember her name."

She saw the three men exchange glances that seemed to have a meaning which evaded her. There was evidently some understanding between them. Was it an understanding about her?

"You say you had never seen this man before you got into his car?" asked another of the three, a young man in a smart black jacket with striped trousers and a thin hatchet face. "Where had you been before then?"

"In the house where the dreadful things happened."

"What dreadful things?"

"The voices," she answered, putting one hand to her forehead. Everything seemed incoherent and vague now. "That terrible laugh, and all the faces. And then when I tried to wake the nurse, and couldn't! Was she dead?"

The man who had brought her there whispered something into the ear of the bearded man, and he nodded.

"What are you whispering about?" she asked sharply.

"Nothing," the bearded man replied smoothly. "You don't remember a trip to the seaside then?"

"No, of course not. I'm positive about that. Surely I ought to know."

"How old are you?" asked the young man in the lounge suit.

She gave her age, and she saw him look quickly at a slip of paper in the palm of his hand.

"You are sure of that?"

"Of course!"

There was a silence, and then, as if at some signal she had not seen, the three men rose simultaneously and went into another room.

"What have they gone for?" she asked her companions, confused. "Why are we here?"

"That's all right, darling!" said the man who had brought her, in a soothing voice. "It's just a little visit we had to pay. Two of those men are doctors. They are going to prescribe a little tonic."

"But I don't want a tonic," she said, and suddenly burst into tears. "I want to go home."

The woman patted her shoulders and spoke to her as if she were a child.

"So you will, Marjorie. Keep quiet. The kind gentlemen will be back in a moment. We'll take you straight home from here!"

In a few minutes the men returned, and she saw the bearded man hand the woman a long envelope. As they went out the eldest of the three, a man who had not asked her any questions before, spoke to the woman. She had been thanking him apparently.

"That's all right, Mrs Easton! It's my job. Although I must admit it's one of the less attractive sides of a magistrate's duties."

As the door closed behind them, and she found herself alone again with the man and woman who had brought her there, Marjorie, in spite of her muddled mind and physical weakness, felt a sudden unreasoning terror. Although the three men had talked so oddly, there had been something comforting about their presence. Now she was alone with these two.

"I don't want to go home! I want to go back there," she said, starting to move back towards the door of the sitting room she had just left. The man grasped her arm roughly.

"None of that nonsense, you little bastard!" he said. "Come on. Get out of it quickly." He put his hand over her mouth and started to drag her along. She caught hold of a bit of furniture and clung to it desperately, panting. She hadn't the strength to scream.

"Better give her another shot, Joe," said the woman, and she felt the skin of her arm pinched. There was a sharp pain, and then she felt the arm go limp. She half walked, was half carried to the car. Everything went confused....

2

Marjorie woke in the afternoon, for the sun was low. She did not know how long she had been sleeping, but it seemed as if it had been for ages.

She was in a strange room.

She went to the window and looked out. An unexpected view met her eyes, which made her wonder if she were still awake.

The house was on a slightly rising ground, and overlooked a huge sheet of water which stretched out, cold and grey, beneath the faint afternoon sun. It was deserted except for the few birds which paddled on its surface or flew out of the huge clumps of reeds which dotted its expanse. Beyond the water could be seen more country—flat, marshy fields which the weather, or the poverty of the soil, had turned a harsh dirty brown.

There was no sign of civilisation in the dreary, flat prospect in front of her except for seven windmills which were placed at intervals in the landscape, and an old black boat, decrepit and ramshackle, which seemed to be sinking at the rotting post to which it was moored. The strangeness of the scene and its deserted, mournful aspect gave her a curious sensation of hopelessness.

There was something foreign about the birds which flitted above the water, about the oily darkness of the vast stretch of water itself, about the windmills, and even about the oddly shaped black boats. She at once had the conviction that she was in another country. Was it Holland?

She found some clothes beside her bed, and she put them on with a shudder. It gave her a physical nausea, now that she was clear headed, to put on these repellent garments. But there was nothing else to be had. The house seemed strangely silent, considering it was the afternoon.

When she had finished dressing, she went to the door. It was locked on the outside. Her efforts to open it were useless, and eventually, to attract attention, she started to shout and bang on the door with a hairbrush.

After some minutes she heard footsteps approaching. The key in the lock turned, and the door was cautiously opened. A little man with a black moustache and a sallow, greasy skin stood in the door. He was smartly dressed in a black morning coat and striped trousers, and his thick black hair was plastered with pomade and looked like patent leather. She was immediately struck by his bright scarlet lips, which stood out in contrast to his sallow face.

"Well, well," he said, with a smile that flickered and disappeared so quickly that it was difficult to be sure it had even appeared. "That *was* a lot of noise. I hope there is nothing wrong?"

Marjorie felt her fury ooze away. There was something sinister and reptilian about his polite remark and it made her afraid.

"Why am I here?" she demanded as boldly as she could.

He shrugged his shoulders.

"It's a little unfair to ask me that! Perhaps life has been too much for you; perhaps you chose your parents badly. I have not yet had the pleasure of looking up my colleague's notes!"

"What do you mean?" asked Marjorie, puzzled. "Why am I being kept here against my will?"

"It is necessary, I'm afraid. In any case, may I suggest it is not very polite to try and kick down the door."

"Well, how else could I call somebody?"

"There is a bell over there by the fireplace," answered the man gravely, pointing to a bell push on the right-hand side of the mantelpiece.

"Well, anyway, now you *are* here, you can at least answer my question. I demand to know why I have been brought here. What happened to me last night? I'm certain I was drugged!"

"It is usual to give drugs to patients! In any case, you must excuse me, Miss Easton. I had just been called to another part of the building when I passed here. If I had not heard so much noise and come in, I should be with my patient now. I hate keeping anyone waiting. It may be serious. A haemorrhage, perhaps! Excuse me."

With a bow, the man closed the door abruptly. She heard the key turn in the lock.

Marjorie pressed the bell and waited. There was no response. She kept her finger on it for several minutes, but still there was no answer. After an hour of futile ringing, Marjorie decided to repeat the expedient by which she had attracted attention, and set up a thundering noise on the door.

After a few minutes of banging, the door was thrown violently open. A brawny middle-aged woman in nurse's uniform burst in, annoyance written all over her hard face.

"What the hell do you think you're doing?" asked this woman, glaring at her.

"I rang the bell and couldn't get any answer, so I had to try another way of attracting attention."

"Rang the bell!" exclaimed the woman, astonished. "Do you think this is a hotel? I've never heard such cheek. Those bells haven't worked since we took over the house, ten years ago."

"I want to know why I am being kept here," Marjorie asked defiantly. "I want to go back to my uncle at once! I warn you it will be the worse for you if you don't let me out. I insist that you get into touch either with my uncle, Mr Michael Crispin or Dr Wood without delay."

The woman stared at her angrily, without troubling to answer her appeal.

"Shut up! Go on, sit down and keep your mouth shut."

"Don't you dare tell me to shut up!" said Marjorie, losing her temper.

"Shut up!" repeated the woman cruelly, striking Marjorie a violent blow across the mouth with one hard fist. She seized the girl's hands and flung her forcibly on the bed.

"We soon tame pernickety people like you here! Any more of this nonsense, and you'll go on starvation diet and castor oil for a month. That'll soon stop your airs and graces. If you behave yourself properly and do as you're told, you'll be all right. We don't want trouble for trouble's sake. But if you ask for it—well, we always win at that game!"

The woman turned and walked out, again locking the door behind her. Marjorie lay on the bed trembling with indignation and shock.

About an hour later, the door opened, and the hard-faced woman brought a cup of tea and two thick slabs of bread and butter. She banged the tray down beside Marjorie. The girl took them without a word.

"Thank you!" prompted the woman warningly.

"Thank you," repeated Marjorie, half choking.

The woman nodded approvingly.

"That's right. You'll soon fall into the way of it."

She seemed to be hesitating for a moment, but then left the room without saying more. Marjorie ate the bread and butter slowly. Her lips had swollen painfully where the woman had struck her, and this made eating awkward. Why was she being kept a prisoner in this house? Where was it? What was the meaning of the events leading up to it—if indeed they had really occurred, and had not been part of some strange, drugged dream. They certainly seemed queerly unreal.

After she had eaten there seemed nothing to do but sit by the window and look out. She watched the birds soaring and swooping above the black waters, which were now faintly rippled here and there by the wind. She envied them their freedom. They were the only living things on the huge landscape in front of her —except for the cat which, a moment ago, she had seen cross the lawn up to the high wall that divided the grounds of the house from the bank of the lake. It had scrambled up a buttress and over the wall. Only a cat could climb that wall, she realised. It was about twelve feet high and was topped with spikes.

Then, as she watched, she noticed a black blur. Was it a log or a floating patch of reeds? It gradually became more distinct. It was a small rowboat with two men inside.

She hoped desperately that they would come within hailing distance of the house. For about a quarter of an hour the boat was hidden from sight by a tall island of reeds, behind which it had pulled. Then it was visible again, now appreciably nearer.

It was coming straight to the house.

Twenty minutes later, it had moored to the same post to which the old rotting black boat was attached. They began to fish. Her chance had come. She went to the window and tried to open it.

She found, however, that it was firmly secured by screws in such a position that there was just enough opening at the top for a draught of air to enter, but that it was too narrow to do more than thrust a hand through.

She was determined not to be baulked of her chance of freedom. Seizing a chair, and holding one arm before her eyes, she hurled it through the window. The glass shattered in all directions, and at once the men looked towards the house. She leaned out of the window as far as she could, and began shouting at the top of her voice.

"Help! I'm imprisoned here against my will!"

To her surprise the men, instead of becoming concerned at

her appeal, stared at her for a moment. She could distinctly see one laugh and nudge the other, who made a mocking gesture towards her. She had a conviction that they were foreigners and did not understand her. The next moment she was seized violently from behind, and flung on the bed. The same woman who had brought in her meal began to rain blows on her face and body with concentrated fury.

"I'll teach you, you little bastard! Trying to make trouble! Just you try that on again!"

Taking some rope from her pocket, the woman began to tie the girl firmly to her bed.

"That'll teach you to try any nonsense. There'll be worse to come next time!"

Unable to move hand or foot, and aching from the blows, Marjorie lay on the bed for two or three hours. Meanwhile her window was roughly patched up with newspaper by the woman. After the lapse of this time, the woman came to her bed.

"I'll let you go now if you promise not to try to attract attention again!"

There was nothing else Marjorie could do but promise, and she was released from her bonds.

The sun set in a blaze, whose colours, reflected in the lake, for a moment relieved its gloom. Then, as it faded, it seemed to leave the scene with a double dose of melancholy. A wind had sprung up, and Marjorie could hear the steady ripple of the water on the lake edge. These sobbing, gurgling noises added to the despair in the girl's heart.

There seemed nothing to do but to go to bed. She got into her night things and was just getting into bed, when she heard a man's voice, followed by a knock on the door.

"Can I come in?"

"No," said Marjorie. "What do you want? I'm in bed."

In spite of her answer, the man opened the door. It was the same little man who had answered her frantic knocking this afternoon.

"There is no need to be embarrassed," he said, with that flickering smile, as he saw her awkwardness. "I am a doctor. I am just making my evening round of inspection to see that all my patients are happy and getting on as well as can be expected."

"I'm not a patient!" protested Marjorie.

"Really, you must allow us to be the judge of that. It's our business to decide, after all. You certainly don't *look* well. You must admit that! In any case, the reason I came round was to find out if everything was to your satisfaction."

"Apart from the fact that I've been brutally attacked by the woman who brings me my food," replied Marjorie sarcastically, "and that I'm being forcibly kept here, I have nothing to complain of."

"Brutally attacked!" exclaimed the doctor in a surprised tone. "But that's impossible! We treat our patients with the greatest care and consideration. Our staff is carefully chosen for their gentleness and patience."

"Look at these bruises," cried the girl indignantly, showing the marks on her arms and face.

The man examined the places she indicated with care. Then he shook his head.

"I'm afraid I can't see anything. It may of course be the light —or my eyesight. May I suggest that you look at them again in the morning—then perhaps you, too, will change your opinion? At present you are a little overwrought and need sleep."

"Do you suggest I imagined this attack?" she asked.

The doctor shrugged his shoulders.

"I leave you to draw your own conclusion. Is there anything else? I have several other rooms to visit. If you have any complaints, I will have them looked into, and see that whoever is responsible is reprimanded; but I must beg of you not to waste time."

"Since I am not allowed out of this room, can I have something to read? Or a pack of cards?"

"I am afraid anything of that nature is strictly against the rules. It is liable to excite the patient's mind."

"Do you mean I'm to be kept here without any distraction? Why, I shall go mad!"

"Impossible," said the doctor with an ironic smile. "Good night, Miss Easton! I will call again tomorrow morning and trust you will be able to say you have had a good night's sleep."

CHAPTER X

Disappearance of a Suspect

Marjorie went to sleep that night after two or three hours' restless tossing. It had seemed to her at first that she would never be able to sleep until she got out of this abominable place; but this first mood gave way to a feeling of resigned helplessness during which she drifted imperceptibly into slumber. She was physically and mentally tired. Her very bones ached.

During the hours of restlessness her mind continually returned to one outstanding question: how had it been possible for these people to do all this to her? She had been kidnapped, taken on that appalling drive, and forcibly imprisoned. Surely those things were not possible in twentieth-century England—if indeed she was in England! More and more this seemed doubtful to Marjorie. It was not merely the quality of the scenery and the behaviour of the two men to whom she had appealed, but the very fact that she was being treated as she was.

Where could help come from? From Michael Crispin? He certainly would be the first to make a move when he found she was gone. And yet now, as she lay there, in some strange way Michael Crispin's figure seemed to take a different shape. It became menacing, acquired a touch of horror, as if it were a piece with all the other horrible experiences of the last few hours. She pressed her hands against her burning forehead. She was becoming confused. Of course this was wrong. Michael Crispin had transformed her life. He was a good influence. Through him she had got into touch with her mother. How confused she was becoming!

And then as soon as Dr Wood heard of her disappearance he would help her. He would get in touch with the police. Then, surely, they would not be long in tracing her! She wished she had been able to leave some indication behind of what had happened to her. But what had happened to her? In some moods the people who were her captors seemed hardly human—they seemed all of a piece with her nightmares of the past few days. It was as if she were still dreaming.

What about her uncle? She knew that directly he heard of her disappearance his first reaction would be "I told you so." But still, she was his niece. He would certainly do his utmost to get her back, if only to have the pleasure of saying to her face, "I told you so!"

Yet, strangely enough, she found no comfort in thinking about these people, who would be sure to be worried by her absence. Her only comfort was in thinking of Ted Wainwright. She had treated him abominably, she thought, tossing restlessly on her bed. Almost certainly he had ceased to love her! Perhaps he had forgotten her existence!

Yet at the same time she had a queer presentiment that he *might* be able to come to her assistance. She felt that if she thought of him with concentration, he could not fail to know her need. She sent out a desperate mental SOS.

The days she had spent with Ted—her old simple humdrum life—all at once seemed vividly attractive. She must have been mad to give it up. And so, thinking of Ted and the quiet past, and somehow comforted by these thoughts, she fell asleep.

In the morning she got up and dressed herself quickly. As she sat in front of her mirror, she could see the grounds of the house through the window, round the edge of the paper which had been stuck over it to mend it. The garden was not deserted this morning. There were several people out on the lawn, and she was struck by their appearance.

There was something odd about the way they went on. There seemed to be two lots—some behaved strangely and were always on the move; others watched these, sitting round on chairs or standing in different parts of the grounds. One or two of the active walked round at a slouching gait with their heads bent. They seemed lost in thought. Occasionally their lips moved, but apart from this they were in a daze, and it seemed a miracle when they succeeded in avoiding flower beds and trees.

Others were just the opposite—they were continually looking round slyly to see whether other people were watching, and grimacing or making queer gestures. One was standing on a seat shouting, but as she looked, one of the watching men came up to him, took him roughly by the arm and made him step down. The shouter cowered away, and Marjorie now recognised the other as the man who had accompanied her in the car.

The full truth sank into Marjorie's mind. The horror of it made her for a moment feel weak. She was in an asylum!

This explained everything. Now she became fully aware of it, she realised that all this time she had half suspected it, but had fought blindly to keep it out of her mind.

She was being kept captive as a lunatic.

Her first and most awful thought was that *perhaps she was a lunatic*. Dr Wood had told her that her symptoms pointed to a mental breakdown. Had this occurred without her realising it? Were all the ghastly events of that night in Belmont Avenue mere lunatic delusions? Was it a fact that she had been taken to the seaside to recover and had forgotten it?

Marjorie felt her whole being shaken. Horrible suspicions reared their heads everywhere. She clung desperately to the slightest shred that proved her sanity.

Wasn't it the case that insane people never queried their own sanity? And wasn't the fact that she was querying hers a sign of her own sanity? Yes, she might be mentally shaken, but not insane!

Insane—the very word sent a cold thrill down her spine. It was some plot; she was the victim of some diabolical conspiracy! A feeling of loneliness and weakness for a time overcame Marjorie, and she burst into tears. A few minutes later she pulled herself together. The only way to prove her sanity was to *fight*. She must fight to be the Marjorie she had been before she met Crispin. She must fight to be the Marjorie who had loved Ted and whom Ted had loved. She must fight to be herself. . . .

Soon there was a knock on the door and the doctor—if he really was what he claimed to be—came in. He looked at her critically.

"Ah, you look very well this morning, Miss Easton! I can see this régime suits you—quiet, fresh air and a complete change! There's nothing like it for building up the constitution!"

"Is there any need to go on with this joke?" replied Marjorie bitterly. "I am in an asylum. That's so, isn't it?"

"You are in the hands of friends!" answered the doctor.

"I insist that my uncle be told that I am here. He's my legal guardian and must be told."

"I agree. He was told yesterday."

Marjorie was startled.

"Why, what did he say? What did you tell him?"

"He was told the truth, of course," replied the little doctor, balancing himself gently on the tips of his toes, with his hands clasped behind his back. "What else do you expect? He was told that you were found wandering the streets in a condition of mental confusion, and that this became so serious that you were certified insane by a magistrate, on the advice of two doctors. We have given him your address, but have told him that it will not be possible for him to see you, as your state of mind is such that it would be dangerous for you to see any near relative. We have told him you are suffering from delusions of persecution. I am sure you will admit, Miss Easton, you have those ideas, even if you do not regard them as delusions. Hence your state of mind would be antagonistic towards him. He quite understands."

"You devils! You've thought of everything, haven't you?"

"However, in fairness to him and yourself," went on the doctor, ignoring her interruption, "and to set his mind at rest, it might be as well if you wrote to him. I will have some ink and paper sent up as soon as I go downstairs."

"How do I know you will really post the letter?"

"My dear Miss Easton," exclaimed the doctor deprecatingly, "what a very suspicious attitude to adopt. I assure you we will post a letter to your uncle from you. If you like, you can hand it to the postman yourself."

Soon after he had gone out, the hard-featured woman returned with ink and paper, and Marjorie wrote a desperate appeal to her uncle, insisting that she was sane, and asking him to get her out of the place at all costs. She put it in an envelope, sealed it carefully and put it on the breakfast tray. The doctor returned before the tray had been collected, and she handed him the letter.

He took it with a bow.

"Excuse me," he said, and without waiting for her assent, tore open the envelope and read the letter. "Dear me, Miss Easton. This won't do at all. Really it won't. This is terribly misleading. You cannot expect us to be a party to this kind of fabrication. It will upset your uncle and give him a totally false conception of your condition and of this establishment!"

"It is true. You know it's true!"

The doctor shook his head. "On the contrary, it is a malicious invention. I must insist on your writing him the truth. Somewhat as follows: You are feeling very weak and ill, and not at all sure what has happened. Your mind is confused. You want to write and tell him you are staying at a very lovely place. You don't know where it is, but you are very happy and everyone is very friendly. Some day, when you are better, he must come and see you."

Marjorie was dumbfounded for a moment by the calm effrontery of this suggestion. At last she gasped out:

"How dare you stand there and suggest my saying that?"

"Why not? It is the truth. Come, be reasonable, Miss Easton. Write this letter!"

"No," she answered firmly.

He attempted to coax her.

"You know, you are taking up an extraordinarily antagonistic attitude towards us! We are only doing this for your own good!"

"Keeping me here against my own will for my good! Hitting me and tying me up for my own good!"

"Dear, dear," he said in a dismayed tone. "These ideas of violence again! Do try and see they are only delusions, Miss Easton. Put up a fight against them! I ask you to put this question to yourself: Why are we going to all this trouble, except for your own good? Our motives are obviously disinterested. This house costs money. Feeding you costs money. The attendants have to be paid. I have to be paid. Pardon my bluntness, but you have no personal money of your own. It is costing us money to keep you here. Would we do it if it were not for your own good?"

The extraordinarily plausible way in which he put forward the argument silenced her for the moment. Then she burst out impatiently:

"I don't know why you are doing these horrible things to me. I only know that you are doing them. I shall not write to my uncle and tell him that I am happy here. I want to get my freedom. I shall never rest until I do."

"Then I am very sorry. It is a pity you should prove such a refractory patient. Let me explain the situation to you simply. Whether you do what we ask or not, you will remain here. That is *quite* definite. But if you do the little things we ask, like writing a reassuring letter to your uncle, and give us your word not to do anything silly such as you attempted yesterday, then you will have a more comfortable room, you will have books to read, and you will be free to go into these grounds. But if you don't——"

He broke off significantly.

"If I don't?" she repeated.

"Then I am afraid it will be necessary to prescribe a very severe régime! You will be shut up here alone, without food, until you behave yourself. If you still resist, then there are various methods open to us. Certain drugs for example . . . You will find your will is not as strong as you think when your body is weakened."

He said this in as casual a tone as if he were prescribing a tonic. Marjorie was unable to answer. He smiled pleasantly.

"I am glad to see you are thinking it over! Believe me, Miss Easton, we should hate to have to use the measures I have mentioned, but as a doctor I am trained to ignore any pain which is inflicted for the patient's good. I'll leave you to come to a sensible decision. If you do, ask the woman who looks after you to send for me. My name is Dr Marsden. I am afraid that, owing to the circumstances of our first meeting, I forgot to introduce myself."

Marjorie was left to her thoughts. She realised that she was in a cleft stick. She had to leave them to post the letters she wrote, so that any letter sent could only be one of a kind they would approve. On top of that, even if no letter came from her, her uncle would not get agitated, because he would have received a satisfactory explanation of her absence already. No doubt he had communicated the news to Dr Wood and Ted. Neither of them would be much surprised. Wood knew that she was on the verge of a mental breakdown; Ted had become alienated from her, and had regarded her as half mad from the moment she had become a medium. The thought of Ted's probable reaction to the news filled her with despair.

Would it not be better to give in to their request and get some peace? If she refused, God knows what they might not do. They had already shown they were absolutely ruthless. If, on the other hand, she gave in, and they in return allowed her more liberty, then there would be some chance of her getting a message to the outside world.

It was impossible to guess what their motives were. It seemed incredible that so much trouble could be taken merely for the sake of making her suffer. What could be the motive? It was better not to puzzle one's brains about that, she decided finally.

When the hard-faced woman came in to her with some dry bread and a glass of water, she asked for Dr Marsden. He came within a few minutes.

"I'll write the letter," she told him, "if you will promise in return to give me some liberty—a daily walk in the grounds—and books."

"Certainly. You must promise not to escape, and we will gladly do that."

"Very well, I promise."

Privately she decided that any promise could justifiably be broken against such blackguards. No doubt they would also regard the promise only as a matter of form. The doctor dictated the letter, and she wrote it. He took it from her, scrutinised it carefully and nodded.

"Fine. We'll see you get a proper meal sent up now, and afterwards you can go in the garden...."

2

On the morning after the odd business of the snake and the dead dog, Morgan received an unexpected letter in the post.

DEAR SIR:
Seeing from the papers that you are in charge of the Crispin case, and that the police want any news of a young chap named Ted Wainwright, I write to tell you that in my opinion my young lodger is this

chap, although he goes under a different name. Please come and see me at an early date, as I don't know how long this young fellow is staying here. I never had any idea till then he was the man you wanted.

EDWARD HARNESS.

The letter came from a small village in Hampshire.

The name of the cottage was romantic—Nightingale Roost—but the place itself turned out, when the inspector's car stopped in front of it, to be one of the pink asbestos-roofed bungalows with which the green and pleasant land of England is slowly being covered, wherever land values are still low and communications bad. It had a lonely, weary air, as if the reproachful spirits of ex-servicemen, who had attempted to make poultry farming pay in it and had failed, still hung over its roof.

Edward Harness was a large, loose-limbed, loose-lipped individual whose breath smelt strongly of alcohol even in the early hour of the morning at which the inspector called. He had come out to the inspector's car, and directly he had introduced himself, Morgan asked him:

"Is this fellow inside?"

Harness nodded.

"Yes, he's still in bed. I've turned the key in the lock."

"That was rather drastic. Are you sure it is him?"

"As certain as one can be from the photographs in the papers. They're not very distinct."

"Well, here's an original," said Morgan, pulling a photograph out of his brief case.

Harness scrutinised it for a moment.

"Yes, that's it!" he admitted. "It's him all right!"

"How did he come here?"

Harness' shifty blue eyes wandered over the landscape without coming to rest on Morgan's.

"Well, I'm going to tell you the truth, Inspector!"

"Yes, it's much better to do that."

"He came here with a recommendation of a friend of mine, a friend what's done me a good turn in the past when I was ill...."

"Name?"

"I'm sorry, sir, but I just couldn't tell you that. I just couldn't.

Why, he lent me the money to set up here—not that I do more than drag a living out of these bloody fowls, but still I live, and thanks to him I can do it. So you see I can't give *him* away."

"All right. There's no need to give your friend away. I think I can guess who it is, Mr Harness. By the way, the name *is* Harness?"

The man flushed slightly and looked at him suspiciously.

"Why?"

"I'm just wondering, that's all."

"Well, if you want to know, it isn't. I don't mind being frank with you on that. I got into a spot of bother a few years ago, so naturally I took a new name when I turned over a new leaf. Harness isn't my name. I'll admit it. My past isn't all it might have been. I admit it. That's why I hesitated a good bit about writing to you. But then I thought——"

"That one good turn deserves another? Quite right. The police are never afraid to be grateful. We'll look after you if you help us."

"That wasn't the reason I sent for you—to set off one thing against another."

"No, I understand. You were only doing your duty as a citizen!" commented the inspector, with scarcely veiled irony. The irony was missed by Harness however.

"That's right!" he said eagerly. "I felt it my duty. I never guessed at first that this chap was the man you wanted! I knew he was someone who was in trouble; but I understood he was some youngster who'd done something a little silly and wanted to keep out of the way until it blew over. You could have knocked me down with a feather when I saw the photograph in the paper, and I said to myself, Bli—I mean, good gracious me! That's Jim Hill! For Jim Hill is the name he goes under here."

Morgan had summed Harness up fairly quickly. One of the seedy ne'er-do-wells without the guts to succeed either on the straight and level path or at wrongdoing. Something shady in his past, then a few weeks of fright as he had realised the possible consequences of his act; and after that, no doubt, a technical righteousness with a general moral degeneration. He walked towards the gate.

"Well, since you're sure of this fellow, I'd better go and pull him in."

"You've got a warrant for his arrest?"

"Yes. We stated in the press announcement that we wished merely to question him; but since then a warrant has been issued."

They went inside the bungalow, and Harness indicated a room on the left.

"He's in here."

Harness went stealthily up to it and turned the key. Then he opened the door cautiously. There was a sudden exclamation from him as he went inside, and a moment later he came out white faced.

"My God! He's gone!"

And it was true. There was no sign of the lodger in the small bedroom.

"But he couldn't have got out!" insisted Harness. "I've been up since five o'clock. I'm always first up. The door's been locked ever since then."

"What about the window?"

"Impossible. The window opens on to the garden in front and I've been out there all the time. He couldn't possibly have got out without my noticing!"

Morgan looked at him suspiciously.

"Well, he's escaped. I'll have to go down to the village to make a few enquiries. You're quite sure this is as big a surprise to you as it is to me?"

"Of course, Inspector. I swear I never guessed," exclaimed Harness with a sincerity in which there was a hint of apprehension. "You surely don't suspect me? Wasn't it I who wrote to you?"

A sulky grunt was the only reply he got as Morgan jumped into his car, pressed the starter button, and started off for the village. But his enquiries there were fruitless.

Wainwright had given him the slip again. Whatever he was, he wasn't the simple young man Morgan had at first believed him to be.

CHAPTER XI

The Escape

Marjorie was now allowed to go out into the grounds and stroll through the garden. But she was always watched by the hard-featured woman who was her jailer. Sometimes she met some of the odd people whom she had seen in the gardens on that morning when realisation of her terrible situation had first come to her.

Her first attitude towards them had been one of instinctive repulsion. After a time this passed off and she began to feel a kind of fellow sympathy for them. Several of them came to speak to her, and she found to her surprise that they often conversed in a normal, even intelligent way.

One day she stopped short in front of one of them. She had seen him before. But he did not recognise her, nor could she immediately remember where she had seen him. All day long she attempted to give a name to him. Suddenly she remembered the occasion when she had seen him before. He was the strange man who had attacked Michael Crispin! She remembered vividly how he had been stopped in the very act of bringing a cleaver down on Crispin's head. Lambert was the name he was given.

The memory came to her with the force of a revelation. Crispin had said at the time that the man was a former friend whose mind had gone, and who had escaped from an asylum. What a strange coincidence that she, too, should be a friend of Crispin's and should now be in the same place as this poor wreck. *Was it only a coincidence?*

A feeling of horror mingled with her amazement. What was behind it all? What *could* be the connection between herself and this mental ruin? How did Crispin form a common link?

She decided to speak to Dr Marsden, who still paid her a regular routine visit.

"I believe Crispin is responsible for putting me here," she said at a venture.

Dr Marsden looked at her sharply.

"What makes you think that?"

"It is merely the conclusion I have come to, that is all."

"You are quite wrong."

Something in his tone made her think she had shot near the mark.

"Does Crispin know I'm here?"

"Crispin has been dead for some time."

This was wholly unexpected. Her first reaction was to treat it as yet another fabrication.

"I don't believe it," she said indignantly. "It's another of your lies!"

"Very well, if you don't believe me, I'll send you up some papers."

Shortly afterwards a newspaper was sent up. It contained an account of Crispin's death. The news that Crispin had been murdered on the very day she had left staggered her. Still more astounding to her was the discovery that Crispin had been a woman. How could she possibly have been so deluded about someone with whom she had been on such terms of intimacy?

The effect on her was perhaps the opposite of what Marsden intended. She saw that her past few months had been one long chain of deceptions. Exactly what the deception had been, and how Crispin had been able to be so convincing, was beyond her. But it was at least obvious that she had been nothing but a dupe. She realised now what terrible havoc had been made with her mind—how she had surrendered all her will power and all her personality to Crispin. Now Crispin was dead. In a way the news was like a release. Her mind was her own. It was like waking up from a dream, in which one has behaved in a ludicrous way, so that one wonders how even in a dream one could have imagined doing anything so absurd.

But, reading on, she had a fresh shock. Ted Wainwright, in some extraordinary way, was *implicated*. The paper did not directly say so, but the fact that the police were asking for his whereabouts was sufficiently significant. Ted was a fugitive.

Up till the last she had cherished some idea that Ted would be looking for her—that he could be her rescuer. Now this hope was dashed to the ground. He had need of help himself.

During the last few days she had become apathetic. She had let the days drift past, hoping for release, and yet with no clear belief in it. The double shock of learning of Crispin's death and Ted's imprisonment, however, had a stimulating effect on her. She determined to escape and not wait for help from outside, for no help from outside could now be expected.

Whereabouts was she? That was the first thing to find out! Was she really in a foreign country, or only in an unfamiliar piece of English land? When next she met Lambert she decided to start conversing with him. Perhaps he could tell her.

Lambert had changed a good deal since she had seen him at Belmont Avenue. All his nervous agitation and distraction had gone. He looked pale, walked about with bent shoulders, and seemed to have no life left in him. His eyes were sunken. At the same time his speech was much saner than when he had called at the house. He spoke little, seeming too tired even to speak, but when he did he spoke clearly and understandably. The only sign of his disordered mind was his tendency to change abruptly from one subject to another. It was hard to hold him to a train of thought.

He did not recognise her, and when she said she had seen him at Crispin's, a sudden look of sly enmity came over his face, which transformed it. But after a time it vanished, and she saw she had won his sympathy.

They had many conversations after that. She never hinted that she considered him abnormal; but one day he said to her sadly:

"Of course you've heard them say it?"

"Say what?" she asked.

"That I'm mad. They all say it. They've been saying it and saying it and saying it until I sometimes almost think I am."

"No, of course you aren't!" she said reassuringly.

"Well, why do they say it?" he said, shouting. "Eh?"

At his shout, an attendant hurried up to them. Lambert quietened down and looked at the attendant propitiatingly. Evidently he was frightened of him. When the attendant went, with a warning word, Lambert's mind had passed on to something else. He was now only a shell of a human being, cowed and weak. It seemed strange to Marjorie that he had been the violent, struggling figure she had seen at Belmont Avenue.

She tried to make friends with the hard-faced woman who was her attendant. But she found this to be impossible. The woman was uncommunicative, and—provided Marjorie "gave no trouble," that is, did exactly what she was told—the woman was not unpleasant. But it was purely a professional pleasantness. As Marjorie found, if there was any trouble, she was unhesitatingly ruthless and savage.

This impersonal ferocity was just what Marjorie found most dreadful. It was impossible to establish any human contact with such a woman. She did not regard Marjorie as a human being, but as some kind of animal under her care.

Marjorie found that the other inmates were treated in exactly the same way—with no "unnecessary" cruelty, but without the slightest regard to their human dignity. Eventually, no doubt, they ceased to regard their dignity themselves, and became the wretched caricatures of human beings she saw.

Now that Lambert had become friendly towards her, it was evident that he had some plot at the back of his mind. He would become absorbed in reflection for hours on end—a time when, he said, he was thinking "secrets." To humour him, she would remain silent while he chuckled and ruminated with himself. She had no idea the plot concerned herself until one day as they sat side by side on one of the long garden seats, he said to her, with a little cackle of laughter:

"You run away from here! That would spite them all."

"There's nothing I should like better," she answered, "but how can I get out of here?"

He gave a stealthy glance round at the attendant who was watching him. They were near the wall and the attendants made a point of keeping a sharp eye on anyone who was near a wall.

"Well, you see this seat we're sitting on now? It's not fixed to the ground, although it looks as if it is. If you were to put it up against the wall, you could use the crossbars at the back to climb up, and then you could reach the top of the wall with your hands.

You'd better cover the top with your coat, rolled up, and then jump down the other side. If you hang on first, and then let yourself go, it's not much of a drop. And the ground is soft anyway. That's the way I escaped."

"But they're bound to see me!"

"Ah, that's where I come in. I'll distract their attention."

It was an ingenious plan, and she wondered at his cunning, although she supposed that insanity only affected a part of the brain. If that was how he had escaped before, it was surprising they continued to leave the long seats about the grounds, not fastened down. Perhaps some inmate had replaced the seat and so concealed Lambert's means of escape. In their sane moments there was a strange camaraderie among the inmates, and mutual enmity towards the attendants.

Once she had seen a combined attack of half-a-dozen creatures on one attendant who had slipped on a piece of lawn. He had been rescued by the other attendants, and next day all except one of those who were concerned in the attack kept to their rooms. Even the one who came out had a face almost raw with bruises and had to walk with the aid of a stick. The attendants evidently had their own way of enforcing discipline.

"Where am I?" she asked. "In England?"

"Dear me, Miss Easton, yes!" he answered in a surprised tone. He looked at her a little anxiously. "Forgive me if I am rude, but do you sometimes feel mentally confused?"

Even in the unpleasant circumstances, the incongruity of the remark struck her, and she could not help laughing. Then, seeing his hurt look, she went on: "Whereabouts exactly are we then?"

"In Norfolk. That is one of the Norfolk Broads—Langdon Mere. The nearest station is at Thorpe. It is a long way by road, but once you are there you will be all right. The railway people are silly about money, but if you creep on the train quietly without saying anything, they will probably let you go at the barrier at the other end, if you give them an address!"

"I don't mind once I get to the station. How far is it?"

But by this time Lambert's mind had drifted to something else, and she could not bring him back to the subject. It was no use expecting help from people like him, she decided hopelessly.

She went on chatting to him and then, quite suddenly, his mind must have returned to the subject of her escape, for, after a crafty, sidelong glance at her, he jumped up and began running across the lawn, yelling and waving his arms. An attendant made a rush at him, but he picked up a garden rake which had been thrown down by a gardener and knocked the attendant down with it. Instantly the whole place was in confusion. All the attendants in the grounds began running towards Lambert, and simultaneously there was a surge of inmates after him. Marjorie was left alone.

As it happened, this place was screened by trees from the house. It was her one chance. She lugged the seat towards the wall, and, with a heave, managed to tilt it against the brickwork. Then she climbed to the top, rolled up the thick overcoat she was wearing, and put it on the top of the wall. It seemed a long drop, but she cared for only one thing—to escape. She held on the top for a moment and then let go.

She found herself ankle deep in the earth, safe and sound.

There was no time to be lost. The main thing was to get away from this terrible place, out of sight of it, as quickly as possible. She hurried along the bank, and, instead of following the road, started to set off across the fields. It was a terrible place to escape from—for miles around there was no cover. The flat land stretched out without trees or hedges for miles on end. The fields were cut up at intervals by dykes, which she had either to jump across or wade through. Soon her breath was coming in pants, and she was already tired. Yet something urged her on to hurry, hurry... She must not be caught again, whatever happened!

If the worst came to the worst she would double back to the lake and swim into the reeds. She was a good swimmer....

Marjorie bent all her thoughts, all her energy, all her hope, on the word "escape."

2

The dog died of strychnine, Dr Tremayne reported, and this made Morgan think hard.

Crispin had died of strychnine. A prussic acid bottle had been found in Wainwright's pocket. It was all getting infernally complex. What on earth did this dog die for, in this unexpected way, without any visible cause? What exactly was the snake doing in Belmont Avenue? Without poison in its glands too?

Morgan paid yet another visit to the house. The cook had left and it had been shut up. The studio, scene of Crispin's death, was dusty.

Morgan went up to the washbowl from which the water had been taken for Crispin's fatal drink. Below the washbasin was a rubber mat, and Morgan rolled this up carefully and put it in his invaluable attaché case, together with the Six Queer Things. Then he got out a bottle and filled it with water from the cold tap.

This was the main object of his visit, but while he was there he made a careful inspection of the carpet. The only things which he thought worth bringing away were a number of pieces of coloured wool clinging to it, which he picked up here and there. Evidently they had survived Anne's broom.

When he returned, there was a certain amount of routine work to be done. The glass of water and the rubber mat had to be sent to Tremayne. The wool had to go to the textile expert.

"Any news of Wainwright yet?" he asked his assistant.

"Not yet. But there's some quite interesting stuff come through on the poison enquiries."

He handed Morgan a sheaf of papers, and the detective took them hopefully.

"They're certainly interesting," he said, after studying them carefully. "I think I'll go round to this address!"

He went round to a chemist's who seemed surprised at the sudden appearance of the law. When Morgan told him it was a murder case, he became alarmed.

"I hope I'm not going to be dragged into this," he said immediately.

"It's impossible to say," answered Morgan. "Naturally if we can get the information any other way, we'll keep your name out of it."

"I wish you would. It doesn't do business any good in this sort of neighbourhood. Although it's not one's fault, something always sticks, and people go elsewhere for their medicines."

"Look here, do me a favour and I'll do you a favour," said the policeman winningly. "Wrap up any bottle of medicine—sunburn lotion, horse liniment, what you like—and send it round by messenger to this address. Get your messenger to ask at the door if it was what was ordered, and wait till he gets the bottle back. See that the bottle is wrapped up—a box will be best."

"How very strange," murmured the chemist, with a disapproving air. "What do you want me to do that for?"

"Do this, and don't ask any questions. In return I'll see you're kept out of it."

The chemist agreed, and by the afternoon Morgan had the bottle back in his hands. It gave him a fine set of fingerprints, which he sent along to records.

He was pleased to find, next morning, on his desk, a fairly full dossier attached to the photographs. The prints were of a known criminal.

He rummaged in his drawer and turned up the list of people who had been present in the fatal séance.

"There seem to have been some nice specimens there," he remarked. The question was, how best to make an approach. He came to a decision.

He would call on Mrs Threpfall.

"I've come round to see you again in connection with the Crispin case," he said, when he had been shown into her elegant drawing room. Mrs Threpfall had evidently been dozing in the armchair—her kindly old eyes blinked at the light as he came in.

Mrs Threpfall nodded.

"Yes, I've been following it in the papers—as much as they print. Have you discovered anything new?"

"Not very much, but one or two new facts have come into my possession, and that is why I came round to see you. I hope I am not taking up any of your valuable time?"

"I'm not a very busy woman, Inspector. When you reach my age and your husband is dead and you have no children, time hangs heavily on one's hands. I'm thinking of moving into the country."

"No amusements or hobbies, eh?"

"None at all. Except music."

"Not even a bit of needlework?"

Mrs Threpfall smiled.

"I suppose you've heard of my passion for knitting and embroidery. Yes, there's always that, although I haven't been doing much lately."

"Well, that's one of the reasons why I came to see you. I came across an odd thing at the Crispins' house, and seeing that you are a needlewoman, I thought you might be able to help me."

The inspector opened his bag and pulled out one of the Six Queer Things—the card with the coloured threads arranged on it.

"Now what would this be?"

Mrs Threpfall took it and examined it closely.

"How queer! I've never seen anything like it. It seems to be instructions for a pattern, but I must say I don't quite follow it. If you would like to leave it with me, I'll see if I can work out a design from it."

Morgan refused her offer.

"No, there's no need. I don't expect it is of importance. I mentioned it in passing; it wasn't the main purpose of my visit. That was to make a few enquiries about Crispin's death. As you know, Crispin was poisoned. An empty poison bottle was found in Robinson's pocket—a bottle which had contained a more than fatal dose of prussic acid. Robinson's real name, as you doubtless saw from the papers, is Wainwright, and he is under suspicion. But at the moment he has vanished, so I have come round to you."

Mrs Threpfall looked at him thoughtfully over her spectacles.

"I don't see what I can do for you, except assure you that this youngster cannot possibly be guilty of murder, or I am no judge of character."

"I believe you are a very keen judge of character," said Morgan winningly, "for all your apparently simple exterior." Mrs Threpfall smiled good humouredly. "Would you be ready to swear that you did not see Wainwright put any poison into Crispin's glass, or make any other suspicious move?"

"Most certainly. As I was seated next to him I should certainly have seen anything of that kind."

"Good."

Morgan got up and stared down for a moment at Mrs Threpfall.

"Then perhaps you can answer another question with equal truth. Why did you buy some prussic acid four days before Crispin's death?"

Mrs Threpfall's hands, which were clasped on her lap, whitened at the knuckles. She remained silent for a moment.

"I buy poison!" she exclaimed at last. "What nonsense!"

"There is no use denying it. I have your signature in the poison book, and a copy of the order for it, which came from Dr Wood. Why did you buy that poison?"

"I refuse to answer. It is my own business."

"Crispin died of poison," said Morgan sternly. "We have positive proof that you bought some, that you were seated next to Wainwright, and that therefore you were in a position to put it in his glass. I warn you that if you do not give a satisfactory explanation of why you bought it, I shall arrest you for the wilful murder of Crispin."

Mrs Threpfall stared back at him defiantly, a spot of colour blazing in each cheek.

"And I absolutely refuse to give you any information. As for arresting me, that is preposterous. You know you haven't the faintest chance of succeeding in a verdict! Not the faintest! I am not the woman to be either bluffed or intimidated!"

Morgan sat down again. When he spoke it was in his normal tone.

"Quite right. I haven't a chance of conviction," he said smoothly. "But how do you know I haven't a chance? Only if you knew a good deal more than has appeared in the papers."

"What do you mean?"

"The precise poison which killed Crispin has not been published. It is only known inside my office. It was not prussic acid, and therefore you are right. In spite of the damning circumstances, it would not be possible to get a conviction against you. All the same, how did you know?"

Mrs Threpfall maintained a stony silence. Her eyes snapped fire and defiance behind her glasses.

Morgan shrugged his shoulders.

"Well, we must find out, that's all."

He got up, put his hands casually in his pockets and strolled up to a large painting on the wall.

"Who's this fellow? Looks a bit under the weather."

"That is my late husband!" said Mrs Threpfall icily.

Morgan contemplated it with a laugh.

"It's a bit different to the photograph of him *we've* got in our files," he said. "His hair's a bit shorter in our picture."

"What do you mean by that remark? It sounds to me to be in rather dubious taste."

"Cut the polite stuff!" said the policeman roughly. "The only husband you ever had, Lucy, is still in Dartmoor. And you ought to be behind prison gates too."

Mrs Threpfall's whole expression changed. The kindliness vanished, and the mouth seemed to coarsen visibly. Her expression changed to one of insolent vulgarity.

"You haven't got anything on me! And please do not call me by my Christian name!"

"Well, you change the other so often."

"The usual flat-footed humour! Think you're clever, don't you? Don't be so damned familiar. This is a respectable house. I want to keep it so."

"Respectable. With a jailbird's wife in charge? That's good," replied Morgan, in a tone as bantering and vulgar as hers.

"I'm not responsible for the sins of my husband!" replied Mrs Threpfall, her expression changing back to that of a kindly and even pathetic old lady. "Here am I trying to keep my end up and forget the past, and you come round here and drag me in the dust again. Have you no heart, no compunction, no pity for a lonely woman who is trying to struggle along in the straight and narrow path—after all the sorrow my poor erring husband brought on my head?

"Besides," she added, with another change of manner, "as crooks go, he was an aristocrat. He sat on the same board of directors as a viscount."

"Sure. And now he's got a cell next to a knight's son. But that doesn't make me any the less interested about your connection with Crispin."

"Pure scientific interest!"

"Don't talk nonsense. Do you think I don't understand the meaning of that chart? How you get friendly with Crispin's victims, and get them talking in the anteroom, and then when Crispin comes in, you signal everything with a bit of embroidery and coloured wools? That's an old stool-pigeon's trick!"

Mrs Threpfall pursed her lips in a grimace of disgust.

"Stool pigeon! I don't know what you're talking about. I wish you would not keep on referring to your criminal experiences, Inspector. Isn't there anything else you can talk about when you pay a visit? The weather, for instance?"

"Confound you!" exclaimed the inspector, rattled at last. He got up to go.

"You think I haven't got anything on you yet. You wait, Lucy! You'll smile on the other side of your face before I've finished."

"I could wait for you forever, Inspector Morgan!" she answered with mock friendliness. "I do so hope you will call again. Why not come round to my next At Home on Wednesday? You are so vigorous and refreshing!"

Morgan's answer as he closed the door with a bang was unprintable.

CHAPTER XII

Death of a Doctor

Marjorie came to London on a train that seemed to stagger never-endingly along the bumpy East Coast railway. She had been able to get on at Thorpe without being challenged by the ticket collector, and was able to evade any ticket inspection until she got to London.

Here she gave a story which she had made up on the way. She explained to the ticket collector that she had been on a trip to the Broads and that she had had her purse stolen. She would be prepared to give them her name and address or wait with them until they had sent for her uncle. The story sounded plausible.

Now she was in London, Marjorie felt safe. She did not mind if the station authorities did detain her or have her arrested. Anything would be preferable to that vile place. Once she was in touch with the police, she could explain the whole thing.

The ticket collector was suspicious and kept her waiting while he consulted the stationmaster. Then he came back to her.

"We've got a message about you," he said, when he came back, with a friendly smile. His whole demeanour had changed. She thought, all the same, that there was something a little strange in his manner.

"A message?" she said in surprise.

"Yes, some friends of yours were expecting you. The message is, not to worry, you'll be in good hands soon. They've arranged to send someone along with the fare, but as a matter of formality, we have to ask you to wait until the money actually comes into our hands."

This amazed Marjorie. How was it that someone had discovered her difficulty. Could it be Ted—or her uncle? Or perhaps Dr Wood had somehow heard of it? Apparently just as she had, for no reason, unknown enemies, without motives, she had equally unknown friends.

She was taken into a room in the stationmaster's office and given some magazines to read. Someone sent up a meal for her. They refused to answer her question, however, as to who the friend was who had sent the message. She was puzzled a little by this air of mystery. Could it be that Ted had sent the message and had not dared to give his name?

Hours passed. She began to get a little uneasy as she waited alone in the office. She went to the door, and found it was locked. Evidently then, in spite of their friendly attitude, they did not trust her until the money had arrived!

Then she heard voices outside. The door opened, and she had a moment of stark horror. For the man who came in with the stationmaster, and who stepped forward with a friendly greeting, was Marsden, his sallow face and scarlet lips one hypocritical look of welcome. She gave a cry, and moved backwards. As she did so she saw the expression on the stationmaster's face, and now realised the whole meaning of her ambiguous treatment. Marsden had obviously telephoned to the station, directly they had discovered her escape, saying that an escaped lunatic might have got on the train, and asking him to hold her.

She appealed to the stationmaster.

"That man has been keeping me against my will. I am perfectly sane, and I demand that the police be called at once. I shall lay a charge against him for kidnapping me."

Even as she said it, she felt the extraordinary difficulty of proving her sanity to someone who already suspected it. There was an obvious scepticism on the stationmaster's face, and her bedraggled look was no recommendation. If only she were tidy, and not wearing this dreadful dress!

"My dear young lady," said Dr Marsden, "it is very foolish of you to take up this attitude! You know we have your best interests at heart. We have a legal document, signed by a magistrate, which I have shown to the stationmaster, and which proves that it is our duty to look after you. Please be reasonable. You must admit that we have done our best for you."

She refused to answer him and appealed to the stationmaster.

"I insist that you get in touch with the police. My name is Marjorie Easton, and I am sure they must be looking for me by now. I was forcibly taken from home."

Marsden whispered something to the stationmaster, and he smiled. She realised that, with diabolical cleverness, Marsden was insinuating that this was one of her delusions. Perhaps he had already warned the stationmaster of it.

"I beg of you to get in touch with my uncle. Surely it is not too much to ask. You have only to send a messenger to him."

"Really, this is only a waste of time," said Marsden impatiently. "I have already phoned your uncle, warning him that you may try to see him, and explaining the danger of this; and he has asked me to plead with you to be reasonable, and to understand that you must put yourself in the hands of your medical advisers."

"There, you see how it is!" answered the stationmaster, a little uneasily. "You take your uncle's advice and go home, like a good girl!"

"Don't treat me like a little child," burst out Marjorie. "Can't you see he is bluffing you? I warn you I will only go back with this man by force. I swear to you that he is keeping me there against my will, in spite of the fact that I am perfectly sane. If he has obtained a legal document it is only by trickery. I make one last appeal to you. Ring up Dr Wood. I'll give you his phone number. Ask him whether he knows a Marjorie Easton, and ask him to come down at once and identify me and testify to my sanity."

The stationmaster hesitated, and then turned to the doctor as if in doubt.

"All this puts me in a very difficult situation," he explained.

"There should be no difficulty," said Marsden brusquely. "The legal position is clear. We are legally responsible for this young girl. However, if it will satisfy your mind, I have no objection to any doctor's coming down to have a talk with her, for, he will confirm that she is insane to put it bluntly."

The stationmaster went away and returned with a report to the effect that Dr Wood was coming down at once. He arrived about half an hour later.

A tremendous feeling of relief came over Marjorie when she saw the well-known face. She ran up to him and clasped his hand.

"Thank God, you've come! Tell these people I'm not mad! They've been keeping me prisoner in an asylum."

Now that safety was so near, she was about to break down.

To her surprise Dr Wood looked at her curiously and withdrew his hand.

"What is all this? Excuse me, but all this is a surprise to me. What exactly is happening, and why precisely have I been called in?"

Marjorie gave a hurried account of her adventures, and at the close of it Dr Wood looked significantly at the stationmaster.

"This is an astounding accusation against a brother doctor, and, frankly, I find it difficult to believe. You claim to be Marjorie Easton, whom of course I knew quite well. While I must admit there is a strong resemblance, I am positive you are not the Marjorie Easton I knew. Quite positive."

The whole world seemed to collapse round Marjorie.

"Do you mean to suggest that I am impersonating her? You, who know me so well!"

Dr Wood shrugged his shoulders.

"I cannot say. There is the other explanation of your claim, which Marsden gives."

"Well, that's clear enough," interrupted the stationmaster sternly. "You've taken up enough of our time. I don't want to have anything more to do with you."

He turned to Marsden.

"Please take her away as quietly as possible. We don't want to have a fuss!"

The betrayal of Dr Wood, which revealed that he, too, was a party to the conspiracy, produced a wave of indignation in Marjorie. She felt like some trapped animal, hemmed in, who suddenly gains courage and turns on her tormentors.

Without any preliminary sign, she made a dash for the door. So sudden was the dash that she had got by them before they realised what she was doing. The next moment she had darted out of the offices on to the platform.

In spite of the shouts of "Stop her", she managed to run out into the courtyard and lose herself among the hurrying throng of people. She passed through a small door and found herself on the main road, near a rank of taxis.

Where could she go to? Mrs Threpfall passed through her mind as the only hope. Her uncle seriously believed she was mad. Ted was in hiding. Dr Wood had betrayed her. The police would believe the doctor's testimony and accept the certificate of her insanity.

Mrs Threpfall was her only hope.

She jumped into a taxi and gave Mrs Threpfall's address. As the taxi moved off, she saw one of the asylum attendants come out of the exit and look round. To her relief, just as the taxi turned the corner, he went in again, evidently satisfied that she had not gone that way.

She was still free....

2

Meanwhile the inspector had received the report of Yard experts on the mat and the bottle of water from the tap in the room where Crispin had died. The report stated that the mat showed traces of considerable quantities of strychnine. The water from the tap was normal in composition, nor indeed had the inspector imagined it would be anything else. What was puzzling was that the mat should have had on it quantities of strychnine. This must be connected with the way in which Wainwright had introduced the strychnine into the glass when he filled it. How could this have resulted in spilling large quantities of the poison on the mat—so large that many days afterwards there had been enough to kill the dog who, presumably, had lapped some up off the mat? Surely this pool of poison would have been noticed and cleaned up? It was an odd circumstance that it hadn't, and it worried the inspector.

Once again he examined the Six Queer Things for inspiration. In spite of their amazing heterogeneity, these had, in actual practice, already proved to have some meaning and some inner connection. He could not see as yet what was the role played by all of them, but he was already becoming increasingly clear as to the sinister nature of the drama in which the snake-charming impedimenta, the balloons and the photograph had each played a part. The sheet had a most unpleasant significance in his eyes. And he had soon grasped the purpose of the chart of coloured wools.

What about the little textbook on "Forensic Medicine"? He took this out of the case and examined it carefully. There was a section on "toxicology", and he turned to the entry relating to strychnine. To his disappointment, he found the leaves had not even been cut.

He was about to put the book away again, when he decided to look up the reference to "hydrocyanic acid." Here he struck oil. Not only were the leaves cut, but the paragraphs outlining the symptoms of hydrocyanic-acid poisoning had been marked with pencil.

The inspector found this a tough nut to crack. An empty phial of hydrocyanic acid had been found on Ted Wainwright, but Crispin had quite definitely died of strychnine poisoning. Crispin none the less had a copy of "Forensic Medicine" in which the section on prussic acid had been carefully underlined and studied. What could be the sense of this?

He turned over the page. At the end of the chapter were two or three words of what seemed gibberish to the inspector, but, after consultation with Tremayne, he found they described certain drugs. He asked what their effect would be.

"Very much the same as the effects of mild hydrocyanic-acid poisoning, except that the symptoms would pass off sooner and would be less harmful. Evidently that is a note of some kind by a doctor, perhaps to remind him not to confuse the two, although I can't imagine anyone taking the drugs in question, unless it were to simulate prussic-acid poisoning."

"That's rather interesting!" commented Morgan truthfully. It was not only interesting, it was revelatory.

"By the way," went on Tremayne, unconscious of the effect of his remarks, "I was able to speak to one of my old colleagues and I mentioned our friend Wood to him. It may interest you to know that Wood left under a bit of a cloud. He was recognised as a clever doctor—indeed if he hadn't been so clever the cloud might have been denser than it was. It was a matter of unethical behaviour—not exactly taking bribes, but something near it. Apparently Wood had the notion that his wealth ought to be commensurate with his brains, and as he started life with none of the former and a good deal of the latter, the idea was bound to lead to trouble!"

This disclosure did not come as a complete surprise to Morgan. As a result of Tremayne's words he looked up his files and compared the handwriting in "Forensic Medicine" with Dr Wood's handwriting.

There was no doubt they were the same. Here was a link, goodness knows what, between the doctor, Crispin, the little book, and the bottle of poison found in Wainwright's pocket. The difficulty was to see how it connected with the actual murder of Crispin.

Morgan decided to go round and see Wood. He phoned him, and thought he detected a certain amount of constraint in the doctor's voice. Did he realise things were getting a little dangerous? However, Wood emphasised that he would be glad to see Morgan immediately.

Morgan had decided to be frank with the doctor. He came straight to the point.

"Look here, Doctor Wood, I have made certain discoveries that demand a further explanation from you. As you know, a bottle of prussic acid was found in Wainwright's pocket. Crispin was found when dead to have a book on 'Forensic Medicine' in her possession. That book belonged to you, and I have discovered that not only was the section dealing with hydrocyanic acid underscored, but you had actually added, as a footnote, the names of certain drugs which would simulate the effect of prussic acid. I want some explanation of these facts."

Dr Wood did not hurry about answering. He took out his cigar box from the drawer and handed one to the inspector, who decided he was justified in taking one. The two men lit up in silence. Only when a dense cloud hung above Dr Wood's rosy features and silvery hair did he decide to answer.

"All things considered, Inspector, I feel I ought perhaps to have been franker with you at an earlier date!"

"That's a remark we often hear in our profession, Doctor,"

replied Morgan, mellowed by the cigar, "and I can tell you it is invariably correct."

"So I can believe! Well, in this particular case, had I been franker, I would have told you that Wainwright was frantically jealous of Crispin's influence over Marjorie, with whom, as you may or may not know, he was at one time engaged. I did not tell you about this incident earlier, because I felt certain in my own mind, on questions purely of character and personality, that Wainwright was innocent; but I knew that if I told you this story, it might increase what I regard as your stupid prejudice against Wainwright."

The inspector nodded.

"Actually, your action has probably increased what you call my prejudice against Wainwright. But go on."

"Well, what happened was this: Wainwright at one time tried to get hold of some poison, with some absurd excuse about killing a pet dog. He did not approach me, but asked Mrs Threpfall to secure it for him. Mrs Threpfall naturally came to me for advice and, in conjunction with Crispin, we hatched a little plot. Mrs Threpfall actually got the poison, and I exchanged it for a drug which would produce all the effects of hydrocyanic acid. I gave Crispin the book so that she would be thoroughly familiar with what was about to happen to her. I counted on the psychological effect of what would follow to clear up the whole tangle in which Wainwright was involved."

"I don't quite see why it should clear matters up. Surely it would make them worse?"

"Minds in a certain condition bend themselves to an act, and the whole psychic energy gets so concentrated on this act, that it is impossible to divert them from it by any outside force. That was the state of Wainwright's mind in relation to Crispin's death.

"Directly the crucial act is performed, however, the tension is released, and the psychic energy flows slowly back into its normal channels. This accounts for the common phenomenon of the criminal who repents of his crime directly he has committed it, although no amount of argument could prevent his committing it beforehand. In the same way the obstinate suicide who has just been snatched back from death's door after an attempt at self murder is often completely cured."

"Yes, I've met plenty of cases like that, I must admit."

"Well, that was the type of cure I attempted in Wainwright's case. I knew that after he had apparently poisoned Crispin, and was confident she was dying, he would experience a great emotional upheaval, in which he would be cured of his obsession against Crispin. This obsession had become so closely interwoven with his love for Marjorie, that I believed it might also alter his attitude to Marjorie, and transform it into a state which would be much more helpful in her then condition. Of course I have not the faintest idea who did ultimately kill Crispin and so upset our plan. That is your problem, Inspector!"

Morgan contemplated the glowing tip of his cigar for some time, before he felt ready to make any comment. Then he said quietly:

"That certainly gives an explanation of the incident, Doctor Wood, although I need hardly emphasise how much unnecessary trouble has been caused by your withholding of it until this date."

"Yes, it was rather an unethical action! To be even more candid, Inspector, although I am a doctor, I am by nature not a very law-abiding person. You may not think it to look at me—I fancy I look respectable—but I have always had a certain contempt for the verbal constructions we human beings externalise and worship, and call Moral Laws, or Right and Wrong. I suppose being a psychologist, and understanding exactly how these gods originate in the subconscious, determined by the experience and objective surroundings of the person who accepts them, breeds a certain nihilism in this respect.

"My brother doctors themselves regard me as a bit of an *enfant terrible*. Some might even call me a charlatan, which, in case you do not know it, Inspector, is the term the rank and file of my profession have always applied to anyone who deviates by an inch from current tradition, and which has therefore been applied to such great pioneers as Lister, Pasteur and Freud. In my own case it led to my being asked to leave the only establishment I have been connected with. However, I don't suppose all this interests you."

"What would really interest me," said the inspector, watching him closely, "would be to know where Wainwright is at the moment."

"You surely don't expect me to know that, do you?" asked Dr Wood earnestly. "I'm afraid you've got hold of the wrong end of the stick somehow. I honestly haven't the faintest idea!"

"Or where Marjorie Easton is?"

"Still less her!"

"Why still less? Either you know something about the whereabouts of one or the other, or you don't."

"Well, there's no use our fencing. I did know for a time the whereabouts of Ted Wainwright after his disappearance. I admit it freely. In fact, I was largely responsible in helping him evade arrest. I am aware this renders me liable to prosecution, but of course if prosecuted I should deny ever making this admission to you.

"I do not regret having helped him to escape, for I am absolutely convinced he is innocent. But I must also admit that he has disappeared even from the sanctuary I gave him. You know that as well as I do, Inspector. You know even the date on which he disappeared. But where he is now, I haven't the faintest idea. But as for Marjorie Easton, in her case I have never had the remotest idea where she has been from the moment of her disappearance, and so in her case, *still less* do I know her whereabouts. You are certainly uncommonly sharp in noticing these turns in phrase. You are more of a psychologist than I thought."

Morgan threw away the finished stub of his cigar.

"Thank you, Doctor, for being so frank. I think what you have told me clears the matter up as far as you are concerned. As for the other question, I don't see any harm in telling you that I have no more idea where Marjorie Easton or Ted Wainwright is than you have."

As soon as he got back to his office, Morgan wrote a note to headquarters, asking that in future Dr Wood's telephone be tapped, and a transcript of all information passed to him.

The next day, he studied Wood's telephone messages carefully. All, with one exception, were apparently on ordinary business.

But the one exception was sufficiently odd. It consisted of a brief message spoken to someone who had called up, apparently by arrangement, from a public call office in Finsbury Park. To him, without any introduction or greeting, Dr Wood had said the following:

"Tell the Director that Morgan has got on the track of the poison racket. Unless he can get rid of Ted Wainwright, we shall all be dished."

Who was the Director? Morgan asked himself, vainly puzzling over the actors in the drama he already knew. None of them seemed quite to fit the title.

His speculations were cut short by an urgent telephone call from Vine Street Police Station.

He was to come at once to Dr Wood's flat.

There he found Dr Wood, or what had once been Dr Wood, for the body was hardly recognisable. The face, and in fact the whole head, had been battered by a bronze statue by Rodin—"Le Baiser"—which stood in Dr Wood's bedroom, not far from his bed.

To all appearances, Wood had been attacked and murdered while he slept, for there was no sign of a struggle.

CHAPTER XIII

The Dreadful Factory

The Inspector's enquiries at Dr Wood's flat soon showed him how the murder had been committed. Adams, Wood's servant, explained that in the evening the doctor had had a caller, a man in a light mackintosh and dirty boots. He had seemed nervous and agitated, and had asked to see Wood. As it happened, Wood had been dining out that evening, but the caller had insisted on waiting until his return, and Adams had given him a chair in the hall.

After about an hour, however, Adams had heard the front door slam. Going out into the hall, he had found that the stranger had disappeared. Adams had naturally concluded that the man had got tired of waiting and had left. He had, therefore, merely mentioned the fact of his having called to Dr Wood, who had shown no particular concern about the visitor.

When the inspector came to examine the bedroom, he found the distinct trace of muddy footprints on the carpet by the bed, and also in a large wardrobe, where the visitor had evidently hidden himself until Wood had fallen asleep. After that he had no doubt murdered Wood and crept out of the flat by the front door.

It was difficult to find any motive for the assault. Nothing in the flat had been touched. There had simply been the murder, sudden and unspeakably brutal. Was it an act of revenge, or was it intended to keep the doctor from talking?

The inspector sent round for a photograph of Ted Wainwright, but Adams was prepared to swear that the caller did not resemble him. Pressed to give a description of the man, Adams emphasised his nervous gestures, his jerky stare, and his habit of darting from one subject to another.

"In fact, he struck me as a bit touched."

"Didn't you feel at all nervous about him in that case?" asked the inspector. "It seems a bit careless to leave a man who behaves like a madman by himself in the hall."

"Well, after you've been with the doctor for a few years, you get used to gentlemen like him," explained Adams. "Most of his patients are either a bit queer or think they are, so it just comes natural to one after a time. I've always found them harmless enough before, I must say. In fact, they're a bit more generous with their money than many of the sane ones."

The inspector was not satisfied of the accuracy of Adams' story about the strange visitor until he had had some confirmation of it. After all, the mud might have been faked. He obtained this confirmation from the hall porter of the flats. A man with queer ways, wearing a light mackintosh, and generally answering to Adams' description, had asked him if Dr Wood lived there. He had told the man the number of the floor of Wood's flat.

It now became primarily a matter of trying to trace the man. The inspector phoned up the Yard and set on foot the necessary arrangements.

The murderer had left the flat either very late at night, or very early in the morning. In either case it seemed certain that someone must have seen him and noticed something strange in his manner.

Meanwhile Morgan ordered all the documents and papers which could be found in Wood's flat to be brought round to his office, where he could go through them carefully. The doctor could hardly have expected his death, and therefore it seemed unlikely that he would have made the same careful preparations to destroy all incriminating evidence as had been made in the case of Crispin.

Yet the inspector had to admit the difficulties he was faced with. Ted Wainwright still stood out as the murderer, for he was the only man who, in the circumstances, could have put the dose of strychnine into Crispin's glass. The evidence of everyone at the séance agreed on the point. Certainly there were other puzzling facts that it was difficult to reconcile—the phial of hydrocyanic acid and the drugs intended to produce the same symptoms. But so far these facts seemed unconnected with the murder.

Still more strange was the complete disappearance from the

scene of Marjorie Easton, Ted Wainwright and Miss Crispin. The inspector was reluctant to give a sinister interpretation to their disappearance, but this fresh incident certainly made him wonder whether any of them were still alive.

He could only issue instructions for a fresh drive to be made to trace them. If they were still in England, sooner or later they were certain to be found.

2

When Marjorie had jumped into the taxi and left her pursuers behind, she had felt that at last she would be safe. The very sensation of speeding on her way, with a taxi under her order, alone gave her a feeling of elation. True, she had no money on her, but she knew that Mrs Threpfall would pay for the taxi when she got there.

If by any chance Mrs Threpfall was out, Marjorie was determined to drive to Scotland Yard. There she would make a last struggle for liberty. She felt sure that, if she did this, she could get this monstrous certificate cancelled, if it were legal, or exposed, if it were a fraud.

When she arrived at Mrs Threpfall's, she asked the taxi driver to wait a few minutes, and went inside. Soon after Marjorie had disappeared inside, a maid came out with some money and paid him. He went away.

Inside, Mrs Threpfall was listening with horror to Marjorie's story.

"But this is terrible, you poor little girl!" she said, as Marjorie told her of her experiences in the asylum. "Surely this is impossible in the twentieth century."

"All the same it has happened!" replied Marjorie bitterly. "What can I do? If they somehow got this power over me when I was drugged, how can I get it upset?"

"Don't you remember what happened when you were drugged?"

"Only vaguely. It was like a dream. I can't even remember the man and woman who were with me, and yet their faces seemed strangely familiar."

Mrs Threpfall got up and pressed the bell.

"The first thing you need is some tea and something solid to eat! You'll feel more yourself then! You look dreadful." Marjorie looked at herself in the glass.

"What I need far more is a wash and some of my own clothes. It is awful having to go about in these things. God knows where they dug them out. Will you come round with me to Belmont Avenue to get them."

"No, that would be dangerous. Anyway, now I come to think of it, all your belongings are with your uncle. He has been terribly worried about your disappearance."

"But they told me that he knew where I was, and that they convinced him it was necessary."

"An absolute lie!" declared Mrs Threpfall hotly. "Why were you taken in? I'll go round to him at once and explain. Whatever you do, don't leave this flat. It may be dangerous. I'll bring you back your clothes, and then we'll go along with you and your uncle to a good lawyer, and get the whole thing straightened out. If I were you, I should have a good rest. You look as if you need it badly."

Marjorie was ready to agree with her. She was physically and mentally exhausted by the events of the day. After a cup of tea and a bath, she was glad to accept Mrs Threpfall's invitation to stretch herself on a bed.

"I'll send away the servants, dear," Mrs Threpfall told her, "just to be on the safe side, in case anyone calls! Don't open the door to anyone. I have the key."

Three hours later, Marjorie heard the door open, and someone come in. She thought she heard voices, and she called out.

"Who's that?"

"Only me," answered Mrs Threpfall's voice.

"Is that Uncle with you?"

"No, I'm alone. That was just the taxi driver I was speaking to."

Mrs Threpfall came into the bedroom and put down a suitcase.

"There you are. Your uncle wasn't in, but his new housekeeper let me come in and take those clothes. Call out to me when you are ready."

It was a tremendous relief to Marjorie to get into the clothes.

She was putting the finishing touches to her hair in front of the mirror when Mrs Threpfall knocked.

"I don't want to hurry you but we ought to be getting off."

"All right," answered Marjorie cheerfully. "Come in. Is this better?"

"My dear, you look sweet," said Mrs Threpfall. "That coat is just a little dusty on the back though. Turn round."

Marjorie turned round, only to feel her throat enfolded in a grip of iron. Mrs Threpfall's strength was astounding, and Marjorie was unable even to cry out. As she began to struggle, she felt herself dragged violently backwards and the pressure on her throat tightened, until the blood sang in her ears. She kicked backwards violently.

"Stop it, you bitch!" hissed Mrs Threpfall. "Come in, Bessie, and help me string her up!"

A terrible feeling of frustration and despair overcame Marjorie when the door opened and her hard-faced attendant from the asylum walked in. At the same time, her drugged swoon of a few days earlier sharpened and became clear. Why had not her muddled brain recollected it earlier? The woman who had pretended to be her aunt, who had accompanied her to the magistrate's, had been no other than Mrs Threpfall herself! Like a fool she had gone straight back into the lion's den.

3

Morgan, after a careful examination of the doctor's papers, found himself in a difficulty. Most of it was the ordinary paraphernalia of the medical man. The only records that he found difficult to explain were the large sums of money which, from time to time, were paid into the doctor's bank accounts, and the *very curious casebooks.*

These casebooks followed in general form what might be expected of the records of a psychologist. They were descriptions of the progress of various cases, designated by initials, and, so far as the policeman could tell from his lay knowledge, were what might be expected of a psychiatrist's practice among wealthy and fashionable neurotics.

But there was one conspicuous exception. Separate from the ordinary casebooks was one which was kept in a locked box, and there seemed something so strange and unexpected about the tone of these records, that Morgan sent it along at once by special messenger to Tremayne for him to study and report upon.

Certainly they threw no direct light upon the facts which Morgan had already assembled in his mind against the dead doctor. Wood's close association with Crispin had been the most damaging item against him, but even more important in its effect on Morgan had been Wood's reaction on seeing the Six Queer Things. He had professed complete ignorance concerning them. Yet one of them, the sheet, was something which any alienist should have recognised instantly. The only explanation for that, as Morgan had long realised, was that Wood had recognised it, but for certain reasons had wished to keep Morgan in ignorance of what it was.

Then there had been Wood's ingenious explanation of the prussic acid episode, and the handbook on "Forensic Medicine" apparently intended to shield Ted Wainwright. It was in fact demonstrably false, for if Ted's phial had really contained not prussic acid, but some drugs designed to produce the same effect, then this would have been revealed on analysis. In fact the analysis had shown that what the phial had contained before it was emptied (whenever it *was* emptied) was hydrocyanic and nothing else. What then was Wood's motive in telling this lie, unless it was to hide something much more serious?

On top of that there had been Wood's association with Mrs Threpfall, with her bad record and obvious function as Crispin's accomplice; Wood's shelter of Ted Wainwright after a warrant for his arrest had been issued; and Wood's own doubtful past. These factors together threw suspicion on Wood, and yet it was impossible to see any link between him and Crispin's murder, nor to see why he should himself be the victim of the second attack.

And who was the Director, subject to the mysterious telephone message? Nothing in Wood's private papers gave Morgan any clue to this. Yet the very fact of the message suggested strongly that there was someone higher up behind the whole chain of intrigue, and that Wood was as much under his orders as was Crispin or Mrs Threpfall. If that was so, the whole affair had the distinct appearance of gang warfare, either between rival gangs, or, more probably, between the leader of a gang and certain of his rebellious subordinates.

Who, in that case, was the leader? And what was the nature of the insubordination?

Morgan's chain of thought was broken abruptly by a telephone call from Tremayne, who asked to come over and see him at once. Naturally Morgan agreed. To his surprise, the medical expert definitely looked upset. There was no other word for it. The grey, precise Tremayne, usually so unruffled, was disturbed.

He slammed the casebook down on the desk indignantly.

"Morgan, never, in all my career, have I read anything so foul and disgusting! If these entries are truthful, if what is described there has really been happening, then all I can say is that Wood got off too lightly. To have his head bashed in while he slept was far too light a punishment! I should like to have attended to his death!"

"Why? What on earth has he been doing?"

"Doing? Simply this. Wood has been using his great scientific knowledge and all the resources of modern psychotherapeutic technique, *not to heal disordered or weakened human minds, but to unbalance them completely!* I know it sounds incredible that any human being could do such a thing, and I should like to believe these entries are pure fantasy. But there is a terrible verisimilitude about them. They chronicle only too clearly the purgatory undergone by a tormented human mind when all the resources of medical science and psychological knowledge—transference, fixation, hypnotism, autosuggestion and drugs—are used, not to heal it, but to ruin it!"

"Is such a thing possible?" asked Morgan, astounded. "Can a doctor really be successful in driving people insane?"

"Of course! Surely you appreciate that the higher nervous system is the most finely balanced part of the complex organism we call the body, that what we term sanity is not something we can take for granted, but a delicate equilibrium of warring forces? You know how easy it is to upset even the most primitive and gross functions of the body, digestion, for example! It is correspondingly easier to play havoc with the finer faculties. A clumsy alienist may do terrible damage merely in attempting to heal. What a skilled one may do in deliberately attempting to *harm*, I hardly dare think."

"Yes, I think I understand."

"Morgan, something unutterably ghastly has been going on here. What the motive was, I can't fathom. I can't see the object of this deliberate ruining of personalities. It might perhaps be that Wood took some perverted sadistic delight in it. Yet it seems more than that. There *must* be other people involved. It is a system. What can be the motive of such a system?"

"The usual motive—cash!"

"It makes me sick merely to think what has been happening here. There's one point, which I think will be of special value to you. One of the cases is under the heading 'M.E.', and from the general description of it and the way Wood describes his development of the subject's suggestibility and dissociation of personality, I believe that it is the case of Marjorie Easton. The only mercy of it is that for some reason Wood has written in at the end, 'Incomplete.' God knows, though, whether by now it is not complete!"

"I must admit I am not quite as much surprised as you are, Tremayne. There have been too many elements cropping up lately and pointing to something of this kind. But I did not expect anything quite so unpleasant. An attempt to exploit lunatics, yes! The Crispins of this world are doing it everywhere in London, if by lunatics you do not mean merely certifiable lunatics, but also all those who are permanently or temporarily weak minded, maladapted, or thrown off their mental balance by some overwhelming private grief. But that's a different thing entirely from a factory for lunatics! That's a new devilry. Yet something of that kind seems to have been going on here."

"What on earth can be the object of it? What on earth is there to gain by it?"

"That remains to be seen. I shall get in touch with the lunacy commissioners and make some investigations. Meanwhile, Tremayne, will you draw up, on the basis of this casebook, a general picture of the persons who are concerned, in so far as you can get any idea of them from the particulars given—details like age, sex, general temperament, and so on? There must be many details of that kind which, together with the initials, will give us the clue to the identity of the people concerned."

"Right. I'll do that. But there is one entry, which struck me as being out of the way. It refers to one 'J.L.', and there is a note towards the end 'Escaped', then a date, and then a little later 'Recaptured.' This escape took place fairly recently."

"That is certainly interesting! 'J.L.', eh? I begin to have a suspicion of who 'J.L.' is!"

"What, you mean you know him?"

"No, but I think that I can guess what his relation to Doctor Wood was."

So sure was the policeman of this, that he went at once to call on Dr Wood's solicitor whose name was among the doctor's papers, but who, according to various sources of police information, was an eminently respectable solicitor.

He regarded Morgan at first with mild disapproval, which became a kind of nervous fluttering when the detective began to hint at the dubious nature of Wood's main source of income when alive.

"But I always understood that my client had a very fashionable practice!" he fluttered.

"It was very remunerative, and he may have had some fashionable clients, but that does not prevent it from being shady. That frankly was what it was. Shady, beastly—devilish, to be precise."

"Devilish! Dear, dear." The solicitor blinked. "I can only say it is very regrettable, and surprising. It was not a side of his nature he showed to me."

"So I should imagine. Anyway, I come here for a definite purpose. Did you at any time help Doctor Wood in taking out a Commission of Lunacy for anyone with the initials 'J.L.'"

The solicitor turned a little greenish about the gills. "I did indeed. I trust there was nothing wrong with that case. Everything was signed and perfectly in order. I saw the man myself, and though I am not an expert, he was certainly *non compos*."

"We don't dispute that," replied Morgan grimly. "And you

have not anything to regret, I imagine. Wood would not have employed you unless he was sure of himself. Who was the man?"

"John Lambert was the name!"

"And I suppose Doctor Wood was made his guardian?"

"Dear me, no. It was a relation of his. It would not have been in order for Wood to have been appointed guardian. Not as his medical man. No, Sir Timothy is a close relation. Everything was quite in order. Lambert was certified independently, and he was taken away to some institution at once."

"Well, I want all the details you can give me about Lambert and his relation, and this institution."

"I will see what we can find, Inspector."

The solicitor bustled out to a kind of anteroom, stacked high with deed boxes and bundles of documents. The floor was spread with letters, and two grey-headed women were crawling about the floor on their hands and knees, apparently engaged in some form of filing activity. They seemed rather pathetic—slowly being engulfed in a deluge of documents.

"Miss Gorringe," said the solicitor sharply, "please find the documents relating to John Lambert, Ward in Lunacy, and bring them to the inspector here at once."

In spite of the sharpness of tone, it took the elderly ladies an hour to find the documents. The records were scanty, but they were still sufficient to enable Inspector Morgan, that evening, to visit a white-faced Sir Timothy Lambert and give him the fright of his life.

"We'll see that this deed is set aside, of course," Morgan warned him. "Relative or not, there's an old legal maxim that no man can profit from his wrongdoing. And that's retrospective. You'll have to render an account of all your stewardship!"

Sir Timothy remained silent for some time before replying.

"All this comes as a very great shock to me . . ." he began pitifully.

"I've no doubt it does," interjected Morgan abruptly. "It was meant to."

"I mean, if I could have given my right hand to save John's reason I would have done it. You don't know the distress——"

His voice died away before the contempt in Morgan's face, and he got shakily to his feet.

"Are you going to arrest me?" he said weakly.

"Not at the moment. I have come for an exact description of John Lambert."

The man gave it to him and Morgan departed, not without a last contemptuous cut.

"Please remain available for the next few days. If you have a passport you'd better let me have it."

Lambert surrendered it without a protest. . . .

Six hours later a man was taken by the police from a Salvation Army Hostel in the Commercial Road. He wore a light mackintosh and his boots were dirty. His eyes were red rimmed from lack of sleep, and there were several bloodstains on the front of his coat. He had refused to go to sleep, but had sat up all night on his bed, occasionally groaning, but most of the time sunk in a kind of daze.

He was charged with the murder of Dr Wood under the name of John Lambert, and, considering he had committed a brutal homicide, there was something curiously gentle in his treatment by the police.

CHAPTER XIV

The Bond of Release

From the very moment that Ted Wainwright drove down to Nightingale's Roost with Dr Wood, he had a feeling that he was losing his grip on events, that he was being simply whirled along like a leaf in the breeze.

This is an uncomfortable feeling for a young man of fairly stolid temperament and normal upbringing. It made him, in spite of his gratitude to Dr Wood, somewhat surly company on the drive down.

When they got to the little bungalow, they found there was no one in.

"I'm afraid I can't wait," Dr Wood told him, "but don't worry. I'll scribble a note for you to give to Harness."

Ted Wainwright waited for some time in the garden of Nightingale's Roost for Harness to return.

He came back soon after ten, and jumped perceptibly when Ted rose out of the shadows of the garden to speak to him.

"It's all right. I've been sent down by Doctor Wood," Wainwright told him. "Here's a letter from him."

"What's all this about?" grumbled Harness. Striking a match, he held the flame near Ted's face. The match also illuminated his own not very prepossessing features—florid, bull necked and sloppy. The inspection seemed to satisfy Harness, for he grunted.

"Come inside."

A wave of alcohol came with the words.

"Closing time must be ten o'clock round here," thought Wainwright.

By the light of an old lamp Harness inspected the doctor's letter. As he read it, he made a half turn away from Wainwright, which for a moment made the young man suspicious. Why did Harness not want Wainwright to see the doctor's letter? Perhaps it was merely a natural caution, however. Ted dismissed it from his mind, for Harness turned back cordially enough, after reading the letter.

"I'm glad to do anything for the doctor. I owe a lot to him, as I expect he told you!"

"It seems a bit thick, parking myself here!" said Ted diffidently.

"Nonsense, lad," answered Harness heartily, slapping him on the shoulder. "It gets damned lonely here, I can tell you, and I'm glad of company! I'll show you where I can fix up a bed for you. It won't be much of one, but I expect it will be better for your health than staying at home—from what I can gather from Doc's letter."

He gave Wainwright a knowing wink.

The days that followed were almost unbearable. On the one hand he had no news of Marjorie beyond the papers, which announced that she still was missing. On the other hand he was concerned about his mother. Early on the morning after his flight, he had posted her a note from a neighbouring village, saying that he was safe and she must keep quiet. He knew it was dangerous to write to her, but could not bear to think of her worrying about him without news.

Fortunately he had been putting by a little money in the Savings Bank for her, against the day when he could get a better job and think of marriage, and so there was no anxiety on that score. Even so, he knew that his flight would be a shock to her. That, coupled with his anxieties for Marjorie and his own terrible position, made the days seem endless. Above all, the inaction nearly drove him frantic.

True, he was able to work in the garden, and he did so in a way that called forth Harness' admiration and surprise. He tired himself out physically during the day, and at night he went down to the pub and tried to forget his pressing anxieties.

But he did not like Harness. There was something unpleasant and soft in the man's manner that repelled Wainwright. Harness was a slacker; that is to say, he was weak willed and lazy. He affected a great friendliness and consideration for Wainwright, but the young man was easily able to see that a good deal of it was put on. Once or twice he had caught Harness' eye resting on him in a manner that made him positively uneasy. Harness, he felt, had some odd ideas about him in his mind.

Wainwright never discussed with Harness who he was or why he was in hiding. He did not even know whether Harness was aware what his real name was, or for what offence he was wanted by the police. It seemed to him odd that Harness never questioned him about his past life, or even referred to it. It suggested that Harness knew the truth; and in some way Ted disliked the idea of his secret's being in the keeping of this loud-voiced, loose-lipped man.

One day Wainwright happened to go into Harness' private study in Nightingale's Roost to find some matches. He routed about in several places and eventually searched in the man's desk. He was about to turn unsuccessfully away, when his own name caught his eye. It was in a letter signed by Wood. His curiosity was at once aroused and he picked up the letter and read it. At first he could hardly believe his eyes. The wording indicated a bland betrayal of himself, in a phraseology which he could hardly believe had come from the doctor's pen. Yet there it was:

DEAR BILL,
> This is brought by Ted Wainwright, who is wanted by the police for murder. It suits us to keep him out of the way for the moment, but it may be necessary soon to hand him over. Wait till I give you the tip by wire with the words, "Uncle ill. Please come at once." As soon as you receive this, get in touch with the Yard. Of course you must do it in such a way that no suspicion attaches to either of us, and particularly not to yourself.
> G. WOOD.

Ted's first reaction to this was one of overwhelming fury, and he wanted to go straight back to London and settle accounts with Wood. But almost immediately he saw the folly of this. He was in a corner. The police were after him, with a first-class case, and he had to lie low. Even the temporary shelter given him by Harness was something.

The question was, where could he go from here without exciting suspicion? He was a wanted man, and although it was possible to dodge suspicion in a country retreat by staying with someone who was known locally, it would be different when he turned up as a complete stranger, without money or any apparent reason for his arrival. That would excite suspicion at once.

Ted happened to be going down the garden path next day when he heard his own name called in a low voice. He turned to see who it was and saw a woman standing on the other side of the hedge, indistinctly visible through it. As he caught sight of her she made a signal to him to be quiet. Puzzled and a little alarmed by this, he went round the hedge.

As he came nearer, he saw to his surprise that the woman was Miss Crispin.

"Good heavens, where have you been?" he asked her, "and what on earth are you doing here?"

"Don't talk, but follow me to the village," she whispered. "We must have a word together. You are in great danger."

"I know that all right! What's the idea, anyway?"

"I'll tell you there. I'll go on ahead, and you'd better keep fifty yards or so behind me, so that if Harness comes there will be nothing to connect us. Meet me at the end of Rook Lane."

Rook Lane was a little byway leading out of the village, and not much used. Evidently Miss Crispin had chosen it because it would be out of the way, and her choice proved that she knew something about the village. Ted felt suspicious. Was Miss Crispin in on the plot, and was this the first move to tip him off? Further reflection made this seem unlikely. No telegram had arrived for Harness, and in any case there would have been no need to choose so dramatic a method to betray him. A word to any policeman would be enough.

Miss Crispin seated herself on a broken-down fence in one of the nooks off Rook Lane and Ted sat down beside her. He had seen a fair amount of Miss Crispin (if that was her real name) during his visits to Belmont Avenue, but her colourless personality had not left much trace on his memory.

She had merely given him the vague impression of a woman who, although not old, was no longer in her first youth, and had accepted from life the role of benevolent self-effacement.

Now, looking at her sideways, he could not help noticing a new quality which, had he been inclined to romantic phraseology, would have drawn from him the adjective "tigerish." It was the kind of tigerishness that meek and gentle beasts show when they are trapped in a corner and their lives are at stake, or when something is threatened which is at least as dear to them as their lives —their offspring, for example. So far as Wainwright knew, neither of these things was true of Miss Crispin, and he was therefore surprised at his sideways glimpse of her pinched, determined face.

"Mr Wainwright, I don't think you know in what danger you are!" began Miss Crispin in a hurried monotone. "You are in the grip of a most unscrupulous man. You think he is helping you, but in fact he is doing just the opposite. At any moment, he may betray you to the police, and you yourself know how little hope you have once you get into their hands!"

"Are you suggesting that I killed your sister—if she was your sister?"

"Yes, she was my sister," confessed Bella Crispin in a low voice. "But I do not suggest you killed her. I am sure you did not."

"You know who really did?"

Bella Crispin hesitated.

"There is no reason why you should not know. Doctor Wood killed her!"

"Wood! But what was his motive?"

"That would take too long to go into now. Indeed, in simple fairness to my poor sister, I do not know whether I shall ever be prepared to tell the whole story!"

"But you must! That is the only thing that will save me," insisted Wainwright eagerly.

Bella Crispin shook her head.

"I'm afraid it's not as easy as that. It's only suspicion, and not the kind of proof the police would accept. How or why he did it, I do not know. Superficially, everything looks as if you killed her. The police have a perfect case. But just as you are sure you did not kill her, I am sure that Wood did."

"Well, that leaves me in as great a jam as ever. Once the police catch me, I'm done. But tell me, if you know so much, do you know where Marjorie is?"

Bella Crispin nodded.

"Yes, I do know."

Ted leaped to his feet in his excitement and gripped her arm fiercely.

"What? Is she safe?"

"Yes, she is safe. That is, she is at present *physically* unharmed."

"What exactly do you mean by that?"

"Just what I say. She is at present unharmed. But she is in danger—grave danger!"

"How? Where is she?"

"At present," replied Bella Crispin slowly, "she is in a bogus lunatic asylum. The director of it is at this moment engaged in trying to drive her mad."

Ted felt a chill travel down his spine as Miss Crispin said these words in a casual, almost callous way.

"What do you mean?" he said, shaking her arm violently. "Are you serious? For God's sake, explain what you mean."

"What I say. Didn't you understand the meaning of my sister's relations with Marjorie and the help given by Wood?"

"It was all deliberately designed to send her off her head?"

"Certainly. Wood would put it in more technical phraseology, of course, but that was the intention."

Ted stared at her as she said this with the utmost coolness.

"You knew this, and yet could help in it?"

"Yes, I knew it," she said wearily. "For God's sake don't start trying to make me repent. You'll ask: how could I stand it? I've been through all *those* agonies years ago, when my sister first started her career, and I tell you my conscience is dead, dead!"

Miss Crispin's cheeks flushed, and her voice rose to a scream as she beat her hands spasmodically on her skinny knees. "Dead! Rotten! Stinking!" she repeated.

There was a pause and then she went on more normally, with a defiant air.

"I'm prepared to help Marjorie now; that ought to be enough for you! And I can help you too."

"Can you really find Marjorie and get her out?"

Miss Crispin nodded.

"I can take you there, and help you get in. You'll have to do the rest."

"Thank you for that. I take back what I said." He clasped her hand, without realising what he was doing, in his excitement.

She interrupted him brusquely, snatching back her hand.

"Keep your thanks. This isn't kindness—I lost any heart I had years ago. It isn't a sudden awakening of my conscience. I told you my conscience was dead. I'm going to do this for a consideration. I shall charge a fee, and a stiff one!"

"But I haven't any money, at least not to speak of. I'm out of a job even."

"It will have to be paid jointly by you and Marjorie."

"But she hasn't any either."

"No, but you're young. You may get on. Pay me when you have some."

Ted Wainwright laughed, relieved.

"If you'll do it on tick, that's all right! I call that sporting, for I don't see much chance of your ever getting it!"

"It's not so sporting as you think. The fee will be a stiff one."

"That makes the chance of getting it all the less likely."

Miss Crispin smiled for the first time since they had been speaking.

"I'll take the chance of that. Here is a document I have prepared."

She opened her handbag and took out a folded paper.

"It commits you to pay the sum of twenty thousand pounds to Bella Crispin should either of you at any time be in a position to discharge the whole sum. This means that until you accumulate at least that amount, we cannot legally press you. If you earn any less sums, we have no claim to them."

"Then it doesn't seem to me that this document is worth much to you!"

"Well, that's my look-out, isn't it? I want you both to sign it jointly. You can sign it here and now, and I will get Marjorie to sign it directly she is released."

"Well, I don't know, it seems a bit funny. Is this kind of thing legal?"

"Perfectly. You see the document mentions the consideration —that we assist in finding Marjorie Easton, who at the date of the agreement is stated to be missing. Therefore it is a contract good in law. Anyway, the legality of it is our responsibility. Here is a pen. Sign it, and I will tell you where Marjorie is."

Wainwright signed it. Miss Crispin outlined her plan, and arranged a meeting place for the next day. When he returned to the bungalow, he found an empty telegraph envelope in the hall. Harness was waiting for him with a false expression of joviality on his face.

"Hello, old chap! I wondered where you had got to!"

"I just went for a stroll round," replied Wainwright, with an equally false cordiality.

He had met Miss Crispin only just in time! He would have to make a getaway that night, so that in the morning Harness would find the bird had flown.

2

When Marjorie woke from a drugged sleep to find the walls of the asylum once more round her, her first feeling was of a dull, aching despair. Impossible as it had seemed, she was a captive, without hope of release. What at first she had thought was some strange mental upheaval had proved to be the active enmity of real human beings.

Why they displayed this cold implacable enmity, why this battalion of foes had suddenly sprung up at every turn, in the place of those whom she thought friends, was more than she was able to fathom. But of the facts there was now no doubt.

This despair presently gave place to a kind of apathy. What was the good of doing anything, when everything had proved so useless? For some reason or other, it had been determined that she should be put out of the way. Now that she had time to reflect, she came to see clearly that at the back of it all must be the figure of Dr Wood. His was the main responsibility for this appalling deed; and it seemed that it could only be a fiendish cruelty, a lust for suffering in others as an end in itself, which could dictate his actions. And this purposelessness of the cruelty made her resigned, as one might become resigned to an inevitable illness. Whether any bromides were administered in her food to produce this resignation, she could not tell. But certainly during the next two or three days a complete apathy came over her.

Meanwhile Ted Wainwright was going through the opposite process.

He had hoped to be able to help Marjorie at once, but instead of that Miss Crispin, who had taken him to a room in the north of London and warned him to go out as little as possible, had kept on putting off the day. He chafed with a fury and impatience which gathered force each day.

He wondered if he had been tricked. But if he had, it seemed pointless. He preferred to accept Miss Crispin's statement in her letters from Norwich that it was impossible to do anything more than she was doing to make contact with Marjorie.

The only consolation he got was that Miss Crispin had seen Marjorie more than once walking in the grounds, and reported that she was quite well, mentally and physically, and that there was no pressing fear for her safety. So the days passed.

"Our only hope for the moment," wrote Miss Crispin frankly, "is that Marjorie should be moved to another room."

Marjorie was much more strictly guarded than she had been before, and though she was allowed in the grounds, she was always accompanied by an attendant, and was not allowed to speak to any of the other patients. Although she looked out for Lambert, she noticed to her surprise that he was nowhere to be seen. This set her wondering. Had his help of her brought some dreadful punishment down on his head; or was he simply ill; or was he being kept shut up in his room?

She asked her attendant but got no answer beyond a resentful stare. Evidently Lambert was a sore point with them, and she thought it more prudent to avoid reference to him in the future.

Matters went on like this until one day, as a result of her constant complaints about the darkness of her room, which gave on to the inner courtyard, she was moved into a room in front. The same day, a strange incident occurred. She was sitting in a seat facing the wall, while her attendant by her side was busy reading. Suddenly she saw a woman's head appear over the other side of the wall, and give her a warning look. A small white object came over the wall and fell into the flower bed below. Then the head disappeared.

Marjorie managed to walk near the flower bed, stoop as if to do up her shoe, and pick up the note. She unfolded it in the privacy of her room. It read as follows:

Marjorie Easton: Find some way of keeping your window unlocked tonight.

This message, suggesting outside help, sent the blood pulsing through Marjorie's veins again. But how could she keep her window unlocked? As a matter of routine, every evening, her attendant came round and locked the casement window by turning the key in a padlock which was fixed on the catch.

At last a stratagem occurred to her. She vividly remembered an uncle who was subject to fits of asthma and who, when he had them, had been forced to lean out of the window half the night, purple in the face. Remembering his symptoms she started to imitate them, and with such success that, towards the evening, her attendant sent for the doctor. Marsden came in and found her leaning out of the window, gasping for breath.

"Have you ever suffered from asthma?" he asked after a brief examination, and Marjorie explained that she had occasionally had it as a child, but this had been her first attack for many years. She repeated some of the symptoms she had often heard her uncle complain of.

As Marjorie had calculated, the attacks of asthma and the visits of the doctor served to postpone the locking of the window, and once the routine time had passed, no attempt was made to do so.

Marjorie was unable to sleep that night. She lay on her bed fully dressed and waiting. When she heard faint noises in the grounds, and scraping sounds, she jumped up and went to the window. It was pitch dark outside, and she could see nothing, but as she leaned out she heard a whisper.

"Are you there, Marjorie?"

Impossible—staggering as it seemed to her—the voice was Ted's! Marjorie's voice almost broke as she answered:

"Yes, here!"

Five minutes later Marjorie was climbing down the ladder which led to escape—and Ted.

CHAPTER XV

Who Is the Director?

Inspector Morgan gained little from an examination of the bleary-eyed fugitive whom he charged with the murder of Dr Wood. Tremayne's examination of Lambert, brief though it was, established definitely that his mind had disintegrated finally under the emotional upheaval involved in his act of homicide. Lambert was now a mere human shell. He was not even harmful now. His last outbreak had drained him of all energy and interest in the outside world. From now on he would live in a twilit world of fantasy and self-exploration. Reality had completely ceased to exist for him. Perhaps this was as well.

A search of his past proved conclusively that, starting from being a fairly harmless eccentric, with one or two curious foibles and a passion for psychic investigation, he had been deliberately driven over the borderline by Crispin. Crispin had made contact with him through the world of psychic research, and had deliberately exploited the psychological mechanism of dissociation to produce a complete cleavage of personality.

In the early stage of this condition, Lambert had come into contact with Wood, who was playing as usual the role of a disinterested investigator. Lambert had applied to him for treatment of the obsessions and compulsions which were manifesting themselves. Wood's treatment—as his notebook showed—had been deliberately directed to complete the ruin. After that, there had been no difficulty in getting an order which put Lambert's affairs in the hands of his cousin, Sir Timothy.

What were the motives of Crispin and Wood for this apparently disinterested fiendishness? An examination of the banking account of Timothy Lambert soon showed that large sums of money had passed from the estate to the medium and the doctor, and even larger cash sums to some personality, evidently concerned in the crime, who had adopted the device of cash payments to preserve his anonymity. Was he the Director to whom Wood's intercepted telephone message had referred?

Evidently Lambert's subconscious mind had retained some inkling of what had been done to the shattered personality of which it was a part. On the occasions when he had made an escape, he had gone straight to his archenemies and attempted to kill them. Now that both were dead, one by his own hand, all resentment seemed to have left his ruined mind. He had become inert and without volition, as the result of a crisis which had brought his insanity to the higher stage of catatonia.

"It's the beginning of the end," explained Tremayne. "Poor fellow, he won't survive long!"

Morgan prepared for the trial which could only result in finding him unfit to plead, and liable to detention at the King's pleasure.

This, however, did not solve the mystery of Crispin's death, for, if one thing was abundantly clear, it was that the murder of the medium was not carried out by a lunatic, but by someone of unusual sanity and acumen. Nothing could be farther removed from the brutal slaying of Wood than the subtle mystery of Crispin's death, in which everything pointed to the complicity of Ted Wainwright and yet where more and more the inspector, in spite of his warrant for Wainwright's arrest, seemed to sense the impress of a more cunning hand.

A vital question for the inspector was: where had Lambert been incarcerated during his "treatment" in an institute? Nothing could be found among the doctor's papers to clear this matter up. Lambert's solicitor was apparently completely ignorant of the address. "All that side of it," he explained with an air of distaste, "had been left to Mr Lambert's medical adviser."

It was impossible, in his present state, to get any response from Lambert. Sir Timothy Lambert professed complete ignorance, and since he was in a pitiable condition of fear, with a criminal prosecution and approaching bankruptcy both hanging over his head, it was unlikely that he would be deceiving the police in this matter.

Morgan was quite prepared to find the place outwardly a respectable, registered institution, with periodical inspections, correct routine, and all the visible signs of authenticity. Cases of bogus mental homes were sufficiently numerous in his experience for such a thing to be well within the bounds of possibility. This made it difficult to know where to begin to look for the place. Morgan contented himself, as an immediate routine step, with making sure that a full list of all registered mental institutes against which any complaints had been received should be compiled and sent to him for checking.

Meanwhile he was still faced with the old problems.

How and why had the strychnine been introduced into Crispin's drink, in full view of everyone in the séance room at that time?

Why was the empty poison bottle, which had contained hydrocyanic acid, found in Ted Wainwright's pocket?

What was the explanation of the lying story which the doctor and Mrs Threpfall had told him about Wainwright, and what was the doctor's purpose in protecting Wainwright, in view of his own guilt?

Unless he could solve these problems, he was at a dead end, for the murder of Crispin had been the starting point of the whole tangle, and must therefore be the end of it. The other mysteries—the disappearance of Marjorie and Miss Crispin—were unquestionably bound up with this problem.

Clear, unpoisoned water had flowed out of the tap in the séance room. By the time it had reached Crispin, it had become poisoned. Under the basin in the séance room there had been a pool of water sufficiently impregnated with strychnine to cause the instant death of the small dog who had lapped it up. What was the solution to these contradictory facts?

Then quite suddenly Morgan—perhaps for the first time in his life—had an inspiration. That is, he saw quite clearly in his mind's eye, without any basis in hard fact, a picture of how the crime might have been carried out. It floated in his imagination tantalisingly clear and vivid. Forty years of routine and factualism demanded that he suppress so wild a vision. If he allowed himself that kind of loose speculation, the forty years reminded him, he would soon be running everywhere on all kinds of wild-goose chases, while the real criminal sat safe and sound under his nose.

But the vision refused to be exorcised. So, with a shamefaced feeling, and saying nothing to his subordinates, Morgan jumped into a car and followed his "hunch." It led him to Belmont Avenue, to the Crispins' home, still shuttered, its rooms full of dust-sheeted furniture. Outside was the notice of an impending auction.

Morgan went straight to the séance room. Then he knelt down beneath the basin and examined the piping leading up behind it carefully. Of course his idea was absurd but——

"Good heavens," he exclaimed aloud, in an awed tone, "I *was* right!"

The piping, and the wall immediately underneath the basin, showed clearly what had happened. A small tank, fitting neatly behind the basin, had been fastened to the rising water pipe in two places. The traces of the two holes, which were now soldered up, could be distinctly felt with the finger tips. It was obvious that this tank could have contained only one thing—poison.

Whoever installed the apparatus was a plumber of no mean ability, for the job had been neatly done and neatly removed, and the unknown had allowed for the pressure of the water by fastening the tank to the pipe in two places, one constituting an inlet, and the other an outlet, so that as the water flowed through the main pipe it would induce a corresponding flow through the feeder pipe and effectually poison the water as it passed. A nice calculation was necessary to ensure that sufficient poison entered the flow without immediately exhausting the tank.

No doubt, the inspector reflected, the poison reservoir had not been a plain tank, but a tightly coiled worm of piping. If he remembered anything of hydraulics, it would have to have been like that.

But whatever it was, it had been fixed up before Crispin's death, and had been carefully removed at some later date. In being removed, some of the poison it contained had been spilt on the mat below, thus accounting for the death of the dog. Perhaps the unknown had crept into the house and removed it that very morning. Perhaps Morgan had been in the house at the same time as the murderer!

Whoever fixed it must have been in an unusual position, in that he had been morally certain that Crispin would drink a glass of water after the séance. This last was a surprising factor. Even given that Crispin generally took a glass of water after a séance, how could the murderer be certain of such a chancy thing?

Even more odd was the fact that the glass of water was handed to Crispin by Ted Wainwright, and Ted Wainwright was found, after his arrest, to have an empty poison bottle in his pocket. Now at first it seemed as if there was a deliberate attempt to make Wainwright the scapegoat. But if this was the case, and the poison bottle was introduced into Wainwright's pocket by Mrs Threpfall, why had such a careless error been made as to introduce a prussic-acid bottle instead of one which had contained strychnine? Why should Mrs Threpfall go to the pain of buying prussic acid when strychnine had already been bought for the slaying of Crispin?

No, it was impossible that such a gross error had been made. From which impossibility one could only deduce that the two complications were set on foot entirely separately, that there was no connection between the poisoning of Crispin and the purchase of prussic acid by Mrs Threpfall on behalf of Ted Wainwright.

Who was the Director? More and more clearly it seemed to Morgan that he was fighting an unknown enemy; and that *this* enemy was the dangerous one. Wood, Crispin and Mrs Threpfall had been exposed; the whole web of horror behind them had been brought to light; but somewhere there still lurked the spider who had spun it all, and of whom Wood, Ted Wainwright, Crispin and Mrs Threpfall were only tools.

Was Marjorie Easton in his clutches now? And if so, why? As he reflected on this, Morgan felt the pattern slip into place, like a missing jigsaw piece when it is turned to fill a gap. He walked out of Belmont Avenue, got into his car again, and drove straight to the suburb of Bilford. He had decided to call on Samuel Burton.

Samuel Burton was in. When Morgan walked into his room behind him he could clearly see, by the line of his back, that

Samuel Burton was afraid. Backs are expressive, and, by the very reluctance with which Burton turned to bring his face towards his visitor again, Morgan could see that he was afraid. Morgan's guess had been right then. Here was the key.

"Mr Burton, I have come—as you have doubtless guessed—about your niece Marjorie," began the detective.

A wavering smile played over the rubicund face of Mr Burton. His eyes remained hard and blue, like little bits of china.

"Have you news of her? Good news? Please don't keep me in suspense!"

"No, I have no news," replied Morgan quietly, and he felt certain that there was a distinct expression of relief in Burton's face.

"On the contrary, I have come to you for information."

Burton gave an exclamation of surprise.

"I? I have heard nothing. If I had, I would have come to you at once."

"I am not asking for any information you may have received subsequent to my last visit."

Mr Burton's eyes narrowed watchfully.

"What exactly do you mean, Inspector?"

"Simply this: that I believe you knew more than you told me on my last visit. It is absolutely essential that you be frank with me."

The other man shook his head in a puzzled reproachful fashion.

"I cannot imagine what you mean—honestly. Perhaps I am a little dense. What more is there that I could have told you?"

He spread his hands wide with an expression of candour.

"You know perfectly well," replied Morgan sharply. "Please stop fencing!"

"Fencing? What *do* you mean? Is this a joke?"

"You refuse to be frank?"

"I have been frank."

"Very well. Mr Burton, will you be prepared to give me an assurance that you do not propose, at any future date, to apply to the Court for the guardianship of your niece on the ground that she is *non compos mentis,* nor to apply on her behalf for the money to which I believe her to be entitled?"

Mr Burton slowly turned white, and he stared at the inspector for a moment, with a face drained of blood. His mouth opened for a moment like a fish's; then it closed. Beads of sweat stood on his forehead, and a little nervous quiver of his hand spread to his upper lip, and made him seem like a jelly, a quivering thing without a solid foundation.

"Come on, speak up, man!" rapped out the inspector, delighted at the success of his shot in the dark.

"Is it a criminal offence?" muttered Samuel Burton at last, mopping his brow.

"It is not committed yet!" said the inspector sharply. "Or is it?"

"How do you mean?"

"Is your niece still sane?"

"I believe so. My God, I *hope* so."

"It's a little late to start praying," commented the inspector contemptuously. "Where is she?"

"I don't know!"

"Don't know?" echoed the policeman incredulously.

"Yes, on my soul I swear I don't know," quavered Burton. "I insisted that I should know nothing at all about that. I didn't want to have anything to do with it."

"Very proper of you! What the eye doesn't see, the heart doesn't grieve about. Let others do the dirty work."

"I simply said, if they liked to do it, it wasn't my affair. Of course I stipulated that my niece shouldn't be harmed and should be made comfortable . . ."

"Cut that out. You knew perfectly well what would happen to your niece. And you didn't mind—so long as you got her fortune. Tell me exactly what arrangements were made."

Mr Burton mopped the sweat off his forehead, which was the colour of cheese.

"Well, it was like this. As soon as I came to hear that Marjorie's Australian cousin had died, leaving her his fortune, I began to think how unfair it was that I should not even be remembered in the will, although I had devoted my life's savings to Marjorie. I ought to explain that Marjorie has always been headstrong and selfish, and I knew well enough that once Marjorie had come into this money she would not have even a kind word for her uncle

—much less anything more tangible. She as good as said plain out more than once that she did not feel she owed me *anything*. That cut me, Inspector, and I could not help resenting it.

"Well, I was discussing it one day with a man I happened to know—although of course I didn't know at the time that there was anything shady about him—and he said that the whole affair could quite easily be adjusted. Adjusted—that was how he put it. It would just be a matter of getting Marjorie declared insane, and then I should have control of the property. Of course directly I had control of it, I would see that Marjorie was released and given a fair share of the property."

Burton smiled nervously at the inspector. "I hope I need not emphasise that fact. Obviously no one would believe that I could keep my niece permanently in such a place, *however* comfortable. It would be a mere paper transaction to ensure that justice was done. It may not be strictly legal, but after all it was only *fair*. I was, in fact, a closer blood relation of this Australian cousin than Marjorie, and if it had not been for me, she would never have heard of him, for the trustees had totally failed to find her."

"So that really you were doing her a good turn?"

"Precisely," said Mr Burton eagerly, and beamed. Then, getting the full force of Morgan's concentrated contempt, he wilted. "I realise now I was doing wrong—*very* wrong. I was playing with fire. I had no idea the lengths to which these people would go. They were very plausible. In fact they utterly deceived me."

"I see," commented Morgan curtly. "That certainly clears up the matter, except for one point. Who was this man you said you got in touch with?"

Burton looked at him furtively.

"I'm sorry, but I forget his name."

"Where did you meet him, and how?"

"I'm afraid it has slipped my mind how I came to see him. I bumped into him quite by chance."

"Where?" pressed Morgan.

Burton passed one hand over his brow, and forgot to remove it. It was trembling. "I clean forget."

"Well, at least you could identify him if he were found."

"I doubt if I could. For one thing I have reason to suppose he was disguised—he wore a beard and tinted glasses. In any case, my memory is bad. All this happened some months ago."

Morgan banged his fist down on his knee. Burton jumped.

"Man, you're lying. You know this man's identity perfectly well!"

"I assure you I don't!"

"It's the man they know as the Director, isn't it?"

"I've never heard him called that," replied Burton guardedly. "Not to my knowledge! As I say, I really can't remember what his name is."

"You're afraid of him!"

"Why should I be?"

Morgan reflected for a moment. It was evident that Burton knew who the Director was but that—perhaps for fear of reprisals—he would not give his name. Yet it was absolutely essential that he be forced to disgorge the secret. It was becoming increasingly plain that the Director was at the back of the whole tangled web. *He* was the spider.

Morgan got up to go and gave a parting warning.

"Look here, Burton! If you will help us to find the Director and turn King's Evidence, I promise we'll look after you. Otherwise, you'll be charged with conspiracy and intent to hurt, and possibly other charges. If you do help us, there's no need to be afraid. We'll give you police protection until the Director is safely in jail! I'll give you two or three days to think it over!"

Burton did not reply, and Morgan left the man sunk into his chair, with a curiously aged and bloated look on his normally rubicund face.

CHAPTER XVI

Home Comforts

It was a moment of pure joy for Marjorie when she felt Ted's arms round her. In spite of the danger she was still in, she forgot the menacing house, the dark garden, the wall still between safety and themselves, and abandoned herself to the pleasure of having his arms round her, of feeling reconciled with him.

She had rehearsed, again and again, what she would say if this moment came to pass and she found herself with him again. She had learned by heart the explanations and the excuses. Now she realised that all these were unnecessary. There was no need for explanation or justification. As in a moment of crisis, the reasoning of ordinary life was set aside. Their quarrel was healed without effort. They had become lovers again.

"Come along, darling," he whispered at last. "We've got to hurry."

He guided her across the garden to the wall. A rope ladder was already swinging there. A moment later, they were over the wall, and Marjorie was too excited to remember how she got over.

In the road stood a saloon car, its lights turned out. Ted opened the door and she got into it. He sat down beside her.

The engine was started up, the car backed and turned, and presently it was purring over the roads to London. Now that the lights were switched on, Marjorie realised there was someone else in the car with them. As they flashed through a village the lamp fell on the person's face, and Marjorie gave a little start of surprise. It was Miss Crispin.

Ted felt her shrink against him, and he gave her a reassuring touch.

"It's all right, Marjorie, Miss Crispin's on our side. She helped to get you out of that place."

Miss Crispin nodded.

"Yes, that is so. We have been fighting on your side."

"Who is *we?*" asked Marjorie.

"Hawkins and myself. You remember Hawkins?"

"The chauffeur?"

"Yes, he is driving now. We have been married for a week. I am Mrs Hawkins now."

"Why did you help us?" asked Marjorie wonderingly. "Of course I am grateful, but I thought——"

"That I was in it too?" Miss Crispin nodded. "Well, my child, I'm not going to pretend to be better than I was. I knew what my sister was up to. I admit it, I've helped her. I loathed doing it—sometimes I wanted to kill myself—but I did it. You may be able to understand and forgive that, Marjorie, because you yourself know that she was an exceptional mind. I've been under her influence since I was a child. She was an older sister, you see, and that gave her a start in my most impressionable years. After that, well, I simply acted as her slave and accomplice!"

"But who killed her?"

Miss Crispin looked aside, and then spoke in a low voice.

"Well, I suppose now I've gone so far, I may as well tell you."

Her voice sank to a whisper. "I told Ted it was Doctor Wood. That was not true. Really the Director did it. He was someone who was a match even for my sister.

"I daren't tell you *his* name. I daren't even give you a clue to his identity. I won't even say if it is correct to describe the Director as 'he.' My sister had always worked in with him, but at last she crossed his will. That was the end of it. Anyone who came up against the Director was bound to come to the same end."

"And who is he? Have I met him?" Marjorie asked eagerly.

"My dear child, it is much better that you should not know. Better for you and for me! If I were to tell you, I might live a few more days and then——" Mrs Hawkins gave an expressive gesture.

"I'm sure you don't want to have a secret that is so dangerous. As for me, I want to forget about the whole thing. George and I are going to leave the country, and forget about it all—make a new start."

"I'm certainly grateful to you both——"

"No, you mustn't be," exclaimed the other woman decisively. "We don't want anything that is not our due, and certainly we are not entitled to gratitude. We are doing this for a reward. It is mean and commercial—but we've got to live."

"But I'm not in a position to give you a reward. I had saved a little money, but it is not much, and I don't know whether it is still in existence. It was in my bedroom."

Bella opened her handbag, drew out a piece of paper, and looked at the girl thoughtfully. Then she said:

"I'm going to ask you to sign this. Mr Wainwright has already signed it. But I'll tell you the truth before I ask you to sign it."

Marjorie read the paper.

"But this is absurd! I shall never have that much money! Neither will Ted!"

"That's what I told her," said Ted.

"You are both wrong. I do not know if you remember your cousin Bob Clemens, in Australia, a relation of your mother?"

"I do seem to remember vaguely. But I don't believe any of the family had heard of him for years."

"He died, leaving you the sole legatee of his estate, which amounts to about forty thousand pounds. So you see, you will easily be able to pay us this sum. You may think we have tricked you into this . . ."

Marjorie hesitated, and then took the paper and pen.

"Ted agreed to it and I stand by him; it's worth anything to be out of that dreadful place. But I make one further condition before I sign this. I think I can fairly make it."

"What is it?"

"That you see Ted gets out of trouble. At present he is still under suspicion of your sister's murder. You must prove to Morgan that he hasn't done it, that the Director did it."

"But that may mean telling him who the Director is."

"Well, why not? If he did do it?"

"I daren't," Mrs Hawkins answered quietly. "He'd get me."

"Not if he were hanged."

"They'd never hang him! He's too clever. He'd keep out of their way. And he'd get me, sooner or later, like he got my sister. No, I'll tell Morgan everything *but* that."

"Very well, as you think fit. But the condition I am going to make is that Ted is cleared of suspicion, whatever story you tell."

"I understand. And of course you are quite justified. George and I will see Morgan and tell him all we know. I think that will be enough to clear Ted. In fact I'm sure it will be."

"But still I don't understand why your sister acted as she did."

"The answer may be a shock to you, but it is better that you should know. She deliberately attempted, with the co-operation of Doctor Wood, to drive you in a condition when you would be certified as insane. The snake, the voice, the drugging of the nurse, those faces, were deliberately designed to frighten you out of the house, so that her accomplices could pick you up in a condition where you could be certified insane."

"But why?"

"She was simply acting under the orders of the Director, who employed both her and Wood. The Director ran the mental home from which you have escaped, and used it to confine insane or eccentric rich people with needy relatives. It was an excellent and profitable legal way of keeping them out of the way while their relatives enjoyed their money. Of course the fees were enormous, but as it came out of the imprisoned people's estates, the relatives never worried.

"As time went on, the supply of mad people with large bank balances and unscrupulous relatives became exhausted, and so the Director widened his field.

"Crispin, as a fashionable spiritualistic quack, and Wood, as a medical charlatan specialising in the imaginary mental ailments of the neurotic rich, were both in touch with unstable rich people, and often enough such people had relatives who thought their rich uncles or cousins were wasting their money and their time, and would be safer and happier under lock and key. It was quite an easy matter to arrange with these two to push some of these doubtful cases over the borderline, for the benefit of their fond relatives. Gradually the Director built up a complete organisation, and of course Crispin and Wood, as they became more and more involved, became more and more his paid creatures."

"But how did he know about me?"

"Quite simply. Your uncle came to him with the problem. It

was rather a tough one, because you weren't even temperamentally unstable. Still Crispin and the doctor were prepared to take it on. Halfway through Crispin quarrelled with the Director. She demanded a larger share of the pickings than had been arranged. As a result the Director killed her. Even to this day I don't know how it was done.

"That meant you had to be smuggled away before you were certifiable—a rather dangerous trick. It was one the Director had never had to try before, for the best part of his scheme was that it is all done in an apparently legal way. He had an efficiently run asylum, with qualified attendants and doctors. Who was to know that the staff had been chosen for their shady past or cruel character?

"By drugging you, and with the help of two incompetent G.P.s, a silly country magistrate, and a cunningly fabricated story, the Director got away with it, and had you legally shut up. The rest you know!"

"But I can hardly believe that my uncle could have been so wicked... How did he come to know the Director?"

"You poor innocent, don't you know your uncle is a crook himself?"

"A crook?"

"Yes. He's a fire assessor—of the shady variety. As such, he's in touch with all the criminal elements of the City, including the Director, who has a finger in plenty of other dirty deals."

"And Uncle knew what would happen to me?"

"Of course he did. It was all fixed up with the Director, in return for half the estate. Now do you understand?"

"I understand.... But I still find it difficult to believe. And yet it explains everything. It's just as well I know, for otherwise I really should believe that I had been mad. So Uncle told your sister all about my mother?"

"Yes. Even including the deathbed speech you thought no one heard, and which he overheard. And about the ring in your trunk. Oh, your uncle was a clever devil! And he gave my sister a photograph of your mother, which came in useful."

"It was all fake? All the things I saw? The voices? And the snake? You were acting all the time?"

"Yes, acting all the time," said Bella in a level tone. Remembering the terrifying power of that acting, in which Bella too had participated from the moment when she had come up to Marjorie in the teashop, the girl felt she could never think of her without repulsion.

How skilfully the attack on her had been launched: the appeal to her vanity; the cunning pressure from her uncle; his pretence of disapproval which, as she now saw, had only been meant to spur her on. She shuddered uncontrollably and Ted, putting an arm round her shoulders, soothed her.

"It's all over now!"

"What a little fool I've been," she answered, smiling wryly.

The car went humming on its way. It seemed to leave behind a strange world of muddled fantasy and broken dreams. It was with a feeling of thankfulness and security that Marjorie realised it *was* dropping behind, that she had passed back into a land of commonplace reality, represented by the familiar presence of Ted by her side. She was going to take up again the life she had left.

But she would take up the old life in a different way. She would be mature and sensible. She had shed her schoolgirlish, romantic notions. She had had a bitter lesson of what the realisation of a daydream meant. Only those people who had known the other thing, who had had life's sharp lesson of reality, could know the full pleasure of living an ordinary life in the ordinary world, and experience the thrill and the glamour of doing ordinary tasks again.

Ted, too, had had the same experience. Ted, too, had been snatched out of his ordinary existence into a world of nightmare and shifting sands, the kind of adventure one reads about in books, but which was so different in real life from the way those adventures tasted in books. He, too, would be equally glad to know again the refreshing certainties of the daily round.

Therefore, perhaps it was as well that they had had this experience, before she learned of this fortune she had inherited. Criticising coolly now the Marjorie she had been, she realised that the surprise might have swept her off her feet and made her yearn for some high romantic life adequate to the new status. She might

—she admitted it frankly to herself—have felt that Ted "was not good enough for her," as she had thought in the first few weeks at Belmont Avenue.

She had learned her lesson. They could never be separated again. She pressed his hand, and an answering pressure told her that it was true—nothing now divided them. She thanked Heaven for his calm stolidity, which in the past she had thought showed a lack of intelligence. Now she had realised how much more precious was character than any amount of intelligence.

Would Bella be able to clear Ted? She herself had no doubt about it. But why was there this absurd fear about the Director?

"Surely, Bella," she said aloud, "if you tell Morgan about Crispin and the asylum, he'll soon be able to discover the Director for himself?"

Bella shook her head.

"No! You don't think the Director left any tracks uncovered? I doubt if anyone but myself and your uncle know who the Director is."

"But are you sure that will satisfy Morgan?"

Bella patted her hand, and it was all Marjorie could do not to withdraw it abruptly from the contact.

"Don't you worry. Mr Wainwright will be absolutely safe! You can count on that."

An hour later they drew up at Ted's home. Marjorie felt she could not face her uncle. She would stay with Ted's mother until everything was cleared up.

As Ted opened the front door, she heard a startled cry from inside. Ted's mother came hurrying out. Her face changed from surprise to joy. Laughing and crying simultaneously, she enfolded them both in her arms. The door closed quietly behind them and Bella moved away and got into the car.

"Come along, George," she said. "We'd better go straight to Morgan."

Her face had a clearly gloomy look. It was as if Marjorie's joy had had an unpleasant effect on her, but that she dared not admit this to her husband.

Meanwhile the reunited three walked slowly into the kitchen. As its cheerful warmth enfolded them, Marjorie felt that a chapter of her life had been irrevocably closed. She had grown up!

To be grown up is perhaps to be happier, but it is also to be less interesting. Ted and Marjorie's future life are outside the bounds of this story. It was left to Inspector Morgan to round off the strange case of the Six Queer Things.

2

Hawkins and Bella duly fulfilled their promise to Marjorie by telling Morgan the full story, so far as Bella knew it, and with due reserve regarding the Director.

"I've been of the opinion for some time that Ted Wainwright never murdered Crispin," Morgan had said at the outset. "My discovery of how the murder was done finally confirmed this opinion. But the discovery has not brought me any nearer finding who did the murder. Or rather I know . . ."

"You know?" asked Bella, with a look of surprise.

"Yes, the Director did it. But I do not know who the Director is. I've got to find out."

"You will never find out!" she said positively.

"We'll see. We've found out a lot that we should never have found out if the Director had been as smart as he thought. We'd have found it all out even earlier if Ted and Marjorie had come to us at the beginning, instead of fighting against the Yard. The influence of all these detective novels, I suppose."

He turned to Hawkins curiously.

"Do you know who the Director is?"

"I don't know positively," admitted the chauffeur, "but I can guess. Bella refuses to tell me whether I am right or not."

"It's bad enough that I should know," replied Bella soberly. "As long as I know I can't feel safe. I wish to God I could forget it. But I'm not going to involve George in the same responsibility."

"This is simply childish. Just look at it calmly. On the one hand you have the Yard, with all its routine, organisation and experience. On the other hand there's this solitary criminal, who daren't show his face, who's already on the run. Do you seriously mean that you are so terrified of him that you won't rely on the Yard's protection?"

"I do. After all, the Yard won't kill me if I *don't* tell, but the Director will get me if I do."

Morgan looked stern.

"The Yard may not kill you if you don't tell, Mrs Hawkins, but you forgot that you are an accessory to this crime. You have concealed material evidence. It is merely for our own convenience that I haven't already arrested you."

"You can't charge me with being an accessory unless you know the criminal. As for that threat about 'your own convenience,' I suppose you mean you are going to have me shadowed in the hope that I shall lead you to the murderer? Well, you are very much mistaken! I never want to see the Director again, and I'm sure he'll keep away from me."

"You absolutely refuse to help?"

"I do!"

"Mr Hawkins, can't you persuade your wife to tell? Surely you can protect her, even if she doesn't trust the Yard?"

Hawkins shook his head.

"I've had this out with her, Inspector! I can't shift her. After all, if I can't even persuade her to tell me, how can I persuade her to tell you? All the same, I think you're rather underestimating the danger from the Director, judging by what my wife tells me."

Morgan shrugged his shoulders.

"We know these romantic, play-acting criminals, with their dark threats! It may be all right to scare children, but we know it's nothing but words. At this moment the Director is not concerned with revenge, but with one thing only, how to save his skin! I bet a pound to a penny that his knees are knocking together with fright and that he jumps like a scared rabbit every time there's a knock at the door. One man can't hold society up to ransom. I'll get him, don't you worry. I won't overlook your refusal to give me this information, Mrs Hawkins, I tell you flat, and in spite of it I'll get the Director. I can make Burton squeak. He's easy meat."

"Burton? He doesn't know who the Director is!" exclaimed Bella.

"He does!" replied Morgan triumphantly. "And, what's more, with a little pressure Burton will tell who he is. Anyway, let's forget the Director for a little. There are other points you haven't cleared up. What was the motive for the crime? And what was the truth behind Ted Wainwright's empty poison bottle?"

Bella looked relieved.

"That's easily told. We never reckoned on Marjorie's having someone who was interested in her well-being. In all our previous cases it's been a lonely person whose relatives are only too anxious to get rid of him or her. As soon as we found that Marjorie had a fiancé, the situation changed. We knew Ted Wainwright would never let things slide, that whatever happened to Marjorie he would want to find out the truth. This would be awkward, for you can imagine how delicate these kinds of cases are! One breath of an enquiry, and the whole truth might come out.

"So Wood and Crispin hit on the idea—or rather it was suggested by the Director—of getting Wainwright put out of the way in such a manner that he would not know what had hit him, and so that Marjorie would be antagonised rather than sympathetic. The idea was for Mrs Threpfall to get some poison, and slip the empty bottle in Wainwright's pocket. Crispin would ask for a glass of water from Wainwright in such a way that Ted would be forced to get it. Then, as Wainwright handed her the glass, she would drop in it the mixture which, as you already know, temporarily produces the effects of prussic-acid poisoning. My sister was an expert conjurer, so there was no difficulty in doing this. As Mrs Threpfall sat next to him, she was able to slip the empty phial into his pocket in the dark.

"The idea was that Wainwright would be accused of attempted poisoning, and get a fairly long stretch in prison for it. This would keep him out of the way for a few years. What with the evidence of Mrs Threpfall and Doctor Wood, and the fact that he was masquerading under a false name, the fact that he had handed Crispin the water, and the fact that he had an empty poison bottle in his pocket, he would not stand a chance in hell of escaping conviction."

"What a diabolically ingenious plot!" exclaimed Morgan. "How did it slip up?"

"Because the Director took a hand in the game, and changed his plans. For some reason, which I have not yet been able to fathom, he decided to get rid of my sister. I suspected once, my sister tried to blackmail him, but now that I think it over, it doesn't seem to me possible. My sister was too much in fear of him herself. Anyway, whatever his motive, this was his opportunity, and he used it. Instead of a fake poisoning, it was a real poisoning, as my sister knew directly she had drunk the water. You remember her death cry?"

"And didn't Wood know anything of this?"

"No, it was a surprise to him! What is more, he did not at first realise it was the Director's work, so the quarrel between my sister and the Director must have been a private quarrel. But I realised whose work it was, and I didn't wait. I got out of the way as fast as possible! When the Director's on the warpath, it's wise to stay out of the way! There was always the chance that I might give something away accidentally to you, and that the Director would hold me responsible for it.

"Meanwhile, George and I had become fond of each other. I had never dared marry him before, I was so much under my sister's influence. Her death seemed to break it, and I wrote to George, and he came to me and we were married. I found out where Marjorie and Wainwright were, and so I saw nothing wrong in bringing them together and getting Marjorie freed for a reward. I tell you frankly I did it for money. I know I can trust Marjorie to see me through."

"But why did Wood shelter Wainwright for a time?" asked Morgan.

"He was in an awkward position. His only chance was to play a two-faced game. On the one hand to appear as friendly as possible to Wainwright, so that Wainwright had complete confidence in him, and so that you thought him simply some innocent friend of Wainwright's who was letting his sympathy run away with him. On the other hand, in his innocent, friendly way, he had to throw as much suspicion on Wainwright as possible.

"He fabricated everything he could which would tell against Wainwright—a whole string of inventions—and in order to focus suspicion on him, he advised him to run away instead of facing up to the music. If Wainwright had stayed on, instead of cutting and running, the whole thing might have been probed to the bottom much sooner."

"Yes, I propose to make a call on friend Wainwright to tell him that!"

"On top of that, as soon as Wainwright practically confessed to the murder by running away, Wood arranged for Wainwright's hiding place to be given away to you. That should have been the last move in the game. Wainwright would have been tried, found guilty, and the investigations would have been closed. After a discreet time, Marjorie's uncle could have cashed in on his niece's certified insanity and the whole business would have been wound up. But we spoilt Wood's plans there by warning Wainwright!"

"In other words you double-crossed Wood for the sake of Miss Easton's money! You thought it was smart to come to the aid of law and order and cash in on it!"

Hawkins' cheeks flamed, but Bella replied defiantly.

"Well, what if we did. We've got to live, haven't we?"

"I don't see the necessity," said Morgan. "However, I may be biassed . . . You absolutely refuse to reveal the Director's identity, even if we promise you full police protection and guarantee not to proceed with the charge of being an accessory? Think it over! Your money won't be much good if you have a ten years' stretch in prison."

"It'll be even less good if we're pushing up daisies! No, if you're so smart, find out who he is!"

They rose to go but Morgan halted them.

"One moment, before you go! What about Burton's connection with Crispin and the Director? Surely it was closer than that of a mere client?"

"Well, he had acted for the Director in one or two fire-raising cases. Apart from that, he was only a client. And a darned mean one! He spent most of his time coming round rowing Crispin over fees and expenses! He wanted Marjorie's money but he wanted it cheap. However, the Director was able to deal with him, even when Crispin wasn't!"

"Right. That's all I want to know. You're very foolish, Mrs Hawkins. I'll get the Director anyway. I've a virtual promise from Burton that he'll squeak. You might as well save yourself the charge of being an accessory."

"Burton won't squeak," said Bella confidently. "He's more

afraid for his skin than I am. Come on, George, and let's beat it. The next time we come in here, we may not be able to get out so easily!"

After they had gone, Morgan opened the drawer of his desk and took out a box of cigars, presented by a grateful friend who knew his tastes. He only smoked them when there was an imperative need for physical comfort. He felt that need now. At all costs he must be able to concentrate.

He closed the windows of his office. Then, opening the door, he hung an "engaged" notice on it. The door was already provided with a draught excluder. Before lighting his cigar, he drew his writing pad to him and scrawled upon it three queries:

1. *Who is the Director?*
2. *Why did he kill Crispin?*
3. *Why, since he had decided to poison her, did he not use prussic acid? The use of this poison would have meant the conviction of Ted Wainwright, and would have immediately brought to an end the investigation of the crime.*

He lit his cigar, lay back in his chair, and contemplated vacancy. The blue smoke slowly formed a giant umbrella above his head.

Like Buddha beneath the bo tree, the inspector wrestled with his soul.

CHAPTER XVII

The Wax Goat

MYSTERY OF DEAD MAN-WOMAN
YARD ANNOUNCEMENT TODAY

One of the most amazing mysteries of modern times will reach a new stage today. Scotland Yard will make an arrest in the case of the murdered man-woman, Crispin, and charge the man hitherto known only as the "Director" with the wilful murder of this strange personality.

"Hitherto the identity of the Director," said Inspector Morgan in a statement today, "has been a complete mystery. As a result of the evidence of Mr Samuel Burton, however, who will be principal witness for the Crown, we are now in a position to lodge a charge against this man."

The case of the dead man-woman, which for various reasons will probably now become known as the Case of the Six Queer Things, will contain many sensational features. Never before has so complex a story lain behind an alleged murder.

Up to a late hour last night the wanted man had not been arrested and the Yard had nothing to report.

"We shall be in a position to make a further statement very shortly," it was declared.

A reporter who called at Mr Burton's house found he was confined to bed with a severe cold.

The above announcement, which appeared in all the morning papers, had been carefully prepared by Morgan in consultation with his chief.

It read very finely and proudly, but in fact it was Morgan's final cast, on which he had staked everything. All other avenues had proved fruitless. The most scrupulous examination of the staff of the bogus asylum in Norfolk had failed to elicit any information as to the identity of the Director. One and all swore that they had dealt only with Wood, although one or two were aware that the Director existed, and that Wood was only his tool. Relentless probing in other directions had failed to bring to the surface a scrap of evidence which could be relied upon as a pointer to the Director's identity.

All this evidence went to show that the Director belonged to the type which Morgan, in his mind, christened the "supercrook." By this he did not mean that this was a type of crook possessed of superior intelligence, for it was Morgan's experience and conviction that the intelligence of all criminals was limited, otherwise they would not be criminals, but would be exercising their talents in some more profitable and glorious sphere of life, such as that of company-promoter or cabinet minister.

By the supercrook Morgan meant those criminals who pictured themselves as crooks out of the ordinary—functioning on a magnificent, storybook scale. The use of the pseudonym, "The Director", the sedulous secrecy, the extraordinarily, even unnecessarily complex web of intrigue, pointed to this type of man. Such criminals, by their abounding self-confidence and the large romantic scope with which their operations were planned, often succeeded for a time in getting away with the impossible. The Portuguese Banknote Case is of course the classic example of this type of criminal, a case where at the end no one knew who was robbed or who had gained, but only that something consummately skilful and astounding had been achieved.

In the same way, the very elaboration of their schemes was often the cause of failure—a magnificent failure, but still a failure. Such types necessarily had the vanity of the ordinary crook developed to an extraordinary degree, often at the expense of the egoism which is usually another distinguishing mark of the ordinary criminal's epileptoid psychology.

Morgan was banking on his knowledge of the psychology of the supercrook as a proven fact. Take a great man by his weakest point, and he proves a very small creature! Take hold of a supercrook by his vanity, and he is revealed as a very stupid individual. Morgan believed that he would be able to touch the Director's vanity, and that he would therefore fall a victim to a stratagem usually reserved for brutes, that of the tethered goat....

Crouching in the scanty shade afforded by the dustbin of the back yard of Samuel Burton's home, Inspector Morgan waited. It was a cold night, infernally cold, and Morgan was no longer young. None the less he waited tensely while the hours dragged past. He was backing his knowledge to win.

Suddenly he stiffened. A small dark figure had detached itself from the shadows. It carried something glittering. The something caught the moonlight and winked wickedly.

The figure moved like a cat. After the moment when it had revealed itself in the moonlight, it sank back into the shadow of the wall, and seemed to melt into the brickwork. By straining his eyes, Morgan could see that the figure was pressed against the drainpipe, and was rising. It clung there like some great bat.

Presently it was leaning, still with two legs curled round the drainpipe, upon the window sill. Morgan could hear his own heart pounding in the silence. The window sill was half in moonlight, and once again Morgan saw the glittering thing wink at the moon in the hand of the dark figure. Then there was a sound like the puff of a suddenly deflated tyre, and a red flash which made the moonlight seem cold and garish.

Morgan did not hesitate but, raising the revolver which all the time had been clasped in his hand, he levelled it at the man. Morgan was a dead-cold marksman, and the weapon was shot out of the hand of the human cat. Revolver and body dropped in the yard almost simultaneously.

Morgan rushed out to pick him up. He did not struggle. Like most supercrooks, he did not mind cold steel or firearms, but shirked hand-to-hand encounters. He gave himself up to arrest without a fight. Only his eyes, burning impotently in the moonlight, snapped balefully as Morgan clamped the handcuffs on his wrists. The fingers of his right hand were shattered by Morgan's bullet.

"Now we'll turn on the lights," said Morgan triumphantly, "and see what fish we've got."

The torch lit up the contorted features of George Hawkins,

former chauffeur of the medium, husband of Bella Crispin, alias the Director....

Upstairs in Burton's room, Morgan inspected the damage. A wax model, with some resemblance to Samuel Burton, borrowed from the outsize window of Gellows, the 30/- tailors, had had its head shattered beyond repair. The waxen fragments were scattered all over the pillow. As he saw this, Hawkins' face twisted in pure chagrin—one of the most painful emotions of the vain man. It was to give place later to a kind of sullen resignation.

He had been trapped....

"Everything you say may be used against you at a later date," Morgan warned him. "At the same time, you are so compromised that I do not see that it would do you much harm to be truthful. Yours was a remarkable—in fact a brilliant—crime. Unless you enlighten us, its details will never be known, and I think it would be a pity if it were lost, and your name did not figure in the annals of crime."

Morgan was sufficiently a psychologist to know that now, when the man's vanity was most wounded, was the time to use it to effect his purpose.

"I am more compromised than you think," answered Hawkins with a snarl. "What is it you want to know? It seems to me you know a good deal as it is!"

"I want to know why you killed Crispin."

"Why does one kill women?" asked Hawkins impatiently. "Any woman? Because she is a damned nuisance! I am prepared to bet that if you go into the details of any big plan that has gone wrong, you'll find a woman in it somewhere, messing it up. They can't keep their emotions and their business separate."

"What do you mean? I don't quite follow," prompted the detective.

"Only that this horse-faced piece of femininity conceived a fatal passion for me!" replied Hawkins bitterly. "She nearly worried the life out of me with her lovesickness. It's possible to discipline most of the emotions of human beings. I've specialised in making the whip crack round their heads and seeing them sit up and beg. Fear is a great tamer! Fear and gold together can do everything—except make a woman in love behave sensibly. Can you imagine anything more foolish and degrading—a woman of her age and experience falling in love like a sloppy schoolgirl—worse, in fact, than a schoolgirl?"

Morgan looked at Hawkins closely, and realised that his small, dark litheness might make a powerful appeal to women. Something in him made him feel even a little sorry for the woman Crispin, utterly devoid of feminine charm, and with a life no doubt completely starved of affection, suddenly falling a victim to the Aphrodite she had flouted and denied so long. Ridiculous —and yet how human and understandable!

"I could have managed her alone, I think," went on Hawkins. "After all, I had only to tell her to do a thing, and she'd do it, if it meant a kind word from me. She had got to that stage! But then there was the difficulty of Bella."

"Of Bella?"

"Yes, Bella had been in love with me for some time. I had encouraged it, thinking it might be useful. I could use Bella to watch her sister, and I always believe in having an observer to check up on one's agents. But these two sisters became jealous of each other. I don't know if you've ever had any experience of the jealousy of two sisters, but if not—well, it's something to terrify Heaven! It didn't terrify *me*, but it irritated me, interfered with my plans, and at last got to a stage where it became definitely dangerous. She actually threatened me that if I did not send Bella away, she would blow the gaff on me! She quite coolly and calmly told *me* that, which showed the state she was in! No one had ever dared to threaten me before.

"Bella was equally mad. She had a fairly tough disposition beneath her outward meekness. Between the two of them I saw that the whole business was becoming impossible, and had better be ended quickly. I wasn't altogether sorry. I had exploited the idea on which it was based for some years fairly profitably, and I was getting tired of it. I never like to run a scheme too long, however paying it is. After all one has an artistic conscience, and a part to play; and these things get boring if they are carried on too long!

"So I poisoned the older sister, and married the younger. Bella was by no means unattractive, and very devoted. I could foresee her being useful. When I say 'married', of course you will realise I speak in a Pickwickian sense. I have long passed the age when I rush into permanent entanglements of this kind, even were I legally able to. But in fact a wife of mine is still alive somewhere. God knows where, but I could have found her if it became necessary at any time to convince Bella that her position was not so favoured as she imagined. That kind of lesson soon brings them to heel!"

"Forgive me if I point out one flaw in your scheme! It puzzles me. Why use strychnine when, by using prussic acid, you could have ensured that the police found a culprit at once—Ted Wainwright?"

Hawkins smiled.

"For a policeman that might be a satisfactory ending. For anyone with a sense of finesse it is not. If Ted Wainwright were to be found guilty, not only might the whole murder come to light, but there would still be the business itself to clear up—the asylum, Marjorie Easton, and so forth. By keeping Ted Wainwright alive, and by posing as Marjorie Easton's deliverer, I was able to ensure myself at least as substantial a share of her fortune as I would have got by acting as her jailer, with the added advantage that I had the whole business off my hands, and could start on a new and larger swindle I had just devised. There was one small mistake——"

"The Six Queer Things?"

"Yes. I cleared out all other clues but those. It was very careless of Crispin to leave a locked drawer."

"But weren't you afraid that one of the people in the racket, Wood, or Mrs Threpfall, or Marsden, might give you away when they found you had betrayed them?"

"No. None of them knew my identity. I had always dealt with them through Bella or her sister. Once Crispin was dead, only two were left alive who knew the secret—Bella and Samuel Burton. Where is Burton, by the way?"

"Safe in a prison cell. He demanded it. He said it was the only place where he would feel safe while you were alive."

A gleam of pride lit the Director's face.

"Quite true. I see he knows me."

He nodded in the direction of the shattered wax model.

"Yes, if Burton had really been there I should have been safe! No one would have been able to give me away!"

"What about Bella?" Morgan taunted him. "Do you still trust a woman after your experiences?"

A gentle, almost childlike smile of self-satisfaction spread over Hawkins' face.

"I shot the bitch dead before I came here."